TA...
THE DAR...

THE PYRUS REACH Sector is under attack! The armies of the orks, eldar, Chaos and the Imperium clash in order to win control of the area. But there are dark and ancient prophecies being revealed behind the scenes and the fate of billions hangs in the balance!

This action-packed collection features work from best-selling authors such as Dan Abnett, CS Goto and Graham McNeill, along with an array of hot new talent. Their stories showcase the Warhammer 40,000 universe in its most dark and brutal glory.

More Warhammer 40,000 from the Black Library

LET THE GALAXY BURN
eds. Marc Gascoigne & Christian Dunn

WARHAMMER 40,000 STORIES

TALES FROM THE DARK MILLENNIUM

Edited by
Marc Gascoigne
& Christian Dunn

A BLACK LIBRARY PUBLICATION

First published in Great Britain in 2006 by
BL Publishing,
Games Workshop Ltd.,
Willow Road, Nottingham,
NG7 2WS, UK.

10 9 8 7 6 5 4 3 2 1

Cover illustration by Michael Komark,
with thanks to Sabertooth Games.

© Games Workshop Limited 2006. All rights reserved.

Black Library, the Black Library logo, Black Flame, BL Publishing, Games Workshop, the Games Workshop logo and all associated marks, names, characters, illustrations and images from the Warhammer 40,000 universe are either ®, TM and/or © Games Workshop Ltd 2000-2006, variably registered in the UK and other countries around the world. All rights reserved.

A CIP record for this book is available from the British Library.

ISBN13: 978 1 84416 418 9
ISBN10: 1 84416 418 7

Distributed in the US by Simon & Schuster
1230 Avenue of the Americas, New York, NY 10020.

Printed and bound in Great Britain by
Bookmarque, Surrey, UK.

No part of this publication may be reproduced, stored in a retrieval system, or transmitted in any form or by any means, electronic, mechanical, photocopying, recording or otherwise, without the prior permission of the publishers.

This is a work of fiction. All the characters and events portrayed in this book are fictional, and any resemblance to real people or incidents is purely coincidental.

See the Black Library on the Internet at
www.blacklibrary.com

Find out more about Games Workshop
and the world of Warhammer 40,000 at
www.games-workshop.com

Find out more about Sabertooth on the Internet at
www.sabertoothgames.com

It is the 41st millennium. For more than a hundred centuries the Emperor has sat immobile on the Golden Throne of Earth. He is the master of mankind by the will of the gods, and master of a million worlds by the might of his inexhaustible armies. He is a rotting carcass writhing invisibly with power from the Dark Age of Technology. He is the Carrion Lord of the Imperium for whom a thousand souls are sacrificed every day, so that he may never truly die.

Yet even in his deathless state, the Emperor continues his eternal vigilance. Mighty battlefleets cross the daemon-infested miasma of the warp, the only route between distant stars, their way lit by the Astronomican, the psychic manifestation of the Emperor's will. Vast armies give battle in His name on uncounted worlds. Greatest amongst his soldiers are the Adeptus Astartes, the Space Marines, bio-engineered super-warriors. Their comrades in arms are legion: the Imperial Guard and countless planetary defence forces, the ever-vigilant Inquisition and the tech-priests of the Adeptus Mechanicus to name only a few. But for all their multitudes, they are barely enough to hold off the ever-present threat from aliens, heretics, mutants – and worse.

To be a man in such times is to be one amongst untold billions. It is to live in the cruellest and most bloody regime imaginable. These are the tales of those times. Forget the power of technology and science, for so much has been forgotten, never to be re-learned. Forget the promise of progress and understanding, for in the grim dark future there is only war. There is no peace amongst the stars, only an eternity of carnage and slaughter, and the laughter of thirsting gods.

CONTENTS

Introduction by *Steve Horvath* — 8
The Falls of Marakross by *Steve Parker* — 11
Vindicare by *CS Goto* — 55
The Prisoner by *Graham McNeill* — 69
The Invitation by *Dan Abnett* — 115
A Balance of Faith
  by *Darren-Jon Ashmore* — 129
Gate of Souls by *Mike Lee* — 147
Fate's Masters, Destiny's Servants
  by *Matt Keefe* — 167
Tears of Blood by *CS Goto* — 203

INTRODUCTION

THE WARHAMMER 40,000 universe has been around for years – I remember when I was first exposed to it as a fan. I eagerly devoured the bits of information I could find, read the stories, and immersed myself in it as much as I could. Now, as the head of Sabertooth Games, I have been able to have a hand in helping to shape that world with our collectible card game *Dark Millennium*, and its previous edition *Horus Heresy*.

We've been able to pair our stunning visuals and great game mechanics with the epic story of Warhammer 40,000. We've been able to not only convey the story through our cards, but also allow players within our tournaments to shape the ongoing storyline by affecting the lives of not only individual characters but entire worlds.

Many of the best Black Library authors have contributed their talents to conveying these events by adding their stories to our website (http://www.sabertoothgames.com).

They have told the stories that our players have written with their victories, carefully crafting the events in stellar written works.

Within this book you'll find other stories set in that area by the same great authors. These stories flesh out the Pyrus Reach Sector of the Warhammer 40,000 universe, the sector that the Dark Millennium Collectible Card Game takes place within. This is a war torn sector afflicted by horrible warp storms that make simple travel within its borders a dangerous affair.

Yet despite this danger, many have descended upon its planets – some looking for power and glory while others seek to stop terrible prophecies from coming to fruition. Each has their own agenda, their own plans and fears.

Once you've read these stories, I hope that you'll come and check out the other stories that have happened within the Pyrus Reach, as well as what happens next, on our website. Or you can help shape future events yourself by getting involved in the Dark Millennium CCG.

Before I close, I want to take this opportunity to thank some of the people who have made this, and all the stories of Dark Millennium, possible. Dan Abnett, Mike Lee and all the other authors included in this book have helped give life to the stories our players have created. I must thank Marc Gascoigne, whose idea it was to make this book, and Christian Dunn and Lindsey Priestley, who did a wonderful job of putting together such a strong collection of stories. I have to give special thanks to Alan Merrett without whom none of this would be possible.

Finally let me thank each and every one who has, or will, play the Dark Millennium CCG and participated in shaping the events that make up these stories. Without you, the characters would not be as alive, the wars as bloody, or the events as dark. You help shape all of our worlds – especially when it means destroying a few along the way.

Steve Horvath
CEO, Sabertooth Games

The Falls of Marakross
Steve Parker

THE RATTLE OF gunfire died off as midday approached. Both sides dug in behind solid cover, neither eager to break the stalemate while the sun burned at its zenith. The air hung hot and still and silent between the deadlocked foes.

Across the city, the streets and market-squares emptied. The citizens of Scala, planetary capital of Cordassa, took shelter in their homes from the searing heat. Not so, the officers of the Praeto Scala – the city's civil defence force. The praetos of Precinct 11 had fought for hours to gain this much ground against a cultist cell called Children of the Merciful Lord. The heretics had overtaken a large territory in the western slums and were drawing tainted water from its deep wells in direct contravention to a citywide Imperial edict.

Though the cultists were able to drink the infected water with impunity, they suffered under the baking sun just as much as the weary praetos.

The sudden, earsplitting scream of jets ripped through the silence. A great black shadow dropped over the contested streets, whipping dust into clouds that raced off down avenues of cheap dirty habs.

Startled men on both sides pressed their hands tight over their ears, desperate to drown out the banshee howling of powerful engines as they worked to hold a great black gunship in position.

These streets were too narrow for a landing. As the incredulous praetos stared dumbfounded, a seam opened in the rear of the gunship's armoured body. A ramp lowered and locked into position. And then they came – a storm of dark, gleaming giants. Dropping in twos from the extended ramp ten metres above, they hit the ground like meteors. The impacts of their booted feet shook the surrounding walls. Each hulking green-armoured figure landed squarely, immediately moving out from beneath the ship and into position, covering the descent of the others.

The last figure to descend wore white robes that whipped and flared around his black armour as he dropped. The ramp closed, sealing the ship behind him. The scream of the jets changed pitch. The gunship banked and slid away over the rooftops, drenching the street in baking sunlight once again.

The praetos blinked dust from their eyes and squinted at the giants standing in their midst.

From under his hood, the monster in white robes boomed, 'Who has command? Step forward at once.'

His voice was harsh. Machinelike. Inhuman. The praetos felt their lungs vibrate with each word.

It was a short, dark woman who rose and moved forward to answer. 'I'm Captain us-Kalmir,' she said, 'of the Praeto Scala, Precinct 11. And I am in charge here.' Her Gothic was heavily accented. 'Who do I address?'

The hooded giant stepped forward, dwarfing her. He raised gauntleted hands and peeled back his hood. Some among the younger praetos gasped and scrabbled backwards, certain that death itself had come for them. The giant's face was a leering bone-white skull.

With deft fingers, the giant detached his skull-helm from its fixings. Cables hissed and snaked away from the masterfully sculpted mask. He lifted it clear.

Beneath, there was a human face. Horribly scarred and pitted, aged beyond its years by the ravages of countless battles, but still a human face. Cold grey eyes locked with the woman's.

'At ease, captain,' said the giant. His voice was deep and compelling – less terrifying than when amplified, though perhaps even more potent. 'I am Interrogator-Chaplain Artemius Grohm of the Dark Angels, First Company, and I serve the Emperor of Mankind.'

He raised a metal fist into the air. His armoured brothers immediately marched off towards the cultist barricades. The air soon filled with gunshots and screaming.

The giant grinned down at the Scalan captain.

'We have come to help,' he said.

'I CAN SPARE a moment only, inquisitor,' said Artemius, squeezing his bulk through a door built for lesser men. He straightened and surveyed the room: luxurious fixings, delicately sculpted artworks, richly curtained glass doors that led onto a wide balcony – the room dripped with the ubiquitous excess of a governor's palace. The Cordassan governor had assigned Inquisitor Heiron fine quarters indeed, though Artemius preferred more spartan accommodation. The air in the room was luxuriously cool after the baking heat of the open streets. 'I did not traverse the immaterium to sit in meetings.'

'Exactly why I summoned you, Interrogator-Chaplain,' replied the inquisitor. 'I wish to know why you traversed the immaterium at all. Particularly to a planet in its death-throes. I doubt you came to end a skirmish between local praetos and a cultist mob.'

Artemius crossed the room to the inquisitor's desk, his eyes on the old man behind it. Inquisitor Mattius Heiron looked ancient – his skin was scarred and weathered, darkened by the relentless sun of this world. His hair was combed neatly from left to right, gossamer wisps of snow white that looked ready to vanish on the next breeze. He wore delicate antique pince-nez on a long, thin aquiline nose. Drowned in the folds of an expensive Cordassan robe, he presented a vision of pitiable frailty.

That vision was a lie. Artemius had only to look into the inquisitor's ice blue eyes to recognise it.

This is the man about whom Brother-Codicier Corvus cautioned me. Very well, inquisitor, let us see what part you shall play.

'Won't you sit?' asked the inquisitor.

Artemius looked distastefully at the ornate wooden chair to which the old man gestured. It looked utterly incapable of supporting a man in power armour.

'I'm sorry. It does look rather inadequate to the task. Perhaps you'll join me on the balcony instead?'

Artemius followed the old man outside.

The heat had grown only marginally less oppressive in the late afternoon. From the balcony, Artemius looked out over the city to the defensive walls that marked its limits. Below him, ringed by wall-walks crawling with members of the Guard-Royal, lay the gardens of the planetary governor. Even now, with half the citizenry dying of thirst, the rare trees and flowers were being watered by ranks of gardeners.

Beyond the gardens spread the spacious properties of the city's rich. Another wall stood between these and the lesser districts. At the outer edges of the city, nearest the perimeter wall, were the slums with which Artemius was already familiar.

'Amasec?' asked the old man, pouring a glass for himself. 'It's a wonderful local vintage.'

'You requested my presence, inquisitor,' said Artemius, declining the drink. 'I'd appreciate it if you would get to the point. There are things to which I must attend.'

'So again I ask: what exactly are these *things*, Interrogator-Chaplain? I'm most curious.'

'It is no great secret, inquisitor,' lied Artemius. 'My Chapter is here in force. The Pyrus Reach faces a dire crisis. Your own Inquisitor Santos brought our attention to the fact. I'm sure you knew that.'

'A predictably evasive answer, and typically unimaginative, Interrogator-Chaplain. You know I refer specifically to Cordassa. What business do the Dark Angels have here, on this world? Answer the question.'

Artemius could feel the inquisitor's words, his tone, his raw will, all working to draw the truth from his lips. But such tricks were for the masses; they could hardly be expected to work on an Interrogator-Chaplain.

A brightly coloured bird fluttered up from the gardens, over the palace wall and away, its shadow dancing across the shining white domes of the city's rooftops.

'We came to assess the situation here, and perhaps to offer assistance to the local forces, should I deem it appropriate. There's little more to it than that.'

'A disappointing half-truth at best, Interrogator-Chaplain. When have the Dark Angels ever descended without some greater purpose? Be honest with me, and I may be able to offer valuable assistance.'

'We waste each other's time, inquisitor,' said Artemius. 'You have asked your question. That the Dark Angels serve the Emperor's Divine Will should be sufficient. We will brook no interference, whatever the source. Now, if you'll excuse me…'

Artemius turned from the view and stepped back into the apartment.

'Why is it,' asked the inquisitor as he followed, clearly fighting to remain calm, 'that the Dark Angels are ever eager to avoid the company of the Inquisition? A question often asked in certain circles.'

Ah, this one cuts to the heart of things. How far will he press me?

'Aimless speculation hardly befits the Ordo Malleus,' said Artemius, turning to face the old man. 'You have far weightier matters to occupy you, I'm quite sure.'

'You presume to lecture me? Live another hundred years before you even consider it. Where the Inquisition appears, the Dark Angels swiftly depart. Is it not so? And here you are, practically running from my apartment, unwilling to answer the simplest of questions.'

'Then I shall ask you a question, inquisitor,' said Artemius. 'I noticed the Ordo Malleus battle cruiser, the *Spear Excelsis*, hanging in high orbit with the Imperial Fleet. I assume you command the ship. Do you intend to authorise Sanction Extremis? With little of Cordassa held by Imperial forces, I wonder that you have held off even this long.'

Inquisitor Heiron walked around his desk, sat down and laced his fingers. 'The Inquisition does not take such matters lightly. My assessment is ongoing. If these people are to die, it shall be because our options have run out. Their sacrifice will preserve the purity of the Imperium. But you merely seek to deflect my question. Perhaps you feel Exterminatus is unjustified? Should I simply concede this world to Chaos?'

He dares question my loyalty? My fervour?

'Have a care, inquisitor,' said Artemius. 'Few, if any, serve the Golden Throne as fervently as the Dark Angels.

We are ready to die whenever it serves His Divine Will. Never doubt it. Never question it. And never again offend me with accusations of leniency where traitor scum are concerned.'

Inquisitor Heiron raised a placatory hand.

'My apologies, Interrogator-Chaplain. The Dark Angels are famously zealous. Of that, I'm well aware. But the very fact arouses my interest. Behind the greatest zeal, do we not often hide our secret shame?'

So, we have it at last. No secret is forever. This bloodhound has picked up the scent. But how much does the Ordo Malleus know?

'Secret shame? Do you wish to confess something, inquisitor?' said Artemius. 'I am ready to hear your sins if it shall help you achieve His forgiveness. Perhaps I can suggest a suitable penance.' Artemius stepped towards the apartment door.

'I wish to formally request your aid, Interrogator-Chaplain,' continued Inquisitor Heiron. 'There is much the Dark Angels could do for the Imperial cause. Will you not place yourself at my service, knowing that I too serve His Divine Will with every breath?'

'I do not doubt your loyalty, Inquisitor Heiron. But ours will be a short stay. You may petition my Chapter if you wish a force placed at your disposal, but the Lord Militant will have sprung his trap long before you have your answer. While I recognise your authority, I remind you of its limitations. Even you, inquisitor, must work within the legal framework of the Imperium. I understand the burden you bear. You have my sympathies.'

'How gracious,' said Inquisitor Heiron bitterly. 'Since you will not answer truthfully, you may go. But my eyes will be on you every moment of your stay. My word on that. I will uncover your mandate one way or another.'

Without a backwards glance, Artemius squeezed through the door and marched off down the hallway, his footsteps echoing from the marble walls.

'Dismissed,' growled the inquisitor, rising from his chair.

The Dark Angel hadn't closed the door behind him.

Artemius marched from the entrance of the governor's palace, back into the pulverising heat and glare of the city. He passed ranks of liveried house guards sheltering in the shadows of massive sandstone arches. They snapped to attention, saluting smartly as the Interrogator-Chaplain walked by. Artemius was the first Astartes they had ever seen.

They look at me as if I were a xenos.

At almost three metres tall, Artemius towered over the Cordassan men. These were a short, hardy people with dark, almond-shaped eyes and hair as black as jet. Under this sun, Artemius didn't wonder that their culture demanded the wearing of the *urut* – the hooded white robe that only non-civilians might shed in public. Before the coming of the Missionarius Galaxia, the punishment for stepping outdoors without the urut was death.

Artemius's own hooded white robes – the robes of his chaplaincy – had brought him smiles and bows from the local people as he moved around the city. They assumed that the giant off-worlder was honouring their customs.

Exiting the main gates of the governor's substantial grounds, Artemius was joined by two of his Chapter-brothers. Brother-Sergeants Syriel and Ogion fell into step on either side.

When Artemius glanced at them, he noted how dark Ogion's skin and hair had become.

As dark as my own must be. The 13th implant is protecting our cells from the assault of this merciless sun.

Syriel, however, had been recruited from a desert world. He had always been dark, his skin contrasting with his gleaming teeth as he said, 'We've commandeered a barracks and arranged a staging area close to the east gate as ordered, Interrogator-Chaplain. There were no objections. Most of the city's garrisoned troops were posted to the front lines to bolster Imperial Guard regiments. The Praeto Scala struggles to keep order among the refugees. For the most part, the citizens hide indoors from the sun. Most are dying of thirst and plague.'

'These people feel the breath of death on their necks, brothers,' said Artemius. 'The Cordassan Guard are stolid and capable fighters from all accounts. I fear the Lord Militant Commander has made a grave error in baiting his trap with Cordassa. Are the Rhinos ready?'

'The Rhinos are fuelled and ready, brother-chaplain,' replied Syriel.

'Ogion?'

The brother-sergeant answered in his distinctive gravelly tones. 'The acting-commander of the surviving guard regiments is Colonel Rhamis ut-Halarr, 3rd Cordassan Grenadiers, First Company. A local man. Both he and Commissar Klauvas Brantine returned from the front lines yesterday. They are preparing the city for an extended siege. They expect the front lines to break any day.'

'That gives us very little time,' said Artemius.

'Both were most eager to make your acquaintance, Interrogator-Chaplain. The colonel has invited you to Command HQ. He wishes to share intelligence in return for our aid.'

'Will he remain so willing, I wonder, when I'm forced to deny him our direct assistance? Very well. Brother-Sergeant Syriel, you may return to oversee final preparations. We move out upon my arrival at the staging area. Have both squads ready.'

'Yes, brother,' replied Syriel with a short bow. He turned down a branching main street and double-timed it back to the barracks, untroubled by the heat.

As Artemius turned to continue, he noticed movement from the corner of his eye and spun. In the shadows, dozens of small figures leapt with fright, scattering to the corners of the surrounding buildings. From their partial cover, the children of Scala peered out at the two giant off-worlders.

The children were dishevelled, dressed in tattered urut more dirt-brown than white. Each was thin to the point of malnourishment.

'Street children so far from the slums?' said Artemius.

'With respect, brother,' replied Ogion, 'these children are of the noble families. Most of the slum children perished from plague months ago. Wealth has merely delayed the inevitable here. These children will soon share the fate of the poor.'

Artemius felt a grain of pity taking root within him.

The moment he recognised it, he crushed it to nothing.

Weak is he who dwells with sorrow on the injustices of the universe. Emperor, guard me from the pitfalls of compassion.

'In death,' he said, 'the shades of rich and poor are equal. Fortunate are we who die in the glory of battle, in the righteous service of the Golden Throne. Only in such service may we rise to His side.'

Ogion bowed. 'As always, brother, your words inspire.' The two Dark Angels turned towards Command HQ. 'We are blessed indeed to serve under your command.'

Small feet stepped tentatively from the shadows. The crowd of children shuffled forwards, eager to keep the strange newcomers in view. None, however, had the energy to keep pace with the Space Marines.

One or two had noticed the shining Imperial eagle on Ogion's breastplate. They began to sing the Hymn of

Allegiance Imperius. Soon all the children had joined in, straining their dry throats to be heard. But the Dark Angels were quickly out of sight and the rasped song fell dead in the hot, still air.

THE MAP-ROOM, deep within the bowels of Command HQ, was even cooler than the inquisitor's apartment. Three figures stood in the darkness surrounding a broad table, their faces transformed into eerie masks by the green glow of the map-screen that comprised its surface. Busy cogitators sat against the black stone walls, their myriad lights winking inscrutably. Much of this technology was centuries old.

Brother-Techmarine Ulvo would be fascinated.

'As you can see, Interrogator-Chaplain,' said a stout, high-ranking Cordassan, 'Scala finds itself effectively isolated from other pockets of resistance. We've only lasted this long because of the spaceport. Scala was built on the equator to facilitate easier launches. It's the only such city on the whole of Cordassa.'

This was Colonel Rhamis ut-Halarr, ranking officer of the Cordassan Guard. The map-screen had turned his smart brown uniform to a sickly green and robbed his fine golden epaulets of their grand dignity. But the man himself stood looking up at Artemius with fine military bearing.

To the colonel's right stood a taller, thinner man. An off-worlder. His eyes studied the map from under the peak of a distinctive cap. An augmetic hand tapped idly on the tabletop as he considered tactical data scrolling across the display. This was Commissar Klauvas Brantine. He cleared his throat and said, 'Would that you had joined us sooner, Interrogator-Chaplain. I mean no offence, but the Cordassan Guard could have used the help of the Astartes long before now.'

Artemius ignored the comment. To the Cordassan colonel he said, 'Our objectives in coming here are, of course, confidential. I cannot enlighten you. But it should suffice that we act for the good of the Imperium. Our actions here will strike at the heart of those who ravage this world. Perhaps you may take some comfort in that.'

Colonel ut-Halarr nodded and said, 'May the Emperor hear my prayers that you will make them suffer, Interrogator-Chaplain. I've seen my people turned into savage madmen by these cults. However, without even vague details of your mission, I can hardly offer relevant assistance.'

'My Dark Angels require no assistance as such, but I seek information.' Artemius tapped a fingertip on the map-screen. 'This river,' he said, 'the Immen. This is the cause of your internal troubles? The unrest in the slums?'

'Indeed,' replied the colonel. 'The river provides the city's only source of water during the dry season. Deep wells throughout the city tap its life-giving supply. It is regarded as a holy river by many.'

'The inquisitor and the local Missionaria tolerate such beliefs?'

Commissar Brantine spoke. 'The worship of the river is regarded as benign. The Ecclesiarchy have deemed it tolerable during the changeover to Imperial rule.'

'Changeover?'

'Cordassa was only rediscovered by an explorator fleet about two hundred years ago,' continued Commissar Brantine. 'Rather than instigate a civil war, the Adeptus Terra decreed that Cordassa's return to the Imperial fold should be a more gradual process. Hence the election of popular local men as interim governors.'

Artemius raised an eyebrow. Such patient consideration was rare in the workings of the Imperium. Out here in the Halo Zone, however, where Imperial presence was by nature thin, there was wisdom in such methods.

'And now the river is taking lives, rather than sustaining them?'

'Indeed,' said the colonel. 'The symptoms of the plague slowly materialise over the course of a standard week. Weeping sores, pustules containing fat white larvae, eventual muscular necrosis – not something to witness before a repast. Thousands were infected before we realised there was a problem.'

'The local Missionaria alerted us to the first cases,' added the commissar. 'Now the city's wells and waterways are covered with razorwire, as you've seen. Drinking the water of the river is banned by Imperial edict. The Praeto Scala run constant patrols, but they're woefully undermanned. Punishment by death hasn't stopped the truly desperate. Your men assisted the praetos shortly after your arrival, yes? Against the Children of the Merciful Lord?'

Artemius nodded. 'I was told the cult were so named.'

'Heretic dogs,' spat the colonel. 'With all their proclamations of immunity to the plague, it's no wonder our civilians are flocking to join them. They recruit the thirsty and the desperate. They organise assaults on praeto patrols. They spread their heresy all over the city.'

'*Are* they immune?' asked Artemius.

'That's the damnedest thing about it. We've autopsied hundreds of them, but to no avail. It's nothing biological.'

'But they bear a mark,' said Artemius. 'An unseemly glyph of some sort? A brand, perhaps?'

'Yes,' said the colonel. 'All who enter the cult bear it.'

'Describe it to me.'

'It is a brand, burned into the flesh of the chest, shoulder or buttock; a circle pierced by arrow-headed spokes that radiate from a central hub. Merely gazing upon it makes one nauseous.'

'I don't wonder that the mark sickens you,' said Artemius. 'Your eyes have beheld the foulest of sigils, the most accursed mark of the unclean. It is the Star of Chaos – the antithesis of all for which the Imperium stands.'

'By the Emperor,' growled Commissar Brantine. 'The Children of the Merciful Lord are daemon worshippers?'

'They have bought their immunity,' said Artemius, 'at the price of their immortal souls. The servants of Chaos are masters of exacerbation. It is all too easy to convert the desperate. The source of the river – tell me of it.'

'The waters fall from the Dhargian Plateau in the north-east, down into the city of Marakross,' replied Commissar Brantine. He pointed to an area on the map to the north-east of Scala.

'Marakross…' said Artemius.

It is as you said it would be, brother-codicier.

'These maps are recent, sent to us from orbit by Battlefleet Gorgorus,' said Colonel ut-Halarr. 'As you can see, Marakross is rather unique – the city is built around a man-made lake at the base of a massive arch dam. The dam is set into a hanging valley, a gouge in the edge of the plateau.'

'Is the city not in a most precarious position? Surely one could wipe out the occupying force by destroying the dam.'

'Certainly, but the dam is a vast structure and built to endure incredible pressure. The Cordassan Guard have nothing that might even crack it. Besides, we'd have to retake the city just to get close enough. Cordassa has a history of war, Interrogator-Chaplain. Our cities are built to last. Marakross stands as a quintessential example of this.'

Artemius studied the orbital pict. Marakross was indeed impressive for both its defensive strengths and its engineering. The city nestled in the crook of a great curving escarpment. Tall cliffs walled the city on two sides. At its rear, the towering structure of the dam stretched to the full height of the plateau. The forward face of the city was a vast defensive wall not dissimilar to Scala's own. The River Immen flowed from outlets in the dam, through the city's canals, and out through a number of watergates.

'How high is the plateau?' asked Artemius.

It was the commissar who answered. 'Those cliffs rise almost two kilometres from the plains.'

'You've conducted aerial assaults?'

'Initially, yes. We don't have the resources now. Everything is tied up at the front line. We're down to ground units for the most part. Besides, if you look closely, you'll see that the heretics have shored up the defences since they took possession. Heavy-bolters, las-cannons, anti-air batteries – weapons salvaged from all over the planet. For all their madness, these dogs are well organised.'

It is no mere heretic behind the occupation of Marakross. Corvus, so far your foresight has been uncanny. But I wonder, were there things you did not disclose?

'So the dam is no weak point. Did you not request an orbital strike on the city itself?'

'Not at first,' replied the colonel. 'We'd hoped to take Marakross intact. With our borders hard-pressed and the plague ripping through our regiments, that quickly became infeasible. When we did request a tactical strike, the Imperial fleet denied us. They didn't deign to justify their refusal.'

The influence of Inquisitor Heiron at work. What does he seek in Marakross? He could end the plague with a single stroke.

'Your water is being tainted by the powers of Chaos,' said Artemius. 'Even now, they sit secure in Marakross, gloating prematurely over their victory on this world. With the paltry water shipments you're receiving from Battlefleet Gorgorus, you'll be hard pressed to last out the coming siege. If the capital falls, the spaceport falls. If the spaceport falls, this planet is lost.'

Artemius turned his eyes to the commissar and said, 'With the Inquisition in primary authority here, you know exactly what that will mean. It is fortunate my own objectives lie in Marakross.' Artemius faced the Cordassan colonel. 'It may be that the Dark Angels will end your plague in the course of our own business.'

Colonel ut-Halarr bowed before the massive Space Marine and said, 'If there is anything you need, simply name it and I will try to provide.'

The man's eyes were filled with hope.

Damn your hope, Guardsman. If it is the Emperor's Will, ending your plague will be a byproduct of my success. It will not distract me from the hunt.

'You can do two things,' said Artemius. 'Two things only. First, I want all maps and information relevant to Marakross copied to a data-slate and given to me at once.'

Colonel ut-Halarr nodded his assent.

'And the second?' asked Commissar Brantine.

Artemius scowled.

'Keep that infernal inquisitor out of my way.'

For almost a day, two Rhino personnel carriers tore across the hard, dusty surface of the Alhaal Plains following the course of the Immen upriver. They passed the carcasses of great gastropods – indigenous land molluscs with shells as big as houses that had died of thirst rather than drink from the deadly tainted water running nearby.

For a long time, the only plants visible were the hardy dry-grasses and thorn bushes that broke the expanse of baked earth. Everything close to the river, plant and animal, was dead. The silvery, bloated corpses of long-necked amphibians littered the riverbanks, stinking in the heat.

In the rear of one juddering transport, Artemius studied his data-slate, searching for weaknesses in the Marakrossian defensive wall. It was futile to consider the outflow pipes and watergates – the pressure of the water made such an entry impossible. Likewise, scaling the cliffs; the traitor armaments were well placed. Attackers climbing the cliff-faces would be picked off with ease. The defences bore all the hallmarks of a veteran commander.

A broad rockcrete highway connected Marakross with towns and cities across the continent, but this was extensively mined.

Instead, Artemius had decided to lead his forces through the thick platewood forest that dominated both banks of the Immen as it cut through the valley.

As if gaining entry didn't constitute enough of a problem, Artemius had yet to consider the untimely disappearance of Inquisitor Heiron. Moments prior to the Dark Angels' departure from Scala's east gate, a messenger from Commissar Brantine had informed Artemius that the inquisitor and his retinue had absconded from the planetary capital. The inquisitor's distinctive Chimera transport was last seen rolling out of the city's south gate and turning east.

So, the inquisitor had given himself a head-start, though what he hoped to gain by it remained a mystery.

How did the old crow know we made for Marakross? The colonel and the commissar would not have betrayed my confidence.

'Interrogator-Chaplain,' said Brother Balthur as he slowed the Rhino, 'we're coming up on the forest.'

'Very well,' said Artemius. He opened a vox-channel to his men in both Rhinos and said, 'Dark Angels, prepare to debark. From here, we travel on foot.'

THE SUN SANK at the Dark Angels' backs, casting its orange glow across the land, throwing out the last of its rays before night came to leech the heat from the ground. Artemius's small force – two tactical squads, each of nine Marines from the sixth company, plus Brother-Apothecary Tarros – moved through the forest. In the sky above, the stars winked on like lights, and Cordassa's egg-shaped moon, ahl-Goluss, began its journey across the heavens.

Artemius could see none of this, however, as the wide circular chloroplates of the trees overlapped each other to form an impenetrable canopy.

The Dark Angels moved swiftly, marching between the thick white boles, their genetically enhanced eyesight attuned to the slightest movement in the deep shadows ahead.

Hours passed, with only the sound of booted feet marching on hard ground.

Then, at the head of the column, Artemius suddenly halted. Between the trunks ahead sat confirmation of his grim expectations. In a small clearing, shrouded in the darkness, unwilling to make a fire that might give their position away to the enemy, Inquisitor Heiron waited with his bizarre retinue.

Artemius motioned for his Space Marines to ring the interlopers and close on them from behind. But before any of the Dark Angels had moved from cover, a familiar voice called out: 'Don't bother trying to take us unawares, Interrogator-Chaplain. It's about time you and your men showed up. My patience has its limits.'

Damn the man's arrogance. His attention may be unavoidable, but it complicates my mission beyond tolerance.

Artemius walked forward into the clearing.

'Should we risk a little light?' asked Inquisitor Heiron.

'Not on my account, inquisitor,' replied Artemius. 'I can see you and your people well enough, would that I could not. What in the Emperor's name do you think you are doing out here?'

'You know full well, Astartes, that we have been waiting for *you*. I've sought entry into Marakross for quite some time. It never occurred to me to request a Space Marine force for the purpose. And here you've fallen right into my lap. The Emperor smiles upon me. But I forget my manners – introductions are in order.'

Artemius growled at the seated inquisitor.

Heiron, who had looked so frail to Artemius back in his palatial apartment, had donned black power armour bearing the Inquisitorial 'I'. The workmanship was exquisite. Even in the shadows, Artemius could see intricate gold filigree describing holy symbols and scripture across the suit's massive pauldrons. Inquisitorial rosettes and purity seals hung from Heiron's breastplate. In one hand, he held an ornate las-pistol; a power sword hung from a scabbard at his waist.

'I have neither the time nor the inclination, inquisitor,' said Artemius.

'Nevertheless,' said the inquisitor, undaunted. He gestured to a large pale figure on his far left and said, 'Biggest first, I think. This is Klegg 66.'

The man was a brute, as big as any Astartes, though his raw bulk was less refined. Size aside, this was no ordinary man. His head was enclosed in a pacifier helm – a complex mask of titanium and plastic tubing. Through the tubes coursed hormones, stimulants and suppressants. His fingers had been replaced with thick adamantine claws terminating in razor-sharp points. This living puppet was the inquisitor's notorious arco-flagellant.

To the left of the giant slave sat a hooded man, cloaked in the robes of the Adeptus Mechanicus. 'Tech-Adept Ossio,' said the inquisitor, 'of the Machine Cult.'

Ossio's unblinking eye-lenses stared at Artemius over the apparatus of a complicated rebreather. From the tech-adept's back rose powerful twin mechadentrites – the invaluable mechanical appendages so beloved of the servants of the Machine God.

On the inquisitor's right sat a scar-faced veteran of the Imperial Guard. This man was almost as old as the inquisitor himself, though far more robust. 'Major-General Adaemus Goodwin,' said Heiron.

The old veteran stood and bowed formally to the Space Marine Chaplain and said, 'Formerly of the 112th Cadian regiment. I've fought alongside the Dark Angels before, Interrogator-Chaplain. I'll be honoured to do so again.'

'I've heard of you, major-general,' replied Artemius. 'Your solid reputation precedes you. But I'm afraid you've been misled. We've no intention of fighting alongside anyone during this operation. The inquisitor makes a grave error if he thinks I've come to facilitate his work.'

The major-general glanced at the inquisitor. Heiron waved off the comment and proceeded with his final introduction.

'This,' he said with evident pride as he indicated a thin woman of middle years in robes of dark purple, 'is Orphia LeGrange of the Adeptus Astropathica.'

The woman sat with her back to a tree trunk, playing with an Imperial tarot deck, seemingly uninterested in the Interrogator-Chaplain.

This is how he knew our destination. She must have plucked the information from the mind of the commissar or the Cordassan colonel.

The psyker LeGrange radiated power. Artemius could feel the faint touch of her mind brushing against his psychic defences, looking for chinks in his mental armour. Looking for the things that had brought him here.

His thoughts turned to his brother Space Marines, unprotected from such intrusions. Though withholding the truth from his brothers sat most unwell with Artemius, the presence of Heiron's psyker only highlighted the necessity for secrecy.

Secrets are the progenitors of all lies. But if these brothers from Sixth Company knew of our quarry, this psyker would have it from them. The shame of our Chapter would be known throughout the Imperium.

No. I have watched brothers fight and die for causes they could not comprehend. The honour of the Dark Angels must be served and the stain removed forever.

Artemius raised his bolt pistol, aiming at the psyker, and said, 'Probe my head and we shall see what the inside of yours looks like. Do you understand?'

'Come now, Interrogator-Chaplain' said the inquisitor, rising slowly. 'There's no need for that. Besides,' he continued with a grin, 'I don't think you want to shoot the one person who can get us inside. Do you?'

It didn't take long.

Artemius had little choice. From the cover of the tree line, shrouded in midnight shadows, he surveyed the great perimeter wall of Marakross and knew Heiron's words for truth: the only weakpoint in the city's defences lay in the minds of the defenders themselves.

That was the territory of Orphia LeGrange.

Silvery moonlight lit the scene before him. From the large water gate in the middle of the city wall, the Immen issued forth. Tonnes of water roared and crashed in great spumes at the start of a journey that ran all the way back to the planetary capital and beyond. It seemed inconceivable that, in the presence of all this water, the people of Scala lay dying of thirst. The taint was invisible; the water appeared to promise life itself. But this foaming torrent brought only death.

Death was written all over the curtain wall, too. Hundreds of the city's civilian inhabitants had been hung from high battlements on lengths of rusting chain. Many of the sun-shrivelled corpses were missing heads or limbs. Their pierced bodies had spilled blood down the height of the wall, streaking the smooth white stone, staining it red-brown.

In that same blood, hideous glyphs had been daubed at the base – a circle pierced by arrow-headed spokes radiating from a central hub.

The Star of Chaos.

There were other markings, most unfamiliar to Artemius, though all were equally offensive in their obvious dedication to the dark gods of the warp. One among them caught his eye, repeated over and over along the broad surface – three circles in triangular formation linked by two angled strokes, all set against a greater circle.

Worshippers of Nurgle – master of disease and bodily corruption. The traitor has allied himself with the God of Decay.

'Well?' whispered Inquisitor Heiron from behind Artemius. 'Do you agree? Only by working together may we breach the city.'

Artemius turned his gaze to the high battlements. Gun towers adorned the crest of the wall, equipped with heavy bolters. Searchlights swept the broad killing ground between the tree line and the main gate.

No chance of rushing that gate without taking heavy casualties. Even then, those doors are solid. Without tripping the mechanism from inside, no one is getting through. How many melta bombs would it take to burn a hole in plasteel that thick? And we have none.

Not for the first time, Artemius lamented the departure of the Dark Angels' battleship *The Relentless* from orbit. Lance batteries would have breached the wall without difficulty.

There was nothing for it. No other way.

The inquisitor's plan was sound, Emperor damn him.

Massi ut-Houda was sitting in the lamp-lit gloom of his gun tower, fingering a pictograph of his dead wife, when he heard his com unit crackle and hiss.

'Open the gate, quickly!' ordered a voice through the static. 'All wall-gunners to stand down.'

'On whose orders?' asked another on the same channel.

'On the Master's, fool. Can't you see him approaching the gate?'

'The Master? Truly?' said ut-Houda excitedly.

He longed to meet the Merciful Lord in person. Ut-Houda, born and raised in Marakross, had always suffered a less-than-solid immune system. He'd contracted plague earlier than most. As the disease ate away at the flesh of his face, his young wife had abandoned him. A family friend had come to him with talk of a man who could offer salvation.

One need only follow the teachings of the Merciful Lord to be saved from death. Ut-Houda, terrified of his own mortality, had followed his friend's instructions and pledged his soul to the God of Rot, begging for clemency. After all, what was a soul worth? A life could be felt and lived, but a soul was such an intangible thing.

His face had become bloated and strange, so disgusting that he'd smashed every mirror in his hab. But while countless others had died moaning and wailing in pools of their own filth, ut-Houda had lived on. Itchy, scratchy, sticky and smelly, but very much alive.

He bore one regret: when the cult rose up to take Marakross for themselves, ut-Houda, driven by feelings of rage and shame, had slaughtered his wife and her family.

He'd skinned them, boiled them and shared their flesh with the others.

He rose from his chair and limped to his post. From beside the mounted heavy bolter, he peered down towards the base of the wall. In the black of night, the searchlights had picked out two figures moving slowly across the killing ground. One, a dark giant whose armour bore the accursed eagle of the false Emperor, was bent over, moving as if wounded.

'Death to the enemies of great Nurgle,' spat ut-Houda, his heart filled with contempt.

The figure at the rear held a whirring chainblade at his captive's back, pushing him forward with his other hand. He was everything ut-Houda had imagined him to be. This was the Merciful Lord in all his splendour. How much taller he stood than the Imperial slave. How glorious he looked, his black armour shining in the searchlights. Ut-Houda felt his lord's uplifting presence wash over him from below.

'Open the gates, my faithful,' said a voice over the comm. 'I have captured a son of the false Emperor.' It was the voice from ut-Houda's dreams. At last, the disfigured cultist would meet the saviour whose teachings had spared him a painful, miserable death. 'Open the gates at once,' came the glorious voice once more. 'Tonight, we share in the desecration and consumption of enemy flesh.'

Along nearby sections of the wall, cultists were abandoning their posts to rush to the city gates, eager to greet their saviour. Ut-Houda turned and hobbled as fast as he could down the tower stairs shouting, 'Open the gates! Open the gates!'

* * *

ARTEMIUS WATCHED INTENTLY from the tree line as Brother-Sergeant Syriel and Brother Phaeton acted out their parts. The watching Dark Angels tensed, ready to break cover and rush the gates early should the psyker's illusion fail.

Beside Artemius, Inquisitor Heiron looked down at Orphia LeGrange with obvious concern. Her veins were bulging with the effort of deceiving a hundred pairs of eyes. Thin rivulets of blood trickled from her nose and ears. Just a little longer. It helped that the cultists were so eager to believe the illusion. If Orphia could just get the two Space Marines inside….

Artemius raised a hand to the inquisitor's armoured shoulder. 'They're in,' he whispered.

All else rested with two brave Dark Angels.

THE MOMENT THE Merciful Lord entered behind the prisoner, the assembled cultists fell to their knees, pressing their scabbed foreheads to the ground. Though each longed to gaze at the face of their lord, none dared until bidden.

And yet, something wasn't right.

As ut-Houda held himself prostrate, he felt something change – something elusive. He wasn't sure when, but all sense of a sacred presence had disappeared. He raised his wretched face from the rockcrete, no longer feeling so awed. His eyes met the broad barrel of a boltgun.

'I am protected,' he said to the massive Imperial slave standing over him. 'The Merciful Lord has granted me immortality.'

'Let's put that to the test,' rumbled Brother-Sergeant Syriel.

Death erupted all around.

'THAT'S IT,' BARKED Artemius on all channels. 'Forward, my brothers!'

Dark Angels exploded from the tree line, charging towards the open gate. Artemius's feet pounded on the hard-baked earth as he raced forward. The psyker's manipulation had only stretched to the area immediately around the city gate. Now that gunshots had been fired, it wouldn't be long until the Traitor hordes began filling the streets. So be it; the Space Marines preferred a pitched battle. Stealth was for scouts and assassins. With hours of night time remaining, the Astartes held the advantage. Their gene-boosted vision, augmented by helmet-visor displays, rendered the midnight streets in daytime clarity.

As the last of the Dark Angels passed the walls, Artemius turned to order the gate locked. Leaving the inquisitor outside would be the smoothest way to ensure his non-interference. But, as he turned, he saw the inquisitor step through the gates followed closely by his people. The exhausted psyker LeGrange was draped over the back of Major-General Goodwin.

Artemius cursed.

'Most dramatic,' said the inquisitor as he surveyed the pile of cultist corpses left by Syriel and Phaeton. 'Mutation appears to be rampant among members of the cult.' The inquisitor kicked a headless corpse from his path – its seven-fingered hand gripped an old pictograph of a smiling woman. 'What do you propose, Interrogator-Chaplain, now that we are finally inside?'

The Dark Angels moved to positions of cover. Brother-Sergeant Ogion sealed the gates, destroying the control mechanism. None in, none out.

'I propose, inquisitor,' said Artemius, 'that we separate. Seek your objective without my interference, and I will seek mine. You have my gratitude for the assistance of your psyker.'

'Not a chance,' said Inquisitor Heiron, grinning at the absurdity of the suggestion. 'Your presence is the very reason I dared finally breach these walls. A Space Marine escort is our only chance of survival in this place. I intend to stay very close indeed. I'm afraid you're stuck with us, Interrogator-Chaplain. Unless you wish to commit treason with the murder of faithful Imperial servants.'

Don't tempt me, Heiron. Hounding me invites death among your people. Should any uncover my purpose here, a bolt-shell will find them. The Inquisition will never have proof of its suspicions.

Still slung over the back of the veteran Guardsman, the psyker LeGrange stirred and said, 'On the far side of the city, I sense a presence dark and sick and terrible.'

That was all Artemius needed.

The Dark Angels moved off at speed.

It is as you said, Corvus. Here at last, we have caught up with him. The traitor will know retribution, at last.

ALARMS ECHOED THROUGH the ruined streets as the Dark Angels moved from cover to cover, scouring the darkness for hints of movement.

Many of the buildings were pocked from the spray of autocannons. No doubt the Praeto Marakross had fought bravely, but the traitor leader boasted almost ten millennia of experience in war. It couldn't have been a fair fight.

On the main streets, many of the corner buildings stood half demolished. Their crumbling facades testified to the ferocity of the conflict. Some were burned out, but the smoke had ceased rising long ago.

Artemius knew the enemy would have prioritised the taking of all praeto precinct buildings. If even one of those precincts was receiving surveillance pict-feeds, the Dark Angels were being watched even now.

A flash lit the streets behind the Dark Angels, followed by the deafening bark of a krak-grenade. Brothers

Thracius and Marhod had run trip-lines between a number of buildings as their brothers pressed on. The cultist horde had picked up their trail and quickly learned how unwise it was to try taking Dark Angels from behind.

Artemius glanced backwards. Despite the pace, the Inquisitorial team was still there, running with great effort at the back of the column. Major-General Goodwin had passed the exhausted female psyker to the massive Klegg 66, but the monster's razored hands had already opened a number of small cuts on her back as he ran.

Artemius sighed and opened a channel to Brother-Sergeant Syriel. 'Assign a brother to carry the inquisitor's psyker before she bleeds to death on the arco-flagellant's back.'

'Immediately, Interrogator-Chaplain.'

Brother Oltos broke ranks and jogged back to the rear of the column. He lifted LeGrange from Klegg 66's wide shoulders, placed her across his own, and resumed his run.

Like any densely packed city, Marakross presented a maze of streets to confound the newcomers. Corners and alleyways were littered with the bones of murdered civilians. Banners of tattered human flesh, painted with sickening sigils, hung limp in the still night air. At street level, many of the walls had been decorated in blood.

The air was thick with flies and a dead-meat stench.

Having memorised the orbital pict-files from his dataslate, Artemius led his men, and by default the inquisitor's retinue, unerringly towards the far side of the city. From this distance, the crashing of the falls could be heard as an unending white noise that drew them on.

Crossing the city's bridges and wide intersections presented the greatest problem. Artemius's auspex showed cultists occupying buildings with good positioning over the streets below.

Snipers on the upper floors and roofs. They'll have raided the precinct armouries.

At the first such crossing, Artemius ordered Syrius and Ogion to pick a single man from each of their squads. Then, he turned to the inquisitor and said, 'If we wish to cross these wide roads, we'll have to take out their watchmen. I want you and your people to dig in and stay hidden until my brothers have cleared the way.'

'That would be a damned waste,' replied Heiron. 'Both Goodwin and Ossio have augmetic eyes and are damned fine shots. Why not use snipers against snipers?'

'As far as I am concerned, inquisitor, this is entirely a Dark Angels operation. I'll not presume to issue orders to your people save to keep them out of our way. If you wish your men to draw enemy fire, I will not object. It would provide a convenient decoy, if nothing else. Are you so willing to sacrifice two of your men?'

The inquisitor paused.

'I thought not,' said Artemius. 'Let the Dark Angels deal with this. Besides, your people need to catch their breath.'

'Don't take us too lightly, Interrogator-Chaplain,' growled Heiron. 'You'll yet see what we're made of, I assure you.'

But Artemius was already turning to give orders to his Marines.

BROTHER METHANDES WASN'T built for stealth. He was large, even for an Astartes, but he moved slowly and surely up the stone stairs, mindful of traps and alarms that might give him away.

Twice he noticed thin wires strung across the stairwell and stepped cautiously over them before moving on. A lone streetlamp buzzed and flickered outside, throwing orange light through shattered windows. For a moment, Methandes's shadow was thrown onto the facing wall. Then the streetlight gave a final electrical death-croak, and blinked out.

He reached the top of the stairs and crossed to the only doorway on the landing. He peered into a wide room. Though the interior was utterly black, Methandes's superior vision picked out the sniper immediately. And more besides.

The man had scattered shards of broken glass around the doorway so that none could take his back unawares. This sniper was no civilian cultist; he was probably a traitor praeto.

Methandes crouched silently, waiting for the pre-arranged signal.

There!

The dark walls flashed bright white as a krak-grenade detonated in the middle of the intersection below.

The sniper reeled back from the window-ledge, blinded by the flash, hands held up to his eyes.

Methandes surged forward and plunged the saw-toothed blade of his close-combat knife deep into the back of the cultist. When the big Space Marine pulled the knife out, the sniper's torso was almost ripped in two.

Before the carcass had even struck the floor, Methandes had dropped his knife and raised his bolter. His hololithic visor-display zoomed in on the roof of the opposite building.

There, shaking his head, desperate to regain his sight, was another sniper. Methandes's bolter gave a single, angry bark, and the cultist's head exploded, leaving a dark, wet mist.

'West corner cleared. North corner cleared,' said Methandes into his comm.

'South corner cleared. East corner cleared,' crackled another voice.

'Good work,' voxed the Interrogator-Chaplain. 'Check your scanners. We have large mobs converging on this position. I want supporting fire from above. Frag-grenades at your discretion.'

'Yes, brother,' replied Methandes. He turned to retrieve his knife, sheathed it and checked the magazine in his bolter.

On the street below, a mob of thousands roared as it pressed towards the intersection. Ugly, twisted faces screamed and laughed in the glow of flaming brands. Madmen fired wild shots into the air, wasting ammunition in their excitement and lust for blood. Some among the heretics carried tattered standards of human skin.

Methandes placed a booted foot on the windowsill, took aim, and said to himself, 'They shall know His wrath. Lion, guide my bolts. Let me smite the enemy in His name.'

His bolter rained death from above.

GUIDED BY THE Interrogator-Chaplain and the maps on his data-slate, the Dark Angels pushed onwards through the city. They faced an enemy that outnumbered them thousands-to-one and, inevitably, there were casualties among their number.

Brothers Kyrris and Lanidei fell to suicidal cultists strapped with stolen meltabombs, but they did not sell their lives cheaply. Throwing themselves at the bombers, the brave Space Marines held them back. The detonations vapourised hundreds of cultists and cooked the selfless Astartes alive in the shells of their armour. Their sacrifice spared the Chapter a much heavier loss. The Space Marines turned and made the surviving heretics pay. Apothecary Tarros removed the progenoid glands of his dead brothers with great reverence. Artemius committed the two brave souls into the care of the Immortal Emperor.

'None that die in his name die in vain,' he told his Space Marines as they saluted their dead brothers. 'Ogion, have the bodies concealed. When the battle is won, we will take them to be interred in the Tower of Angels.'

During a skirmish in a broad market square, Brother Oltos fell to concentrated las-fire as he covered the retreat of the inquisitor's retinue. The Dark Angels took bloody and vicious revenge on those responsible. Even Heiron had difficulty stomaching the brutality of the response.

The psyker Legrange knelt weeping over the Space Marine's body until the inquisitor gently pulled her away. Oltos had carried her on his back after her psychic efforts gained them entry.

Now he was gone.

But the Dark Angels could allow no grief to weigh them down as they pressed on. Instead, they opened their hearts and minds to a howling anger, and unleashed even greater fury on those who opposed them.

Inquisitor Heiron marvelled at their speed and savagery. His own people fought hard alongside the Astartes, but the only member of his retinue to even approach the lowest number of kills among the Dark Angels was the mindless Klegg 66.

The arco-flagellant threw himself into the deepest knots of mutated cultists at a single word from Heiron's lips, unmindful of the cuts and bullet wounds that marked his pale flesh. His razor-sharp adamantine talons raked the gibbering hordes of the damned. Klegg 66 loosed no battle-roar – not a single word – as he hurled the broken bodies of his master's enemies high into the air.

As night gave way to the coming of day, the Astartes finally broke free from the maze of city streets. They had reached the falls of Marakross.

Artemius imagined he could smell his enemy on the air – a rancid, nauseating latrine stink. 'Inquisitor,' he called, beckoning the old man forward. Together, they crouched in the shadow of a burned-out warehouse. Artemius pointed, watching as the inquisitor gaped. There, reaching up to the sky, stood the vast white wall of the Marakrossian dam.

'Quite something,' said Artemius.

Inquisitor Heiron nodded wordlessly.

The great concave surface of the dam stretched all the way to the top of the escarpment, almost two kilometres tall. A third of the way up the wall, at a height of about seven hundred metres, outflow pipes disgorged tons of foaming white water that crashed to the man-made lake below with a ceaseless roar. A cool wet mist rose from the pounded surface of the lake and drifted across the rockcrete quayside.

Canals spread out from the water's edge, many blocked by closed flow-gates during the dry season. These would be opened at other times of the year to prevent the lake breaking its artificial banks. Warehouses and manufactories were abundant on the quayside, dominated on the north-west bank by the cyclopean bulk of the hydropower station, and on the south-east bank by a desecrated Imperial cathedral.

Artemius saw the inquisitor's face flush red with rage as he looked upon what the cultists had done to the Sacred House of the Emperor. The gold eagle had been torn from the stone face of the building. It lay on the ground, covered in mounds of human excrement about which buzzed clouds of fat black flies.

In its place there hung the twisted sigil of Chaos, wrought from human bones, bound together with bloodstained razorwire, adorned with sun-bleached skulls. From the cathedral's many spires swung the desiccated bodies of hundreds of sacrificed Marakrossi.

'We have come almost to the end of our journey,' said Artemius, 'and I must reiterate my earlier warning, inquisitor. It is imperative that you do not interfere in Dark Angel affairs.'

Before Heiron could respond, Orphia LeGrange spoke from nearby. 'Lord,' she said, 'it is here, the dark and terrible presence.' The woman looked pale. Her hands were shaking.

'Will you not level with me now, Astartes?' said Heiron to Artemius. The Interrogator-Chaplain's expression was masked by his fearsome skull-helm, but the tension he radiated was palpable.

'Something unnatural,' whispered the female psyker, 'cloaked in absolute evil.' She gasped and turned her head in all directions, searching frantically. 'He sees us even now!'

Heiron's gauntleted hands took hold of LeGrange's own as he said, 'Go back among the Dark Angels. They will not let you fall.'

Artemius said nothing.

The psyker walked back down the line on unsteady legs.

'She is not ready for this,' said Heiron to himself. 'The evil here is overwhelming her.'

'You should take your own advice, inquisitor,' said Artemius. 'Stay among my Space Marines. Fight at their side. Your survival depends on it.'

Artemius saw the traitor's plan: the hunted had laid a trap for the hunter. The traitor had chosen this site for their confrontation, knowing that the Dark Angels would be pressed back, right to the water's edge. There was nowhere else to go. His auspex showed massed bio-signs converging on them from every part of the city. A full attack had been ordered now that daylight had robbed the Astartes of their night-vision advantage.

I alone must face the traitor. I alone can bring redemption to our Chapter. My brothers must guard my back. The inquisitor and his people must be kept busy with the mad horde.

It would be foolish to play the traitor's game, to fight on the open quayside. Ammunition was running low; they weren't carrying anywhere near enough for a sustained firefight against such numbers.

'Brothers,' voxed Artemius, 'the slaves of Chaos are amassing at our backs. Move in twos, protect each other. Brother-Sergeants Syriel and Ogion, you have squad command. I want everyone in position on nearby rooftops and high balconies. Try to force the enemy into bottlenecks and utilise your grenades.'

'Yes, Interrogator-Chaplain' replied the brother-sergeants simultaneously.

'I must conduct the business with which I have been charged. Cover me, brothers. Let no heretic dog slip through to take my back.'

The dark-green colossi bowed to their leader.

'The Emperor is watching over us,' continued Artemius. He felt righteous zeal wash over him as he spoke. 'The Lion stalks beside us. His fangs shall pierce, his claws shall tear. You are those fangs. You are those claws. Let the Emperor's wrath fill you. May every one of you be a storm of death descending on the enemy in His Name.'

'In His name,' came the group response.

'Bless your weapons, brothers.' Artemius turned to the inquisitor and said, 'Take cover, inquisitor, for now the battle truly begins.'

Don't make me kill you, Heiron. Don't make it a battle of wills.

* * *

Behind him, even over the roar of the falls, Artemius could hear the constant screaming of the dying cultists, the sharp crack of grenades, and the ceaseless low barking of Space Marine bolters as his brothers punished the Chaos horde. But despite the great cacophony, his every sense was focused like a laser on the figure that threw open the double-doors of the desecrated Imperial cathedral and marched across the quayside towards him.

'You've caught up with me at last, little brother,' rumbled the figure. The words came, not from his jawless ruin of a face, but from vox-speakers sunk into corrupted power armour. Even through speakers, the voice was wet and sickly. 'I only had to wait here on this planet for, oh, about a year.'

'I almost had you on Tranteth V,' replied Artemius. His stomach was knotted with all the hatred he carried for this blasphemous figure. 'If you hadn't bombed that bridge...'

They stood face to face in front of the cascading water.

Artemius was tall, but the traitor was even taller.

Borroleth the Corruptor. Borroleth the Fallen. Traitor Captain, servant of Nurgle the Unclean. Finally, it ends.

The sun peeked from the rim of the high cliffs, painting the figure before Artemius in disgusting detail. The Chaos Space Marine wore black ceramite covered with pustules and blisters as if, somehow, the hard surface were subject to the same diseases as his rotting face.

Borroleth's shoulders and knees were adorned with leering daemonic faces carved from the bones of his victims. Some of those victims had been Artemius's brother Astartes.

A cape of tattered human skin hung from the monster's back – faces flensed from the dead and sewn together.

'My appearance pleases you,' laughed the Fallen.

I must try. It is my duty to try. If he can be made to repent, perhaps he will guide us to the others. Perhaps...

'Your appearance saddens me and sickens me,' said Artemius. 'You were once a chosen son of the Emperor Himself. You stood beside the Lion, the primarch. Your deeds shone in the annals of our Chapter. How could you have come to this? How could you have fallen so far?'

Again, that wet chuckle rendered toneless through the vox-speakers. 'You wish me to repent. I see those black pearls on your rosarius. How deeply you desire to add another. The desire consumes you. We are not so different. I too feel powerful desires.'

'What could such a wretched being desire but to return to the light of the Holy Emperor? Do you not wish to bask in his forgiveness? You can be redeemed, fallen one. I can offer you this.'

The Traitor Marine's brow creased in a scowl, bursting fat pustules that dotted his head. Pus ebbed slowly out and down over his rotting features.

'Forgiveness for what? For surviving? When Caliban was sundered, I was cast into the warp, there to die in the jaws of unspeakable things. But the Master of All Decay found me, saved me, and bestowed his great gifts upon me. While your pathetic false god gasps for every breath, kept barely alive by machines and sacrifices, the Lord of Rot has granted me immortality. Ten thousand years have I lived, and for ten thousand more shall I dedicate myself to the undoing of your precious Imperium! Even now, the Dark Angels couch their actions in lies, and yet you talk of light and redemption. Hypocrite! Your brothers die behind you, the truth kept from them. Your guilt gnaws at you, burning in your heart, eating you alive. You are sick of the charade, are you not? How long can Azrael and Ezekiel prolong this unworthy deceit?'

I must not let his words reach me. He merely seeks to undo my will. I shall not listen...

The stinking figure glanced over Artemius's shoulder, laughed again and said, 'Here comes another who lives by lies. Here comes another filled with hypocrisy. Another pathetic dog lapping eagerly at the vomit of your crippled, incontinent false Emperor.'

Artemius heard several pairs of booted feet on the rockcrete. He knew without turning that the inquisitor and his people were approaching.

'So this is your quarry, Interrogator-Chaplain,' said Heiron.

'Welcome to our little family gathering,' rumbled Borroleth.

Behind the inquisitor, LeGrange was vomiting violently, unable to tolerate such proximity to the Chaos Marine's malign aura. Tech-Adept Ossio stood unable even to look upon the disgusting abomination.

'Family gathering?' said Inquisitor Heiron. He glanced at Artemius.

Artemius watched in disgust as the jawless Traitor tried to smile.

Time is up, inquisitor. I warned you not to get in my way. I have to take the traitor alive. All else is meaningless. You should have stayed with my brothers.

Artemius moved forward in a blur, his fist flashing out at the Traitor Space Marine's face. Borroleth caught the strike on a massive armoured forearm and countered, kicking Artemius hard in his plated abdomen. As Artemius was thrown backwards with the force of the blow, he lashed his foot out at the traitor's weapon, sending it clattering to the rockcrete before it skittered over the edge of the quayside and into the lake.

The traitor screamed with rage, a sound like grinding metal, at the loss of his ancient bolter. He moved towards Artemius, raising a booted foot to stomp on his skull-helm.

A las-blast caught the Fallen on the shoulder. At such close range, the blast punched right through the traitor's black ceramite pauldron to the diseased flesh below, sending him reeling backwards.

Artemius looked up. Heiron's laspistol hissed as it cooled.

Borroleth howled and spun, sprinting for the doors of the defiled church. On Heiron's order, the inquisitor's retinue gave chase.

'No!' barked Artemius. He leapt to his feet and sprinted after them, but as he began to close the distance, something huge exploded from the water, almost knocking him over.

Artemius leapt backwards and rolled to his feet, drawing his bolt pistol. He smacked a gauntlet to his chest, activating the power-conversion field of the sacred rosarius that hung from his neck.

There before him, writhing and squirming on the rockcrete quay, was a bloated abomination to rival even the horror of Borroleth the Fallen.

Its fat white body was sectioned like a great maggot over thirty metres long. Each fleshy segment was ringed with obscene, pink-lipped mouths from which poured stinking torrents of effluence. Rockcrete bubbled and hissed where the acrid brown liquid splashed the ground.

This, then, is the source of the Scalan plague?

Artemius tried to dash around it, desperate to prevent a dialogue between the inquisitor and the Fallen, but the creature vomited at him every time he moved.

Artemius fired his bolter into the fat flesh. Shells thundered into the soft body leaving holes as large as fists, but though high screams sounded from many of the mouths, the beast continued to writhe and vomit and block the Dark Angel from his prey.

No time to find another way around. Let us see how you handle this.

Artemius fired again and again into the creature's body, this time grouping his shots, opening a wide, bloody hole in the pallid tissue. Gouts of blood splashed the ground, mixing with the brown excreta.

Artemius pulled a frag-grenade from his belt, tore out the pin and hurled it into the open wound.

Seeing this, the monstrosity began shifting its weight, writhing frantically, trying to roll towards Artemius with some vague plan of crushing him or catching him in the blast.

But the thing was too slow.

There was a muffled boom and a section in the middle of the beast exploded outwards.

Artemius threw himself down.

A foul brown mist descended, hissing where it touched his armour. But Artemius had no time to worry about that. The creature was still alive, or rather, it was now two creatures, each severed part squirming and screaming with a life of its own.

Artemius sprinted through the space he'd created in the massive body, too fast for the fiend to bring its jets of vomit to bear.

Within seconds he reached the double doors of the cathedral. He raced through.

Don't let it be too late.

The scene that lay before him stopped Artemius dead in his tracks.

HOT SUNLIGHT FILTERED through holes blasted in the high vaulted ceiling and through the shattered remains of intricate stained-glass windows. The remains of smashed wooden pews littered the stone floor. Dust motes sparkled and danced in the air.

Framed in the golden light, Inquisitor Mattius Heiron stood, breathing hard, with his humming power sword pressed to the neck of the Chaos Space Marine.

Borroleth the Fallen knelt only metres from Artemius. Blood poured in streams from great jagged rents in his ancient armour. Flesh had been cut from his cheeks and hung in raw, bloody flaps at his neck.

How did they…

Then, Artemius saw how.

Even now, the inquisitor's powerful arco-flagellant, Klegg 66, lay slowly dying, his life running in red streams from grievous wounds.

Ossio, the servant of the Machine God, had had his augmentations torn from his body in the battle. Parts both mechanical and biological lay where they had landed on the floor. He had been spread over quite an area.

Of the old veteran Guardsman, there was no immediate sign.

But the psyker LeGrange was there. She lay unmoving on her back, her eyes rolled up into her head, her skin discoloured where blood vessels had ruptured during her psychic assault on the traitor.

Artemius reached up and removed his skull-helm. He locked eyes with the inquisitor. There was no victory, no gloating, in the inquisitor's glare. Only bitterness, regret, hatred.

Hatred towards whom?

'So,' said Heiron through gritted teeth, 'the Inquisition achieves what the Dark Angels could not. And it seems I hold all the cards at last, Interrogator-Chaplain. Would that we could have worked together. However, the book belongs with the Ordo Malleus.

Explain to me now what business the Dark Angels have with such a thing?'

He thinks we came for a book?

'What book?' asked Artemius.

'You still play games? It belongs with the Inquisition, you must see that. Molchoi's *Liber Nefestum* is of great value to the forces of Chaos. My order will turn that very power against them for the glory of the Golden Throne.'

There came again that toneless laugh from one remaining undamaged vox-speaker on the traitor's chest. 'He thinks you came for the book,' gurgled Borroleth. 'Let me live, inquisitor, and I will give you the book and much more besides. I will tell you of the Dark Angels. You think them heretics? Ah, let me share their deepest secrets.'

So, Brother Corvus, now comes the moment of choice about which you would not instruct me. I must choose which path to take. Our secret has brought me to this. Who shall it be: the traitor or the old fool?

'And just how would you know the deepest secrets of the Dark Angels, treacherous dog?' asked Heiron.

The question was never answered.

The deep crack of a gunshot echoed off the walls of the desecrated sanctuary.

A single fat, brass shell-casing rang like a tiny bell as it struck the stone floor.

Thick blood and gore spattered Inquisitor Heiron's face. He gasped and tossed his head, unable to see, trying to shake the blood from his eyes.

Where Borroleth's head had been, only a stump of flesh and exposed spine remained. The Chaos Space Marine fell lifelessly forward.

Forgive me, brothers. I could not kill the inquisitor. Detest him as I may, I cannot stain our honour further with such a death.

So it ended – years of hunting, years of obsession. Borroleth the Corruptor, Fallen One and Traitor Captain, was no more.

Artemius turned and strode from the cathedral, his sacred rosarius unusually heavy around his neck. The two black pearls he'd already earned winked at him in the sunlight, taunting him. Behind him, Heiron roared with rage.

'This is only the beginning, Interrogator-Chaplain. I will bring the resources of the Inquisition to bear on your Chapter. If you are engaged in heresy, I will uncover it. Do you hear me? You have my word on that, Astartes.'

Keep your damned word to yourself.

OF AN INITIAL force of twenty Dark Angels, seventeen remained alive after the operation on Cordassa. The dead were brothers Artemius had known all his life. These heroes were interred in the Tower of Angels, where their names joined so many others in the Books of Remembrance and Honour.

Though Marakross was purged, Artemius could never come to see it as a victory.

He kept his oath to Colonel ut-Halarr of the Cordassan Guard. The Dark Angels saw to the destruction of the foul Chaos abomination that had tainted the water supply. They burned its screaming, vomiting body with promethium.

Upon returning to Scala, Artemius discovered that Colonel ut-Halarr had died, victim of a lasgun blast to the head. Commissar Brantine had survived to bury his friend and companion. The city was under full siege from the planet's Traitor Legions, but the morale of the local forces had returned with the end of the plague and the renewed flow of drinkable water. The Cordassan Guard dug themselves in and prepared for a long fight.

Heiron hadn't given up searching for his unholy book. The man was convinced it was hidden somewhere in Marakross. Of his retinue, only Major-General Goodwin survived, having stayed among the Dark Angels during the final battle. Heiron dedicated himself to pushing back the enemy, buying more time to search for the accursed *Liber Nefestum*.

As his gunship lifted into the air above the spaceport of Scala, bound for high-orbital rendezvous with the Dark Angels cruiser, *The Relentless*, Artemius prepared to explain his failure to his Deathwing brothers.

How much might Borroleth have divulged under the Blades of Reason. How many of the Fallen might he have given us? Emperor, save us from the meddling of the damnable Inquisition.

He gazed at his brother Astartes sitting silently with their thoughts. He could not tell them what the sacrifice of their brothers meant. Only the Deathwing could ever know. And yet, these survivors would do it all over again without complaint, go through hell on the order of their grand master, never needing a greater motive than to serve the honour of their Chapter.

That is what it means to be a Dark Angel.

VINDICARE
CS Goto

THE ROCK CUT into her thigh, pinching a long crease into the synskin that enwrapped her body like a membrane. Beneath the clinging rubberised suit, a trickle of blood seeped out of the pressure wound, but she ignored it. She could feel the delicate chill of the dawn breeze as it breathed over her, caressing each tiny bead of dew and creating minute, silent cascades down her taut muscles. Shifting her weight slightly, to ease the tension in her leg, she pressed her back against the moist stone surface behind her. As she moved, a fragment of rock worked itself loose from the cliff and bounced down towards the ground, sending tiny rains of dust sprinkling into the morning air. Nyjia held her breath, cursing herself inwardly – that was an amateur's mistake. But there was nobody there to notice her error, and she exhaled quietly, letting the tension release from her body.

The dawn brought some welcome heat to her muscles, warming her body and making her privations more bearable. She could feel the energy of the sun beginning to soak into the chemicals of her membranous armour, thawing her frigid limbs and returning suppleness to her carefully set joints, feeding her organs with nutrients. For the sleepless Assassin, the morning was a refreshing respite. She had been jammed into the crevice since the Imperial Guard rode out to confront the enemy six days before, utterly motionless. Waiting.

The Bahzhakhain, the eldar Swordwind army, the Tempest of Blades, had descended onto Orphean Trine seven days before. It had swept across the planet's surface and driven the last remnants of the Imperial population to Pious IV, the colossal hive city that dove down into the depths of the planet core and pierced the clouds at its distant apex. The city had been built at the end of a long, deep ravine, with the sheer rock walls acting as a natural defence on three sides. The south side was the approach through the valley, and it was peppered with giant monoliths of hard rock, left standing like great stalagmites after the terrible storms of Orphean Trine had whipped through the valley and eroded the rest of the channel.

Some of the huge rocks had been carved into statues of the great soldiers who had first brought the light of the Emperor to the planet. A monument to Orphean himself bestrode the valley floor, with a broad, two-handed force sword pointing valiantly into the sky. The explorer had taken the sword from the dead hands of an eldar warrior, one of a small number of aliens that the Imperium had been forced to purge in order to purify the planet for assimilation into the proud Imperium of Man. Etched into the base of the monument were the defiant words of the great founder: *Never again will we suffer the pollution of the xenos on Orphean Trine.*

Local legends tell of how Orphean had battled with the last eldar on the planet, matching him blow for blow, before running his own blade through the creature's neck and severing his spine. As the alien slumped to the ground, he had gurgled some barely coherent words: *I am not the last*. Orphean had laughed at the arrogance of the eldar and taken his head... and his sword.

Now it seemed that the eldar had been right. He had not been the last. Many centuries had passed, but the eldar had finally returned to Orphean Trine, this time in tremendous force. The Swordwind army of the Biel-Tan craftworld had blazed down through the atmosphere in a maelstrom of lightning and power, scything through the pathetic resistance offered by the agrarian settlers and ploughing on towards the capital. And now, after six days of war, the Swordwind was thundering through the long valley like a tidal wave, crushing the paltry defensive encampments of the Imperial Guard at the mouth of the ravine, and preparing to crash and break against the walls of Pious IV. Orphean had once laughed at their arrogance, but now the eldar laughed at the weakness and stupidity of the mon-keigh. Nyjia never laughed.

The great statue of Orphean was now cracked and weathered, and Nyjia had squeezed herself into a slim vertical rift in its structure. She twisted her body deeper into the crevice and braced the long barrel of her rifle against the rock, holding a tight angle of depression so that the reticule focussed on the sandy ground next to the statue's base. That was the precise point that the psychic Inquisitor Lord Parthon had indicated a week before from the comfort of his chambers on the top of the Spire of Piety, near the apex of Pious IV, and Nyjia had held her rifle trained on it for the last four days. She was simply waiting, listening to the distant rumble of the inevitable eldar advance and the futile rattle of the Imperial Guard's defence. It wasn't only the eldar who could play games with fate.

The rifle was almost weightless in her hands, adding nothing to her discomfort, as though it was part of her. It was her best friend and truest ally. She called it *Shlaereen* – an eldar name that meant silent death. Long ago in the Vindicare temple, she had made *Shlaereen* herself, and she had maintained her ever since – caring for her with the same devotion that she had offered to her body. Together, she and her rifle were entire, and entirely dedicated to the Emperor's will. In return, the Emperor offered her soul salvation, permitting her to bathe in the most sinister predilections of her nature.

The Inquisition had augmented her body and provided technology for her to augment her weapon. *Shlaereen* contained an eclectic mix of alien parts, including an eldar gravitic accelerator, which removed all recoil from the weapon and rendered it almost silent in operation. Nyjia's master, Lord Parthon, was a radical inquisitor, and he enjoyed the irony of hunting aliens with their own technology. Alone together, motionless for six days, Nyjia felt the presence of these enhancements, and she was certain that the eldar components had given *Shlaereen* a soul of her own.

As THE SUN pushed low across the sky, sending a great shaft of light blasting through the valley towards Pious IV, the tips of huge shadows reached for the city walls like the fingers of massive daemons. Squinting her eyes against the sun as her ocular implants glossed into blackness, working to filter out the dazzling light, Nyjia could see the vanguard of the eldar Swordwind cresting the horizon.

A bank of Falcon tanks skimmed over the rough valley floor, silhouetted against the rising sun. Dark, flickering shapes suggested jetbikes and Vyper gun-platforms. Here and there, standing on top of the vehicles, Nyjia could see the distinctive outline of eldar warriors, with the stretched shadows of their elongated helmets fingering the city walls behind her. As they drew closer, the dust cloud that billowed around them started to dissipate, and the greens and whites of the Biel-Tan craftworld became visible. Stuck on the long barrels of the lance arrays and banner shafts, Nyjia could see the heads of the commanding officers of Orphean Trine's Imperial Guardsmen, displayed in a grotesque testament to the eldar's inhuman rage.

Nyjia tensed the muscles in her shoulders, letting them flex and then relax. She inhaled deeply, exercising her patience as though it was also a muscle. Was she really all that was left to defend Pious IV? Parthon had mentioned the Dark Angels – experienced eldar slayers after the Tartarus affair – but there was no sign of them.

A roar in the sky made Nyjia snap her head back, staring up through the top of the crevice in which she was secreted. The tear-shaped crack in the side of the statue was widest in the middle, where Nyjia had climbed in after the Imperial Guard had vanished out along the valley a week earlier, and it narrowed to a fine line at the apex, just above Orphean's forehead. High above her, she could see a cluster of black pods hurtling towards the valley, accelerating down through the stratosphere like meteorites. On the edge of her hearing, she could hear the people on the walls of the hive city let out a cheer of relief. The Adeptus Astartes were on their way.

The drop-pods crashed down into the floor of the valley on all sides of Orphean's statue, punching deep craters out of the sandy ground and shattering the other rock protrusions like glass ornaments. The impacts rocked the valley, sending avalanches cascading down the sheer walls of the ravine, and forcing Nyjia to tense her legs against each side of the fissure in which she was hidden, struggling to keep her balance and to maintain her firing line.

Three squadrons of Dark Angels Space Marines spilled out of the pods, the bright morning sunlight bursting stars off their immaculate, spectral green power armour as they wracked their weapons in readiness. With a few hand signals, the captain sent his Marines storming across the valley floor, falling into formation behind a number of the monoliths, where they worked to establish emplacements for their heavier weapons.

Meanwhile, the eldar advance had paused midway down the valley. The Falcons and Vypers had stopped before reaching the field of monoliths, allowing the jetbikes to zip through between them and rip over the desert that separated them from the Dark Angels, leaving the bulk of their forces in reserve, as though toying with the Imperium's finest. One of the bikes pulled ahead of the others, bearing a rider with a great plume running down its long helmet. The jetbike shot through the monoliths, banking and swerving at incredible speed and with impossible ease, filling the air with showers of shuriken from its nose-mounted catapults.

The Dark Angels returned fire, tracking the speeding forms with their bolters, strafing fire through the sand in their wake. A rattle of shells punched along the flank of a bike, rupturing its stabilisers and sending it spiralling on its axis, smashing into one of the monoliths and exploding into a fireball. Out of the sun, sudden blasts of fire erupted from the Falcons and Vypers, crashing into the monoliths behind which the Space Marines held cover.

Nyjia watched the battle unfold. The eldar ordnance flashed across the valley floor, punching into the monoliths and shattering them into vicious shards, annihilating the already sparse cover afforded to the Dark Angels, leaving them clear targets for the speeding jetbikes. The Dark Angels may have arrived just in time for a last-ditch defence of the city, but Nyjia reflected that the battle was over already. She looked lovingly along the slender barrel of *Shlaereen*, checking her line of sight down to the base of the statue, and she settled in for the wait. If only the Adeptus Astartes were as well prepared as the Vindicare.

A HIGH PITCHED whine made the Dark Angels captain turn and drop as the jetbike soared over his head. The captain rolled onto his back and raised his bolt pistol, firing off a chain of shells into the rear of the speeding eldar, climbing back to his feet without breaking the rhythm of his fire.

The bike spluttered and jerked, spitting smoke from its engines before losing balance and diving down into the sand, ploughing a runnel into the desert. The eldar warrior flipped off the back, turning an elegant, twisting somersault, landing into a crouch facing back towards the Marine. The alien drew a long, double-handed sword from a holster on its back and started to run towards the Dark Angel, the plume on its helmet fluttering in the rush of air.

Casting his bolter aside, the captain pulled his chainsword free of its fixings on his leg, feeling its power splutter into life as he held it in both hands in front of him. The rest of his squad had already fallen, and he was the last Dark Angel standing in defence of Pious IV. The desert was strewn with the ruined bodies of Space Marines and the smoking remains of eldar jetbikes, interspersed around the shattered remnants of monoliths.

Far above the battlefield, Nyjia could see the heavy black silhouette of a Thunderhawk gunship plunging down out of orbit. She looked back down towards the Dark Angels captain, and knew that he would not last long enough to see the arrival of his reinforcements. Reluctantly lifting the barrel of *Shlaereen* and twisting her body in the heart of the statue, Nyjia tested the aim against the figure of the charging eldar exarch. But even without checking, Nyjia knew that the shot was out of range. Just as she would know whether the blades fused into her fingertips would reach the neck of a heretic, so she knew whether her bullet would reach the head of a distant alien. And the exarch was just out of reach. She resigned herself to wait, rolling her shoulders and exhaling slowly, returning *Shlaereen*'s reticule to the target point.

The exarch sprang into the air, flying through the last few metres separating it from the Dark Angel. Its sword flashed into a blur of motion, scooping and spinning in ritualised patterns before turning into a vertical arc. The captain stepped in towards the eldar, breaking its timing and stooping inside the cut, raising his own whirring blade in a horizontal parry.

The two swords clashed in an explosion of power, with the teeth of the chainsword grinding and sparking against the shimmering alien material of the eldar blade. But the exarch pushed off the collision, using its power to flip into another somersault without even touching its feet to the ground. The Dark Angel spun on his heel, bringing up his sword into a guard just in time to meet the parallaxed horizontal sweep of the eldar force-weapon.

As the blades clashed once again, the captain braced his muscles and the servos in his power armour, struggling to repel the inhuman power of the eldar. But the exarch was ineffably light on its feet; its legs bicycled out to the side, as though running up an invisible wall, pivoting around the clashing swords, and landing a punishing kick against the side of the Dark Angel's head. The captain stumbled under the sudden impact, dropping his guard for a moment. As he did so, the exarch withdrew its force sword from the clash, dipped its tip, and then thrust it forward like a spear, skewering the Marine through his neck, straight through the hairline seal at the base of his helmet.

As the Dark Angel slumped to the ground and the eldar exarch brayed its victory into the rising sun, Nyjia could just about discern the collective sigh of despair that arose from the walls of Pious IV behind her. She pressed herself deeper in the crevice, narrowing her shoulders slightly in order to move further back into the heart of the great stone, away from the keen eyes of the eldar.

Echoing her silent movements, the Swordwind of the Biel-Tan, held in reserve on the edge of the field of monoliths, slipped into motion and advanced down the valley. The Falcon tanks slid effortlessly over the debris and corpses that were strewn over the killing zone, hardly even disturbing the sand beneath them as their antigravitic engines pulsed with mysterious energies. The remaining jetbikes from the vanguard peeled around in giant arcs, bringing themselves to rest in flanking positions alongside the triumphant exarch. Soon, the entire width of the valley was blocked by a single, slender line of eldar vehicles and warriors, with the exarch standing gloriously in the centre, the red sun rising above its head.

A wind-whispered silence breathed through the valley, and Nyjia held her breath. Then a piercing whine started to build out of the wind, growing steadily and rapidly into the roar of engines. Without moving her body, Nyjia cast her eyes up through the slit in the top of the statue and saw the Thunderhawk charging down out of the sky, thundering towards the brief clearing between the eldar line and the walls of Pious IV. Sheets of fire erupted from the eldar position, peppering the green armour of the Space Marine gunship, which returned fire with the splutter of heavy bolters and javelins of lasfire. About one hundred metres from the ground, the Thunderhawk's retros kicked in, blasting a huge cloud of sand into the air and obscuring its own landing.

Even over the continuing roar of the engines, Nyjia's perfect ears could pick out the clunk and hiss of the hatch opening, and then the incredibly heavy footfalls of something terrible descending into the desert of Orphean Trine. As more and more footsteps sounded against the metal ramp, the engines were injected with a touch more power and the Thunderhawk rose back into the air, its weapons batteries flaring with power, spraying the eldar line with a vicious assault. Then, as the dust began to settle beneath it, giant forms started to emerge from the sand-filled fog.

The Swordwind army was poised, motionless, waiting for their next foe to be revealed. And Nyjia could feel the tension on the walls of the besieged city, as the people struggled to understand what hope they might have left now: after a week of war their Imperial Guardsmen had been slaughtered and even the fabled Adeptus Astartes had been defeated.

As the dust cleared, the eldar and the people of Pious IV were treated to a glorious vision: a full Terminator squadron stormed across the desert towards the alien invaders, supported by the lumbering forms of three massive Dreadnoughts, their weapons blazing and their intent resolute. And overhead, hovering as best it could in the eddying winds of the valley, the Thunderhawk roared with power, punching its fire into the line of xenos creatures. From the city walls beyond, Nyjia could just about make out the cheers of the people once again. She exhaled slowly and rolled her neck, settling in to watch the battle, and to wait a little longer for her turn to come.

The twin-linked shuriken catapults on the emerald-green Falcons hissed and whined as they spewed hails of projectiles into the faces of the advancing Dark Angels Terminators. Meanwhile, their heavier weapons angled up into the sky to confront the Thunderhawk: starcannons convulsed with power, bright lances spat javelins of energy, and missiles spiralled, roaring through the air before punching into the thick armour of the deep green gunship.

The Thunderhawk reeled under the onslaught, pitching and yawing as though adrift on the most violent of seas. Its own weapons were a constant blaze of fire, as the gun-servitors struggled to compensate for the erratic motion of the ship itself. Hellfire rounds cut down through the air, exploding into vicious shrapnel as they smashed against the wraithbone armour of the Falcons and the eldar warriors.

Meanwhile, three giant, green war walkers stomped out from behind the eldar line, breaking into a run as they cleared their own forces, scattering lasfire, lance javelins, and plumes of flame as they pounded across the desert to meet the oncoming Dreadnoughts.

The Dark Angels Terminators began to outpace their heavier cousins, and they vaulted into the midst of the eldar line, crashing chainfists into green armour, brandishing great thunder hammers, and slicing with chainswords, all the while loosing constant tirades from their storm bolters.

The lumbering Dreadnoughts lashed fire against the war walkers, splintering their elegant legs with blasts from parallel-tracking autocannons, before stamping giant feet down on their scrambling pilots as they struggled to clamber free of the wreckage. As the war walkers exploded beneath them, the Dreadnoughts turned their attention to the Falcons, leaving the Terminators to plough through the eldar warriors. But it was already too late.

The Thunderhawk convulsed hugely, staggered by a well-orchestrated volley from three Falcons at once. The rockets and lance fire punched home simultaneously, rupturing the gunship's armour and detonating its engine core. The dark green ship erupted into flames and plunged down out of the sky, exploding into a massive fireball as it crashed into the sand, sending concentric concussions rippling through the desert towards the battle.

With the Thunderhawk downed, the Falcons lurched into motion, sliding forward of the attack line and dispersing around the valley floor, depriving the Dreadnoughts of static targets. All the time, their gun turrets swivelled and their fire tracked the laborious motion of the Dark Angels Dreadnoughts – until two of them exploded into infernos of rage.

The Terminators were pinned, surrounded by superior numbers of lighter and faster eldar warriors. Despite cutting down dozens of the alien creatures, the Dark Angels were on borrowed time.

Suddenly, the Falcons broke off their attack on the last Dreadnought, and the eldar exarch leapt clear of the melee with the Terminators, sprinting across the desert towards the lumbering machine-warrior. The exarch flipped and somersaulted around the stream of shells that flashed out of the Dreadnought, tumbling and dancing until it reached the great machine's feet, unscathed. It vaulted into the air, flipping and twisting, before coming down on the roof of the ancient war-engine. Spinning its huge sword into an ostentatious flourish, the eldar drove its glowing blade straight down through the armoured plates, right up to the hilt. A great hiss jetted out of the machine, and then its legs gave way as it crashed to the ground.

Nyjia felt a slight tension build in her shoulder blade as the Dark Angels Terminators were finally destroyed. The valley floor was a bloodied mess of Guardsmen and Space Marines, interspersed with the ruins of

Dreadnoughts, Terminators and even a downed Thunderhawk. Speckled in amongst the corpses of the Imperium's finest were the bodies of eldar warriors and the smoking remains of some jetbikes, but the Swordwind was unbroken, and, after a week of impatience, the exarch stood once again in the centre of its offensive line, waiting to take the city. Nyjia flexed her arms delicately – she had been waiting too.

The afternoon passed slowly, as the eldar moved through the killing field and collected their dead. They were in no hurry to sack the defenceless city. Nyjia watched the aliens carefully remove the spirit-stones from each of their fallen brethren, and then pile the bodies into a great pyre at the base of the huge statue of Orphean. Each time a warrior approached to sling a corpse onto the growing pile, she tracked their movements with *Shlaereen*, imperceptibly. But none of them looked up.

By the time night fell, the pyre was complete, obscuring the defiant text etched into the base of the statue. And the Swordwind fell into silence, preparing a temporary camp in which to await the first rays of the morning sun. Settling in for her seventh motionless, icy night, Nyjia found herself ensconced in the heart of the eldar camp.

Keeping her eyes trained on the camp below her, she ran her hand along the barrel of her rifle, blindly working her fingers across its slick, icy surface, checking it for abrasions or defects. She knew every last fraction of it, as though it were part of her, and she could perform the required ritual purifications in perfect darkness if she needed to. Making the checks whilst braced into a rock fissure above a camp of eldar warriors was nothing.

The first glow from the morning sun broke the horizon, and with it came a flurry of activity in the eldar camp. It was as though the light brought them back to life, thought Nyjia, smiling inwardly at the irony. The warmth flooded into her muscles once more.

Waiting on the clear sand below the statue of Orphean was the exarch's retinue, resplendent in the emerald greens of the Biel-Tan, each on one knee with their heads bowed. As their war leader strode across the camp towards them, they raised their heads to face it and clasped their hands to their chests in gestures of loyalty. The climax of their eight-day effort was at hand.

The exarch stood before them and raised its blade into the air, a gloriously cynical mirror of the statue at its back, and the Swordwind began to beat their weapons against the ground, sending out thunderous waves of sound that rippled through the desert, signalling their intent to the people of Pious IV. A female seer stepped forward and touched her fingers to the funeral pyre, bursting it into flames.

Nyjia shifted her weight onto her right leg, pressing her left against the rock-face to brace her position, as the growing flames lapped up towards her feet. With a tiny motion, she caressed her rifle into life and *Shlaereen* hissed a potent whisper into the morning air.

The exarch's head exploded into a rain of shattered fragments. The magnificent emerald warrior slumped to its knees in the sand, its blade falling from its grip and crashing into the desert. For a moment, its body teetered on the edge of balance, swaying in the morning breeze, before it fell forward into the dust with the faintly smoking mandiblasters all that was left of its head.

'Never again will we suffer the pollution of the xenos on Orphean Trine,' whispered Nyjia, silent and motionless in Orphean's heart, as the Swordwind fell into disarray.

THE PRISONER

Graham McNeill

ORINA SEPTIMUS WAS a world dying a slow, but inevitable death. Thousands of years of exposure to corrosive oceanic vapours had turned its single continent into a rolling dune sea of blackened steppe. Its mountains were little more than slowly disintegrating knolls, eaten away over the millennia by airborne pollutants and rendered smooth as glass by the caustic atmosphere.

Acid seas covered ninety per cent of the planet's surface, and great ore ships of the Adeptus Mechanicus would periodically enter low orbit to suckle from the burning oceans. These monstrous vessels then transported the chemical-rich seawater to the mechanised hell of a forge world where it would be refined into vehicle fuel, propellants and war materiel of all description.

The planet's only other exportable commodity dwelt in the oceans, tiny desquamating invertebrates that swam the acid seas in continent-sized shoals. Ironclad trawlers crossed the oceans harvesting swathes of the minuscule creatures, whose hyper-efficient metabolisms were ultra-rich in proteins that could be processed into Imperial Guard ration packs.

And with many of the Hyrus system's supply lines cut by wolf pack squadrons of Arch-enemy ships, fresh sources of food for the defenders of Obereach and Illius were needed more than ever.

Such commodities were valuable, but dangerous to exploit and only those obliged to come to Orina Septimus ever risked venturing upon such a lethal world.

The Zhadanok Prison Complex housed the sector's most notorious criminals. One of the few man-made structures on Orina Septimus, it sat on the slopes of a black-walled valley at the mouth of a wide bay, the majority of its bulk carved deep into the decaying rocks and battered by waves from the acid sea. Gun towers and utilitarian landing facilities were all that remained above ground, protected from the planet's deadly vapours by a series of energy shields.

There was a grim saying amongst the indentured guards of Zhadanok that no one came willingly to Orina Septimus, they only ended up there.

As though in defiance of that saying, a sleek black cutter dropped through the misty skies towards Zhadanok, its hull streaked silver by the falling acid rain. The ship bore no insignia and flew with an escort of gunships, insectoid craft with gimbal-mounted assault cannons and racks of missiles slung under each wing.

No sooner had the craft entered the airspace of the prison complex than defence emplacements irised from the rocks and acquired the cutter and its guardians.

Invisible transmissions between the cutter and the prison swiftly established its authority and the guns retracted into the rocks as a series of winking lights illuminated to guide the cutter towards a newly revealed landing platform.

With a speed and precision that spoke of a highly skilled pilot, the cutter skimmed the rocks and touched down as the gunships peeled off and streaked towards the sky.

The landing platform retracted into the prison complex, swallowing the cutter in darkness. Contrary to the guards' proverb, the cutter's owner had not merely *ended up* on Orina Septimus, he had come here willingly and with all possible speed.

All because of the prisoner.

WARDEN PENDAREVA SHIFTED uncomfortably from foot to foot as he watched the landing servitors hose the acid-streaked cutter down with corrosion-retardant fluids. Stinking vapours hissed from the pitted surfaces of the aircraft and Pendareva wrinkled his nose at the acrid stench.

He reached up with a faded handkerchief to mop his sweat-beaded forehead and turned his pale, creased face to Chief Gaoler de Zoysa.

'Damn it, but we could do without this,' he said. 'As if we don't have problems at the moment. The inmates are spoiling for trouble, I can smell it.'

De Zoysa, a shaven-headed, bull of a man in dented bronze mesh armour with a face that mirrored the landscape beyond the prison walls, nodded and said, 'Let them. I've got my enforcers itching to break some heads.'

'I don't doubt that's true, but it would be better if it didn't happen while we have such an august personage here, don't you think?' said Pendareva, gesturing at the cutter.

De Zoysa shrugged, as though he couldn't care less, but Pendareva saw real fear behind the gaoler's bravado. Pendareva had seen de Zoysa wading through blood in the midst of a prison riot with nothing but brute strength and a power maul to protect him. Until now, he had never seen him afraid.

It spoke volumes for the reputation of the new arrival that even a psychotic thug like de Zoysa was nervous, and Pendareva mopped his brow once more as the servitors finished hosing down the cutter and began laying out grilled matting from the iron doors of the prison towards the dripping craft.

Pendareva normally worked hard to avoid attracting the attention of organisations beyond Orina Septimus, content in maintaining his own private little empire, but the capture of the prisoner had made that impossible.

As protocol demanded, Pendareva had notified his superiors of the capture, expecting a response in the normal period of months, but within days, an omicron-level communication had arrived instructing him to expect the arrival of Lord Syphax Osorkon of the Orders of the Emperor's Holy Inquisition.

Even isolated on a backwater planet such as Orina Septimus, Pendareva had heard of Inquisitor Lord Syphax Osorkon.

There were few in this part of the galaxy that had not.

Syphax Osorkon was a man of fearsome reputation, a man who had uncovered the secret heart of the Pyrus Reach for nearly three centuries. From Hyrus to the outlying systems of Verdis and the Sorien Delta, Inquisitor Lord Syphax Osorkon had unmasked and destroyed scores of sinister cults, quashed innumerable alien incursions and cut out the root of heresy and sedition from uncounted planets. No one was above his scrutiny, and paupers and planetary governors had felt the full wrath of his judgement.

'I want this done quickly and smoothly,' said Pendareva. 'No trouble. You understand me? From the inmates or the enforcers.'

'I understand,' said de Zoysa. 'But you know damn well there's ugly trouble in the air. The scum know something's happening and they're spoiling for a chance to kick off.'

'What have you done about Finn?' asked Pendareva. 'If anyone's going to start something, it will be him.'

'Don't worry, he's secure,' promised de Zoysa.

'He had better be,' warned Pendareva. 'What about his gang, the Brothers of the Word?'

De Zoysa shook his head. 'Ever since Finn attacked Reyan, they've been keeping a low profile. They're smart enough to know that with Finn out of the picture for a while, they're vulnerable. The Devil Dogs and the Red Blades are all looking for a piece of his gang, so they're the ones to worry about now.'

Further discussion was halted by the whisper of the pressure lock on the cutter's side disengaging and the hiss of the hatch sliding open. The hatch was inordinately large, thought Pendareva, but seconds later he saw why.

A shape moved within the cutter and a giant figure in gleaming battle plate bearing an enormous sword blotted out the light from inside.

Pendareva heard de Zoysa gasp at the sight of the Space Marine, marvelling at the shining plates of silver steel armour and the expressionless, red-eyed faceplate. The warrior's massive width blocked the hatch and his sheer physical presence filled the landing facility. Pendareva had never seen a Space Marine this close and every hyperbolic slogan he had heard of them seemed now to be absurdly understated in the presence of such a magnificently proportioned warrior.

His shoulder guard gleamed silver, with a device of a black sword piercing an open book displayed upon it. Numerous scrolls hung with the same symbol hung from his pauldrons and breastplate. A golden, basket-hilted sword hung at his waist in an etched scabbard of shimmering bronze.

'Are you Warden Pendareva?' asked the Space Marine as he marched down the cutter's landing ramp, the metal bowing under his weight. Despite the vox distortion, the Space Marine's voice was deep and sonorous.

'I am,' replied Pendareva once he'd found his voice. 'Welcome to Zhadanok Prison Complex. And you are…?'

The Space Marine said, 'I am Justicar Kemper of the Grey Knights.' Pendareva nodded as four more Space Marines came after him, giants with long halberds fitted with wide-muzzled weapons below the blades, and armoured in burnished steel plate that eerily reflected the red glow of the landing platform's guide lights.

Finally, with the five Space Marines debarked, Inquisitor Lord Syphax Osorkon emerged from the shuttle, followed by a coterie of brass-fingered scribes, augmetic warriors in form-fitting armoured bodygloves and a trio of white-robed astrotelepaths with their hoods drawn up over their faces.

Compared to the Space Marines, the inquisitor lord was something of a disappointment to Pendareva. The terror of the Pyrus Reach was clad in a long robe of deep, selpic blue and wore his Inquisitorial rosette pinned over his heart. The inquisitor eschewed ornamentation where his servants appeared to celebrate it. Tall and smooth-skinned from extensive juvenat therapy, Osorkon's features held a blandness that Pendareva guessed was easy to underestimate. The inquisitor lord's hair was thinning and cut close to his skull, his gimlet eyes a cold, icy grey.

Osorkon came down the boarding ramp at a calm, unhurried pace, as though he were descending the stairs at a debutante ball rather than the cold, stinking depths of one of the sector's most notorious prisons.

Pendareva stepped forward to greet the inquisitor, bowing expansively before him.

'My Lord Osorkon,' he began, 'welcome to our humble facility.'

'Is the prisoner secure?' asked the inquisitor, brushing aside Pendareva's greeting.

'Ah, yes, he is indeed,' said Pendareva, masking his irritation at the inquisitor's abruptness. 'My chief warden here has him locked in the Hell Hole.'

Osorkon nodded and said, 'How many guards maintain a vigil on him?'

De Zoysa answered the inquisitor, saying, 'I have thirty enforcers watching him round the clock. All armed with lethal force ordnance and weapons free rules of engagement. If the bastard so much as makes a move I don't like, he's dead.'

'Only thirty? Double it. Immediately,' said Osorkon. 'Believe me, if he made any kind of move then all your men would be dead before they could cry for help. In fact, I am surprised that any of you are still alive.'

The inquisitor rounded on Pendareva and said, 'Take me to the prisoner. Immediately.'

FINN LAY ON his back on the hard floor of the cell, smiling as bubbling pools of acid leaking up through the cracked tiles scorched his skin. The air tasted acrid from the chemical burns, but he enjoyed the sensation of his skin blistering.

It meant the first stage of the plan was already working.

The next stage depended on the psychotic violence of his fellow inmates, and he knew he could rely on that. Zodiac and Wrench had promised him a riot he'd be proud of, and *that* would be something worth seeing.

The Brothers of the Word were ready to fight and the Dogs and the Blades couldn't wait to get bloody. He was only sorry he wouldn't be there for the best of the killing.

He pulled his mind from the slaughter to come and focussed on his current situation, locked in the deepest pit of Zhadanok Prison – the Hell Hole.

The enforcers claimed that anyone put in the Hell Hole would break, that they would be dragged out weeping and soiled and less than human.

Finn knew that it wasn't the hardship of the Hell Hole that broke prisoners; it was simply that they hadn't accepted pain. It might be boring stuck here in the deepest cell of Zhadanok for days on end, but it sure beat working the acid pumps in the lower levels that kept the deadly oceans beyond from flooding the prison complex.

Finn had suffered worse pain than this and not broken, and they weren't going to break him here. It had been three days since they'd thrown him in here after gutting Reyan for looking at him funny in the mess hall. Putting some hurt on the Devil Dogs was always fun, but it had been an incidental bonus to his real reason for wanting put in the Hell Hole.

Countless spells in Imperial Guard stockades had taught Finn all he needed to know about surviving solitary confinement and only his value to his numerous commanding officers had saved him from a commissar's bullet.

For Guardsman Finn was a man with a truly singular talent for killing – above and beyond that possessed by even the most feral soldiers of his regiment, the Kanak Skull Takers. Finn had an uncanny ability to walk out of some of the most intense fire-fights and brutal close quarters actions without so much as a scratch on him, his claw machete bloody and the light of murder in his eyes.

But his talent for murder and mayhem, so very useful on a battlefield, were liabilities when underemployed during down time between fighting.

At his court martial, no one, probably not even Finn himself, could say for certain how many people he'd killed, but the number was reckoned in the hundreds.

He rolled to his knees as he saw the patterns of light around the edge of the trapdoor in the ceiling of his cell shift. Someone was moving around above him in the enforcers' corridor.

'Hey!' he shouted. 'Hey! Who's that up there?'

'Shut your mouth, Finn,' came the response.

Finn recognised the voice as belonging to Enforcer Dravin, a weak man with a thin neck that would part easily from its skull. Dravin was a stickler for rules and Finn smiled as he realised he couldn't have asked for a better gaoler.

His plan was working, but its ultimate success relied on the true Brothers of the Word returning to Orina Septimus as they had promised in his visions.

Looking at the growing pools of acid on the floor, he just hoped it would be soon.

PENDAREVA LED THE way into the Zhadanok Prison Complex, de Zoysa and Inquisitor Osorkon to either side of him and the Grey Knights of Justicar Kemper following behind. They passed through the armoured gates and into the antiseptic, tiled halls of the prison itself. Numerous isolation halls and double gate entries slowed their progress, but Pendareva didn't mind the wait, sure that this display of his facility's security would impress Osorkon.

As if hearing his thoughts, Osorkon said, 'Tell me again how the prisoner came to be here, Warden Pendareva.'

'Ah, yes, inquisitor, of course,' replied Pendareva, 'though I thought I had enclosed the details of his capture in my report to sector command.'

'You did, but I wish you to tell me.'

'Very well,' said Pendareva as they passed through the main gate into one of the main viewing halls that traversed the length of the main cellblock. 'Though I don't see what will be different.'

'Indulge me,' said Osorkon in a manner that warned Pendareva not to protest again.

Pendareva cleared his throat and said, 'Some six standard weeks ago our system augurs detected a craft approaching low orbit and heading towards us.'

'Did you identify this craft?' interrupted Osorkon.

'Not at first,' explained Pendareva. 'Our equipment here is rather temperamental and it is only thanks to the favour our resident tech-priest is held in by the Machine God that it functions at all – at least that's what he tells me.'

The group passed opposite modular cells stacked upon one another ten deep and which were reached by means of removable walkways run on a complex series of rigs and suspended cables. Teams of enforcers lined the parapet between the cells and main thoroughfare, shotguns cradled in their arms and power mauls hanging from their belts.

'Carry on,' said Osorkon, looking up at wretched prisoners slumped against the doors of their cages, their legs and arms dangling between the bars as they glared with naked hostility at the group passing below them.

'Well, the craft entered our exclusion zone and refused to answer our hails, which is when the guns acquired it,' continued Pendareva, raising his voice as word of their passing spread along the cellblock and hurled insults and the clamour of tin cups rattling against iron bars filled the air. 'It kept coming, so they shot it down. It crashed about thirty kilometres from here and I despatched a team of enforcers to investigate.'

'And they found the prisoner in the wreckage?'

'Yes, he was the only survivor,' said Pendareva, 'the rest of the crew were killed in the crash. We have them in our morgue if you wish to see them.'

'No,' said Osorkon. 'Destroy them. Tell me about the craft you found.'

'It was too badly damaged to tell what kind of craft it was, but from what we were able to recover, it looks as though it was an orbital transport of some kind.'

'So where did it come from?' asked Osorkon.

Pendareva shrugged, 'That is a mystery I fear only the prisoner knows.'

'And it didn't occur to you to wonder how a ship that size could have reached Orina Septimus on its own?'

'Frankly no,' said Pendareva. 'I leave such matters to men such as yourself.'

The inquisitor frowned and said, 'It is beholden to all citizens of the Imperium to question the suspicious. I will remember this laxity of alertness when I file my report with my superiors.'

Pendareva was too surprised at the idea of someone like Osorkon having superiors that he nearly didn't register the demerit he was soon to accrue.

'Well, what I mean to say is, we wondered where it had come from, but could not answer that conundrum. System surveyors detected nothing, so we ascribed it to one of the mysteries this cosmos is all too full of and awaited your coming to enlighten us.'

'If there is an answer to be had, then I will get it from the prisoner,' said Osorkon, 'have no fear of that.'

'But if I might ask, lord inquisitor, this prisoner... he appears to be–'

'Don't even ask, Pendareva,' warned Osorkon. 'The true identity of the prisoner is something you are not cleared to know. Such knowledge is dangerous.'

Pendareva nodded, though he was deeply unhappy at his exclusion from such information. Osorkon might be an inquisitor, but this was *his* prison.

'I fail to see how–' he said.

'I have had men killed for less,' said Osorkon, looking him square in the eye.

Pendareva believed him and asked no more on the subject as the group passed from the main detention halls of the prison, leaving the clamour of inmates behind them. They began travelling along a maze of twisting corridors hacked from the black rock, heading down towards the deep levels of the prison. Occasionally, their pathways took them from beneath the rock along shielded walkways with curved transparent plasteel walls that travelled beneath the acid seas.

Weak grey acid-filtered light filled these walkways and Pendareva enjoyed the worried expressions that stole across the faces of Osorkon and his retinue.

'Have no fear, Lord Osorkon, the shields protect us from the sea, though if they were to fail, the acids would eat through the plasteel in seconds, killing us all,' said Pendareva, enjoying the discomfort he saw on Osorkon's face.

The relief in the visitors' faces was clear as they passed back into the rock and then into vaulted tunnels that were reassuringly metal-walled and sealed with thick steel blast doors.

Soon, Pendareva stopped before a security station manned by six enforcers armed with combat shotguns and glossy black power mauls who stood before a heavy blast door. The image of a yawning abyss had been painted on the door, the lick of flames just visible at its base, and across the width of the door were the words 'Welcome to Hell'.

Each enforcer wore thick, padded body armour with all-enclosing helms of bronze, and each man had his gun trained on the approaching group. Pendareva could feel the snap of tension from the warriors of the inquisitor's retinue and, to his credit, Pendareva's men appeared to be unfazed by the presence of the massive Space Marines.

Pendareva said, 'Lieutenant Grazer. We are here to see the Prisoner.'

Grazer nodded and stepped forward saying, 'Access permissions?'

Both the Warden of Zhadanok and its chief gaoler produced control wands from their uniforms and were escorted towards panels either side of the blast door.

'Insert your control wands when I give the word and then step back,' ordered Grazer.

Pendareva nodded and readied his wand as the lieutenant dialled in the code known only to him that would allow the door to open.

Grazer said, 'Insert,' and Pendareva slid his control wand into the panel, keying in his personal identification code once it clicked into place. De Zoysa did likewise and the blast door rumbled as internal locks disengaged and the massive portal descended slowly into the floor.

Pendareva removed his control wand and beckoned to Inquisitor Lord Osorkon.

'Welcome to the Hell Hole.'

'Hey up there!' shouted Finn, registering the pain in his feet, but shutting it off from his conscious mind. The rising acid pooled across the entire floor, diluted since it had come through filter traps, but still painfully corrosive. Fumes drifted from his blistered feet and the drain in the centre of the floor dripped molten gobbets from its sagging metal.

'I told you to shut up, Finn,' said Dravin. 'I won't tell you again.'

'Listen,' said Finn. 'Something's wrong. This place is filling with acid, it's not good.'

'What are you talking about, Finn?'

'I'm telling you, this place is filling up with acid!' called Finn, injecting a note of pleading into his voice. He had to bait the hook just right. 'You're gonna be hosing me down the drain soon.'

He smiled as the silence stretched. Neither Warden Pendareva or his pet psycho, de Zoysa would shed a tear if Finn died in the Hell Hole, but Finn knew that Dravin was a stickler for the rules. And in Dravin's ordered world, you didn't leave prisoners to die in their cells, mass murderers or not.

'There's acid in your cell?' asked Dravin.

'Sure as I'm down here and you're up there,' replied Finn. 'The soles of my feet are damn near burned through! You gotta get me out of here!'

Finn heard muttered conversation from above and reached down to grip an acid-burned shard of metal from the drain. He pulled and the metal bent, eventually coming away from the drain. Not much of a weapon, but it was still a sharpened fifteen centimetre length of metal. Finn had killed men with less than this.

He blinked in sudden brightness as the trapdoor above him was hauled back and a square of light shone down into the cell. He could see the helmeted head of Dravin above him and he pointed to the floor.

'See, I told you,' he said. 'I ain't lying.'

'Shit,' said Dravin to someone out of sight. 'He's right, the cell's filling with acid. The pumps to this part of the prison must be playing up.'

'You gotta get me out of here!'

'Hold on,' ordered Dravin and vanished from the square of light.

Finn fought to hold back a feral grin of anticipation and secreted the jagged needle of metal in his palm, feeling the acid coating it hiss against his skin.

'Okay, Finn,' said Dravin, reappearing at the trapdoor. 'We're getting you out of there, but you so much as twitch a way I don't like, I'll shoot you and leave you down there to melt. Are we clear?'

'We sure are,' said Finn as a battered steel ladder was lowered into the cell.

PENDAREVA LED THE way along a bare corridor with a succession of passageways branching off that led along flickering, dismal tunnels with guards stationed at each junction.

'I can see why this place is called the Hell Hole,' muttered Inquisitor Osorkon.

'A name of our inmates' devising, but it seems to fit, yes,' agreed Pendareva.

Their journey continued to the end of the corridor, where it passed through a wide opening in the wall that led into a long, vaulted chamber filled with humming machinery and the stink of ozone.

'Our most secure area,' said Pendareva proudly.

A gleaming, metallic circle filled most of the chamber, a crackling column of light rising from its circumference to form a domed web of lighting through which nothing could penetrate.

A hybrid of power field and void shield technology, it formed an impregnable barrier of lethal energy that would incinerate anything that attempted to pass through it.

Thirty enforcers surrounded the shimmering energy field, their guns trained on the solitary figure that knelt in prayer at the centre of the circle.

He was a hulking brute, his bulk clearly that of an Astartes warrior, but one clad in unclean red plate armour hung with scorched scrolls and snapped chain links. Vile sigils and blasphemous catechisms were carved into one of the armour's shoulder guards, while the other bore a horned, daemonic head worked from dark iron.

His shaven skull was bowed and Pendareva could see the light of the energy fields dancing over the strange scripture-like tattoos that covered his skull.

The prisoner looked up from his devotions and Pendareva shivered, feeling the aeons of hatred and malevolence distilled within that gaze.

Inquisitor Osorkon stepped towards the edge of the circle of light, and Pendareva was put in mind of a predator that closes on its snared, helpless prey.

The Grey Knights moved to surround the prisoner, their weapons aimed at his head as Osorkon said, 'Erebus...'

THE HEAD COUNT was the last thing to be done before lockdown. The cells were opened en masse from the suspended control booth as a barked command ordered the inmates onto the movable gantries that slotted home before them.

Automated weapon mounts swivelled to cover the cells as hundreds of the sector's most dangerous men and women stepped out to be tallied.

Squads of enforcers covered the cells with their shotguns, but none of the prisoners failed to notice that their numbers were conspicuously thinned thanks to the extra manpower detached to guard Zhadanok's newest inmate.

WORKING IN THE depths of the mechanical plant cavern of Zhadanok Prison was a detail most inmates thought worse than the Hell Hole. Deafening machine-pumps and perforated walkways suspended on thick steel cables filled the cavernous space with the stench of oil, sweat and acid.

Below the walkways, breakers of the acid sea churned and foamed, crashing against the black rocks and dripping from the base of the suspended ironwork.

Those prisoners sent to work the acid pumps that kept the prison complex from flooding were sent in wearing flimsy corrosion-resistant oversuits and rebreather apparatus that looked as though they had come from the earliest days of the Imperium.

Prisoners shuffled around the stinking ocean cavern maintaining the machinery under the watchful gaze of a skeleton crew of enforcers. No one could escape from this place – save by leaping the safety rails into the acid sea – which hadn't stopped desperate inmates from trying to swim to freedom in their oversuits. Each of those attempts had failed as the escapees swiftly discovered just how little protection the oversuits really offered.

This shift was a mix of prisoners from various parts of the prison, but amongst them were three members of Finn's Brothers of the Word. Two were simply violent men who had killed fellow members of their regiments, but one had been an indentured Skitarii who previously served with work details of the Adeptus Mechanicus and had learned much from his time there before being sent to Zhadanok for tampering with holy machinery in an attempt to learn its secrets.

All of which would have meant nothing were it not for the fact that he had sabotaged the main controls that regulated the acid pumps. Two of the pumps that cleared out the lower levels, including the Hell Hole, had already been deactivated.

But that was only the beginning.

As the shift changeover klaxon sounded, a red light winked to life on the console, indicating that several of the pumps were failing, but they went unnoticed as the enforcers concentrated on moving the prisoners.

The first light was swiftly followed by another, then another and another. A whining alarm sounded, but was swallowed by the roaring breakers below and the noise of the shift change.

Red lights spread across the console as, one by one, the pumps that kept the deadly acid from Zhadanok Prison shut down.

And the ocean rushed in.

Inquisitor Lord Osorkon laced his hands behind his back as the prisoner rose to his feet and glanced with disdain at the Grey Knights surrounding him. His presence was enormous, greater even than the Astartes warriors, though he was surely no taller or broader than them. Pendareva grimaced as he studied the prisoner, who now had a name if what Osorkon had given voice to was indeed his true name.

Erebus.

A name that carried with it a weight of ages and dark myth. If the tales were to be believed, Erebus was said to be one of the ancient leaders of the great rebellion that legend told of in ages past. Erebus had been one of its chief architects, a warrior priest from one of the ancient Space Marine Legions that rebelled against the rule of the Emperor and were cast down almost ten thousand years ago.

Pendareva had never put much stock in such tales; after all, how could a being exist for ten thousand years? Such a thing was ludicrous, but looking into the twin pools of bitter malice of Erebus's eyes, he found it all too easy to countenance that the prisoner had nurtured hatred for so long.

'Five?' said Erebus. 'You think so little of me, you only come with five Astartes?'

'They are of the Grey Knights,' replied Osorkon. 'More than enough for the likes of you, traitor.'

'Traitor?' laughed Erebus, his cruel features twisting in a snarl. 'That word no longer has any meaning for me. It is you and your pathetic shadows of warriors who are the traitors. You and men like you betrayed the Imperium long ago when you fought against the Warmaster.'

'Do not speak his name,' warned Osorkon. 'Your time is over. Within the day you will be suffering the torments of the damned in an Inquisition cell.'

'Torments of the damned?' said Erebus. 'What do you know of such things?'

'Enough to make you rue the day you fell into my hands.'

'You know nothing,' snapped Erebus, pacing within his energised cell. 'Wait until everything you have striven for is naught but ashes and the gods you once walked amongst are legends to be reviled. When you feel the weight of betrayal on your shoulders for an age of eternity. Then you will be fit to speak of such things.'

Osorkon laughed. 'Spare me your theatrics, Erebus. You are finished, you and your dreams of conquest. Without you, the invasion of the Hyrus sector is over. I know it and you know it too, so shall we dispense with the tedious grandstanding?'

Erebus snarled and hurled himself at the inquisitor and the enforcers racked their shotguns, but not before the Grey Knights each had their long, crackling halberds aimed unerringly at his head.

Osorkon didn't flinch as Erebus was hurled back in a blaze of light, his armour scorched and his skin blistered from the discharge of his enclosing energy field.

'Tiresome,' sighed Osorkon, as Erebus rolled in pain on the ground within the energy field. He turned to face Pendareva and said. 'Disengage the field. We will assume responsibility for the prisoner.'

Pendareva nodded dumbly, sharing a glance with de Zoysa that spoke of his unease at releasing Erebus.

'Warden,' said Osorkon. 'Now, while he is disorientated.'

Pendareva nodded as de Zoysa moved around the circumference of the energy field, ensuring that each of his enforcers were ready should anything untoward occur. The Warden made his way towards a bank of controls maintained by a white-robed adept and a trio of hard-wired servitors.

The adept bowed as Pendareva approached and within moments, the bass hum of machinery faded and the ever-present stink of ozone diminished.

Erebus was on one knee, surrounded by Grey Knights, their silver plate reflecting the ruddy red of his spiked and chained armour. Each warrior had the glowing blades of their halberds aimed squarely at the prisoner and though each wore a full enclosing helmet, Pendareva could feel their hatred for Erebus. Justicar Kemper stood behind the prisoner with his sword raised to strike.

'Up,' commanded Osorkon and Erebus painfully forced himself to his feet, glaring with undiluted hatred at the inquisitor.

'You think you can break me, Osorkon?' said Erebus. 'You haven't even begun to suspect the depths of pain I can show you.'

'Spare me your threats,' said the inquisitor, turning away from Erebus. 'I have no wish to hear anything you say for now. Bring him.'

Surrounded by the Grey Knights and de Zoysa's enforcers, Erebus was led through the arched entrance. Previously, Pendareva had thought that such numbers were ridiculous for one prisoner, but faced with the sheer physicality of Erebus without the protection of the energy field, he wasn't sure it was enough.

* * *

FINN CLIMBED THE first few steps of the ladder, the metal feeling blessedly cool on the burned soles of his feet. He squinted in the light from the corridor above, taking more time than he needed to allow his eyes to adjust and give the impression of weakness. He'd been in the Hell Hole for three days now and they'd expect him to be weak.

That would be their mistake.

'Come on, Finn, get a bloody move on!' snapped Dravin.

'Alright, alright, I'm almost there,' replied Finn, lifting his shoulders beyond the level of the floor. He could see three pairs of boots and lifted his head, squinting theatrically and shielding his eyes to get a better look at the enforcers around him.

Dravin in front of him, one to the left and one behind him.

'Little help here?' said Finn. 'My feet are all burned to hell.'

'My heart bleeds,' said the enforcer behind him.

Gimme time, thought Finn.

He hauled himself over the lip of the trapdoor and sat on the corridor floor with his legs dangling into the cell. The level of acid was really beginning to rise quickly, reflecting the wan light of the corridor in rippling waves.

'On your feet,' ordered Dravin.

Finn nodded and pushed himself onto one knee. He made a pantomime of climbing to his feet, letting the pain of his burns free of the force of will he'd placed around it for a brief instant.

He stumbled and Dravin instinctively reacted by reaching to grab him.

Finn's hand shot out and grabbed Dravin's wrist, wrenching him off balance and pulling him forward. Even as the enforcer fell through the trapdoor, Finn was moving.

He spun low, kicking backwards and hammering his fist to the left. The long needle of drain metal in his fist stabbed into the second enforcer's thigh tearing through his coveralls and ripping open his femoral artery. The ball of Finn's foot connected squarely with the kneecap of the enforcer behind him. The bone shattered, shock and pain driving the man to the floor.

Finn dived left as a shotgun blast tore up the floor and landed on top of the screaming enforcer with the sliver of metal jammed in his leg. He swept up the man's fallen weapon and rolled, racking the slide and firing shot after shot at the other enforcer.

Deafening booms and stinking, acrid smoke filled the corridor, and Finn yelled with the thrill of combat. The enforcer was pitched backwards, his body armour ripped up where the shotgun shells had torn it up.

Though the man Finn was lying on was bleeding to death, he still fought as blood gushed from the wound on his leg. Finn smashed the butt of the shotgun into his face and slithered off him, rising to his feet and swinging the weapon into his face like a club to shut his screaming up.

The enforcer he'd shot was struggling to push himself into a sitting position in order to use his weapon. Finn didn't give him a chance to fire, calmly walking over and planting the barrel of his shotgun in the centre of the enforcer's chest.

'Let's see if your heart really does bleed,' said Finn, pulling the trigger.

The enforcer's body armour was designed to resist knife thrusts and bludgeons, not a point-blank shotgun blast, and the grey floor of the corridor was sprayed with a fan of blood and bone.

Finn could hear painful curses and splashing from below and risked a glance through the trapdoor. A shotgun blast ripped through and shattered the glow-globe above him, but Finn had been expecting the shot and ducked back with a whooping yell of laughter.

'Emperor damn you, Finn!' shouted Dravin. 'You're a dead man! You hear me? When I get out of here, I'm going to kill you, regulations be damned!'

'Whatever. Enjoy drowning in acid, Dravin,' said Finn, hauling the cover back over the trapdoor and muting the enforcer's shouts.

He quickly gathered up a pair of boots and the rest of the ammunition from the dead men, feeding a full load of shells into the shotgun then stuffing the rest into his pockets.

Getting out of his cell had been the easy part, now he had to get to the landing platforms and that wasn't going to be easy unless the rest of the plan kicked in soon.

As though on cue, the sound of the acid alarms screamed from the battered iron klaxons mounted on the walls.

'Music to my ears,' chuckled Finn. 'Music to my ears.'

THE MAIN HALLS of Zhadanok resounded to the deafening howls of the acid alarms, the blaring tones catching everyone off guard. The Brothers of the Word were the first to react, sprinting across the suspended walkways and rushing the enforcers before the first peals finished echoing.

Cries of pain and booming shotgun blasts followed, as old scores were settled and bitter rivalries flared up in the wake of the alarms. The Red Blades went for the Brothers of the Word and the Devil Dogs fought anyone in reach of their makeshift shanks. Hundreds of prisoners on the lower levels hurdled the railings to the main floor of the viewing hall and charged at one another in the confusion. Enforcers shot down prisoners and the automated weapon mounts opened fire, spraying the rampaging inmates with bullets.

Blood sprayed as shards of mirrored glass or sharpened lengths of metal were used to open veins and rip out throats and blasts of gunfire knocked prisoners back from the suspended control booth. A team of enforcers kept inmates at bay with disciplined volleys of shotgun blasts, but the rushing bodies of prisoners reached closer with every charge.

Hundreds of rioting prisoners hacked and stabbed at one another, filling the viewing halls with blood and screams. Splintering glass rained down from above as frenzied prisoners stormed the control booth and stabbed the enforcers to death. Bodies fell from above as inmates and enforcers alike were hurled from the high walkways to smash headlong onto the hard floor of the viewing hall.

Psychotic violence reigned within the main prison halls of Zhadanok, but the real bloodshed was yet to come.

Justicar Kemper of the Grey Knights was the first to register that something was wrong. Pendareva shot de Zoysa an interrogative glance. Zhadanok's gaoler shrugged, but slipped his shotgun from his shoulder and racked the slide.

'What is the matter?' asked Inquisitor Osorkon, halting their procession with a raised hand.

'Gunfire,' said Justicar Kemper. 'Shotguns.'

'From where?' asked Pendareva. 'I didn't hear anything. Are you sure?'

'I do not make mistakes,' said the Grey Knight, and Pendareva believed him.

Pendareva looked through the wall of plate armour to where Erebus stood and felt a shiver travel the length of his spine at the gloating smile he saw there.

'Who else do you have locked in here?' demanded Osorkon, turning to Pendareva.

'Finn...' said de Zoysa, answering the inquisitor's question for him. 'Emperor damn him! It has to be.'

'Who is this Finn?'

'He's no one,' said Pendareva. 'A murderer from some feral regiment of Guard who claimed the voices in his head made him kill a great many hivers. He's a troublemaker, but no one to worry about really.'

Pendareva jumped in surprise as the acid alarms went off, sudden dread filling him.

Lord Osorkon looked him square in the eye and said, 'Are you sure? What are these sirens?'

'It's the acid alarms,' said Pendareva, hurriedly. 'Some of the pumps must have failed, but I'm sure it's just a coincidence.'

'There's no such thing,' stated Osorkon, turning to Justicar Kemper and pointing to Erebus. 'Watch him.'

'I'll take some men and check it out,' said de Zoysa, forming a detachment of armoured enforcers around him. 'If it's Finn, then I'm going to take pleasure in blowing his brains out.'

Pendareva nodded as de Zoysa led a group of ten enforcers off into the corridors of the Hell Hole towards the sound of the shotgun blasts. The vox-unit on Pendareva's belt chirruped and he unhooked it, saying, 'Pendareva here.'

'Warden, this is perimeter control.'

'Yes?' asked Pendareva, with a sudden sense of events beginning to unravel.

'We, uh... we've picked up a vessel moving into low orbit that looks like it's on an intercept course with us.'

Pendareva glanced over at Osorkon and said, 'Yours?'

The inquisitor shook his head. 'No, my vessel remains in hiding behind the third moon.'

'Perimeter control,' said Pendareva, returning his attention to the vox. 'Can you identify this craft?'

'No, sir, it doesn't match any vessels in our registries, but then they're not exactly complete.'

Inquisitor Osorkon said, 'It's his...' and turned to face Erebus. 'They're coming for him. Justicar Kemper. Where is your vessel?'

'On the dark side, lord inquisitor,' answered Kemper. 'As you requested,' and Pendareva thought he detected a note of reproach in the Space Marine's tone.

Erebus chuckled and said. 'You are all going to die.'

'Know this, traitor,' said Osorkon. 'I'll kill you before I allow you to be rescued.'

'Fool,' said Erebus. 'I was alive when the Emperor and the Warmaster bestrode the galaxy, your threats mean nothing to me.'

'Sir,' came the distorted voice over Pendareva's vox once more. 'We've detected a number of incoming signals from the approaching ship.'

'What are they?' asked the warden.

'I... I'm not sure, sir,' said the officer on perimeter control, unable to keep the fear from his voice, 'but I think they're orbital torpedoes.'

FINN LOPED THROUGH the tunnels of the Hell Hole with the familiarity of one who had been marched along its corridors many times before. The shotgun felt natural in his grip, but he wished he had his familiar claw machete for the up close killing that was sure to come before he met up with the Brothers of the Word and got off this damned planet.

The acid alarms continued to screech and he knew that within the hour this level of the prison would be knee-deep in deadly acid. He followed the dismal corridors back towards the security station, knowing that evac crews would be on their way to remove inmates incarcerated on the lower levels.

With his shotgun, he should be able to cause enough bloody confusion to get past the evac teams and any security detail they had with them.

After all, they wouldn't be expecting an armed prisoner with nothing to lose.

THE FIRST ORBITAL torpedoes struck the molten landscape above Zhadanok Prison, smashing through the acid-softened rock and exploding with terrifying force. Burning scads of debris rained down as a cascade of searing lance strikes hammered the landscape. Most just cratered the landscape, forming deep bowls in which acid lakes formed that would, in time, melt great sinkholes through the mountains.

Buried beneath this region of the mountains was a heavily shielded mechanical facility not dissimilar to the cavernous machine plant of the acid pumps. Its structure was designed to withstand the slow, but inevitable erosion of the climate, not the horror of an orbital barrage and, when the first shells broke apart the mountainous cover, it was a matter of moments before the facility was smashed to a tangled ruin of metal, oil and flesh.

The machines lay in a million pieces, their turbines shattered and transformers vaporised.

And without them, the power in Zhadanok failed.

PENDAREVA STIFLED A yelp as the corridor was plunged into screeching darkness, feeling more than hearing the Grey Knights close in around Erebus almost at the same moment. The ceiling-mounted lumen strips flickered dimly as low-wattage emergency batteries kicked in and Pendareva fancied he could sense a rumbling vibration through the stone floor over the howls of the acid alarms.

'Torpedo impacts,' said Justicar Kemper, matter of factly. 'Close.'

Lord Osorkon nodded and said, 'They'll be coming soon,' before turning to Pendareva and adding, 'What measures are in place to prevent a forced entry to this facility?'

'Entry?' said Pendareva, shouting to be heard over the alarms. 'Uh, well, the guns and the thickness of the doors. Generally our defences are geared to preventing the inmates from leaving, rather than people trying to get in.'

'Not good enough,' snapped Osorkon as Pendareva's vox squawked to life again. Even over the hiss of static and screech of sirens, he could hear the gunshots, screams and the clang of metal through the vox.

'Code Imperator!' screamed a voice. 'Code Imperator! We need help here. Now, damn it, now!'

The vox barked one last hard bang of static and went dead.

'What is Code Imperator?' demanded Osorkon.

Pale-faced and shaking, Pendareva said, 'It's a full-scale prison riot.'

Six gunships, their blood-red hulls streaked with the scars of re-entry and the acid storms, swooped like raptors towards Zhadanok, their prows curved and cruel. Blue jet-wash flared from their engines and silver contrails spiralled in energetic vortices from their wings.

Of ancient design, they resembled the Astartes Stormbirds of old, but with added embellishments of unclean runes and sigils.

They streaked through the rain-lashed air towards the prison complex, the warriors within grim-faced and ready to visit death upon their enemies. Without power, the guns of the prison did not track them or open fire, their auxiliary batteries long since depleted and never replaced.

The lead vessel broke away from the pack and circled low on an attack run directly at the recessed prison gates. Four missiles leapt from the underwing rails and streaked towards the gate, exploding in quick succession and blowing a path within.

Even as the smoke cleared the others were circling in to land, each disgorging twenty warriors of such discipline and methodical precision that they could only be Astartes.

Or had once *been* Astartes…

DE ZOYSA CHECKED for signs of life on the two downed enforcers, even though he could see from the blood and pallor of their flesh that it was useless. Both were dead, though he had no idea what had happened to the third enforcer on duty in this section.

A faint, acrid smell of burning metal came to his nostrils and he looked down at the lip of the cell trapdoor that led to the oubliette below. Streamers of brackish liquid oozed from around the edges and hissed with faint wisps of steam.

'Shit,' he said, hauling on the chain that opened the trapdoor.

Stained acid spilled from within and sloshed over the raised edges in a sudden flood. A battered and mostly corroded helmet was carried clear and the fate of the third enforcer was no longer a mystery.

De Zoysa and his men backed away from the bubbling, frothing trapdoor as foaming runnels of acid bloomed into the corridor. Hissing trapdoors along the length of the corridor leaked streamers of acid as they too were burned through from below.

'Shit,' said de Zoysa again.

THE MAIN HALLS of Zhadanok were awash with blood. Until the power had failed, an uneasy peace had fallen over the complex with the bulk of the enforcers having drawn back within sealed internal bunkers and the inmates contenting themselves with random acts of vandalism and the settling of old grudges.

Firelight danced from makeshift bonfires, and burning rags fell like bright leaves from the highest cells as prisoners set light to bedsheets or anything combustible they could lay their hands on. Whooping yells, tribal and feral, echoed from the high cloisters of the prison as those unfortunate enough to have fallen victim to the savage prison gangs were beaten and hung from the high platforms, their entrails hanging in gory ropes from slit bellies.

The enforcers that had fallen into the hands of the inmates suffered far more gruesome fates, tortured beyond endurance with makeshift blades and flame. Those who didn't die immediately were dismembered and their limbs feasted upon by the more barbaric prisoners.

Zhadanok had become a charnel house, a temple to degradation and blood, its inhabitants its supplicants in search of a high priest.

From somewhere higher, a huge detonation shook the prison, but amid the chaos of the riot no one paid it much mind, too intent on wreaking as much bloody havoc as could be done in these precious moments of freedom.

Between the running battles between the gangs, the occasional attempt would be made to assault the enforcers' position, but with only short-bladed shanks to their name, the booming shotguns of the enforcers hurled back every attack in smoke and blood.

But once the lights went out, all bets were off.

Lights failed, the blaring acid sirens were silenced and the motorised wheel locks disengaged with harsh clangs that were clearly audible in the sudden silence.

Slowly, the internecine battles between the prisoners halted as they realised that the hated enforcers were no longer secure in their bunkers and a gathering mob began to encircle each lonely bastion.

Though there were no leaders left alive by now, a hierarchy of the strongest and most ferocious prisoners had established itself, and they now led the screaming charge towards the enforcers' bunkers as a new light broke upon the main halls of Zhadanok.

The main gate at the far end of the hall vanished in a blinding detonation, hurling killing blades of metal spinning through the air. Prisoners milled in confusion and dozens were cut down by gunfire from the enforcers.

The smoke of the explosion billowed and whipped in the freezing air that knifed into the prison from high above. Shapes moved in the fog of debris and fire, massive forms swathed in brazen plates of armour the colour of coagulated blood.

Like daemons of the abyss they marched into Zhadanok Prison, spreading out and forming an unbroken line of red warriors. They each carried a monstrous, unwieldy-looking weapon before them, the eyes of their snarling helmets glowing with the fires of the warp.

Some prisoners wept and soiled themselves, seeing only death in these horrible figures, while others cheered, seeing liberty. Such optimism was hopelessly misplaced as the intruders' guns barked bright flames and blew apart those who ran towards them, bursting them like wet, red blisters.

Screams of fear and rage erupted from the prisoners as this new enemy gunned them down. Primitive knives and looted shotguns were no match for boltguns and power armour and all who came near these warriors were slaughtered in seconds.

The enforcers, likewise not knowing the identity of the intruders, but sensing nothing but ancient and terrible purpose in their implacable march, fell back in a rout, abandoning their posts and fleeing deeper into the prison.

'What's happening above?' said Osorkon. 'We need information.'

'I don't know,' snapped Pendareva, his patience with the inquisitor lord finally wearing thin. 'Nobody's answering their vox. At least not with any sense.'

'Inquisitor Osorkon,' said Justicar Kemper. 'We should move back down into the prison until we can gain a clearer understanding of the situation above.'

'There's a damn riot going on above!' shouted Pendareva, an edge of panic in his voice. 'That's the bloody situation above! If you hadn't come for this bastard, we'd be sitting pretty. This is all your fault!'

'Be silent, Pendareva,' snapped Osorkon. 'Without the Grey Knights here, we would not even have a fighting chance. Now unless you have anything pertinent to say, keep your mouth shut. Justicar Kemper, you are sure of this strategy?'

'Yes,' nodded the Grey Knight, 'if the vessel above is truly of the Word Bearers, then it is likely they come in strength to retrieve this traitor. We will need to wait until my men are in position to launch a counterattack and we can trap them between us.'

'Agreed,' said Osorkon. 'We move deeper into the prison.'

'That would be a very bad idea,' said de Zoysa, reappearing from around a bend in the tunnel and jogging back to join them.

'Why?' asked Osorkon.

'Because the prison's filling up with acid from below. You heard the sirens. The pumps have failed and the lower levels are already full.'

'How long?' asked Pendareva.

De Zoysa shrugged. 'The oubliettes are full and the acid's coming in at a hell of a rate. If the blast doors hold... then we've got an hour, maybe less.'

FINN PEERED AROUND the corner and saw the sealed blast door that led from the Hell Hole. He'd been waiting anxious seconds, but nothing had yet come through and he knew he didn't have long. Someone must have found the bodies he'd left behind him by now and they'd be on his tail like spoorbugs on a fresh turd if he didn't get moving.

Then, as though in answer to his prayers, the door began to rise and he tensed himself for action.

He heard running feet and screams of panic and fear, watching in amazement as a bloodied, terrified mass of enforcers streamed past him.

Finn slid down the wall, drawing himself into a tight ball and keeping the shotgun clasped tight to his chest, as the enforcers fled down the corridor he'd been about to turn into, oblivious to anything except their own terror. He saw their faces and knew that this was more than just panic from a riot – something had seriously freaked these guys.

Hard barks of gunfire followed them and Finn was sprayed with fine mists of red as enforcers exploded from within. He looked back through the door to see red-armoured daemons following the enforcers, malevolent and implacable, fire and death blasting from the roaring muzzles of their weapons.

'Holy shit...' breathed Finn, seeing that these guys were seriously bad news. Then he saw the insignia on the shoulder guards of their armour, a dark daemonic face with curling horns... the same as he had seen in his dreams and he knew then that these were the true Brothers of the Word.

But as he watched the slaughter of the enforcers, he realised that these were not the liberators of his visions and that they'd kill him just as happily as they were killing the enforcers.

He pushed himself from the wall as the red-armoured warriors slaughtered the last of the enforcers. On one level, they were so very like the devotional picts he'd seen of Space Marines, yet horribly different. As uncaring as Finn had been to the majesty of the Astartes, he saw on a very basic, instinctual level these warriors were just… *wrong*, plain and simple.

Finn turned tail and ran, taking off in the direction the enforcers had been heading.

He doubted it would lead to safety, but it sure beat staying here.

Pendareva could see that Osorkon was rapidly running potential scenarios through his head, but was coming up dry. They couldn't go deeper into the prison thanks to the acid pumps' failure and their enemies were coming from above. Pendareva now knew the full implications of being stuck between a rock and a hard place.

'Are there any cells near here that aren't below the acid line?' barked the inquisitor.

'Not now,' said de Zoysa. 'All the oubliettes are flooded and the corridors between here and the lower levels will be full of acid by now.'

'There are interrogation chambers on this level,' added Pendareva. 'Not as secure as cells, but they'll do in a pinch.'

'Take us there,' commanded Osorkon.

Pendareva nodded and indicated that de Zoysa should lead the way.

The party moved off with a hurried desperation, de Zoysa leading them back through the Hell Hole towards its upper levels. Twice they passed beneath areas of transparent plasteel, their surfaces now a worrisome concave bow as the acid rain softened them almost to the point of bursting.

They heard distant shots and screams echoing weirdly along the tunnels, their proximity impossible to pinpoint due to the twisting acoustics of the lower levels. Each time de Zoysa led them along another corridor, Pendareva expected to meet fiends from the pits of his worst imaginings; beings like Erebus.

Thinking of the traitor made him turn his head as he made his way towards the interrogation chambers. For someone so dangerous, Erebus was about as docile a prisoner as any warden could hope for. Perhaps it was the acceptance of his fate or the prospect of potential rescue that kept him calm, but whatever it was, Pendareva was thankful for it.

They made their way into a wide corridor. The turning that would take them to the interrogation chambers was fifty metres ahead of them, the corridor travelling onwards for half that again.

'Halt,' said Justicar Kemper and everyone jumped. Without words, the three of the Grey Knights moved to the front of the party and braced themselves with their be-weaponed halberds held out before them.

'What's going on?' he asked.

'Something's coming,' said Kemper, by way of explanation.

Pendareva bit his lip as the sound that had alerted the Grey Knights came to his own mortal senses. The sound of running feet and panicked breathing. A lone figure skidded around the corner of the tunnel far ahead and Pendareva saw that it was no daemon or monster, but an inmate.

An inmate carrying a shotgun.

'It's Finn!' shouted de Zoysa, raising his own weapon. 'Put him down!'

Pendareva watched Finn hear de Zoysa's shout and throw himself flat as a hail of shots sawed the air from the Grey Knights' weapons, ripping a line of gouged rockcrete in the wall above him.

Finn slammed into the wall, losing his grip on the shotgun and the weapon skittered away from him. He rolled onto his front, knowing that trapped like this, there was no way he could avoid another fusillade.

De Zoysa racked his own shotgun, but before he could fire, Osorkon said, 'Hold your fire. He may know what is ahead of us!'

'What?' shouted de Zoysa. 'He killed three of my men!'

'Irrelevant,' said the inquisitor. 'Bring him.'

De Zoysa looked pleadingly at Pendareva, but he could only shake his head.

'Do as he says.'

Cursing under his breath, de Zoysa led a team of enforcers forwards and hauled Finn to his feet none too tenderly, sweeping up the fallen shotgun and returning to the main group.

'Man, you don't want to hang around here,' coughed Finn. 'They're right behind me.'

'Who?' demanded Osorkon. 'How many?'

Finn shook his head. 'Don't know. Big guys like them,' he said, nodding warily at the Grey Knights, 'but bigger and with red armour. The Brothers of the Word. I saw about thirty, maybe more. Look, gimme a gun, they're gonna kill me just the same as you.'

'Shut your mouth, Finn,' snarled de Zoysa, and Pendareva could see the man's lust to do Finn harm.

'The Brothers of the Word,' said Osorkon. 'Where did you hear that?'

'I don't know,' said Finn, casting nervous glances over his shoulder. 'Look, they'll be here soon. They killed all the others and they're gonna kill you if we don't get the hell out of here.'

Osorkon seemed to consider this for a moment, and Pendareva willed him to speed his thought processes as the rhythmic tramping of marching feet echoed from ahead.

'Come on, for the Emperor's sake!' shouted Pendareva, running towards the corridor that led to the interrogation chambers. 'Even I can hear them coming!'

The rest of the group followed him down the turning, the corridor eventually opening out into a wide, semicircular chamber with iron doors spaced at regular intervals along the curved wall opposite them. A thick transparent dome of armoured glass spilled a bleached light into the chamber, its outer surface slick and sheened with acid rain.

Pendareva ran to the door in the centre of the wall and slid his control wand down the locking mechanism before he realised that the power was out. Only an unknown time of battery life remained and there obviously wasn't enough to power secondary locks.

He pulled the door open with a squeal of rusted metal and said, 'This is as secure a location as we have that isn't under the acid.'

A dim glow filtered out from the interrogation chamber, where a silver gurney sat in its centre, surrounded by trays of excruciation implements and banks of innocuous-looking machinery.

Justicar Kemper pushed the compliant Erebus inside, turning to one of his warriors and Pendareva could hear the click of inter suit vox. The Grey Knight nodded and braced himself before the door, readying his halberd at the same time.

'Spread out,' ordered Kemper as de Zoysa and his enforcers opened the other chambers and began dragging out gurneys, tables or anything that could be used as a barricade or shelter. Finn was unceremoniously tossed against the curved wall, still protesting that he needed a weapon.

The sound of approaching warriors was even louder now and Pendareva felt his terror suddenly seize hold of him in a bone-crushing embrace. Until now, he had felt that the Grey Knights would protect them without giving the matter a second thought, but hearing the inevitable, drum-regular footfalls of their enemies drawing nearer and nearer, he realised that they were all doomed.

'Here,' said de Zoysa, pressing a shotgun into his damp palms.

'What?' he said numbly. 'I don't know how to use this.'

'It's easy,' growled de Zoysa, racking the slide for him. 'Just point it at any bastard that tries to come along that corridor then pull the trigger. Pull the stock tight into your shoulder, 'cause it's got a kick like a grox to it.'

Pendareva nodded and pulled the weapon in tight, though he was shaking so much he didn't know that he'd have a hope of hitting anything. De Zoysa moved among his men, barking words of encouragement and promises of the rewards they'd get once this was all over, but Pendareva was sharp enough to hear the lie in them.

Osorkon drew an exquisitely tooled boltpistol from beneath his robes and his augmetically enhanced warriors took up position, crouched low to either side of the entrance to their refuge.

'I'll not let them take him,' hissed Osorkon. 'By the Emperor I won't.'

'You may not have much choice,' pointed out Pendareva.

Osorkon shook his head. 'If they want him out so badly, then it is our duty to deny them that if we can't hold on until our reinforcements arrive.'

'Do you really expect them to?'

'If we can hold on long enough,' answered the inquisitor. 'And do not forget, we fight alongside the Grey Knights, the finest fighting warriors of the Astartes. Anything is possible.'

Osorkon's optimism gave Pendareva hope and stilled his shaking hands a little. The inquisitor was right. The Space Marines were the greatest warriors of humanity and if anyone could hold against such dreaded foes, it was surely them.

The first warning the enemy was upon them was when Justicar Kemper raised his arm and opened fire with the weapon fitted over his gauntlet. The report was deafening and Pendareva almost dropped his own weapon. The rest of the Grey Knights fired a heartbeat later and Pendareva yelled in released fear as he saw red shapes jittering in the strobing flashes of gunfire.

He squeezed the trigger of his shotgun, grunting in pain at the power of the weapon's recoil. He didn't know if he'd hit anything, but racked the slide as de Zoysa had done and fired again.

In the lull between shots, the inquisitor's augmetic warriors leapt to their feet and danced amongst the red-armoured figures still standing, shimmering swords and energy sheathed daggers cutting through armour, meat and bone. Even Astartes plate was no protection from such esoteric weapons and limbs were lopped from torsos, heads from necks and arms from shoulders.

They killed six of the red-armoured enemy before the first of them fell as one of the armoured killers trapped his glowing sword between pierced armour plates and snapped the blade with a twist. A daemon-mouthed bolter was rammed into the warrior's chest and his back exploded in a halo of splintered ribs and shredded meat. The second of the inquisitor's warriors spun away from a brutal clubbing blow and ducked beneath a slashing sword, but was unable to avoid a thunderous boot that hammered into the side of his head. The impact split his skull from jawbone to temple and he dropped, limp and dead, bone and oozing matter spilling from his burst brainpan.

More gunfire lanced out and Pendareva flinched as thunderous impacts hammered amongst them, ripping through the space like horizontal rain. Enforcers were hurled back, torn apart by explosive bolts that were little short of missiles and Pendareva was struck by how ludicrous an idea it was that these gurneys and tables might offer protection from such weapons.

More red warriors were pushing up the corridor, heedless of the fearsome casualties they were sustaining plunging headlong into this firetrap. Only the weapons of the Grey Knights and the inquisitor were having any real effect, the gunfire of the enforcers' shotguns pattering like rain on their enemies' armour.

Numbers were telling as more and more of the red warriors gained the interrogation chambers and, without seeming to give any verbal command, Justicar Kemper led his Grey Knights forward with their halberds lowered. Red and silver warriors clashed in a din of plate armour, the fighting close and brutal. The Grey Knights spun their long, be-weaponed halberds in practiced motions, stabbing, hacking and bludgeoning the enemies with disciplined strikes.

An enemy warrior fell, his head a splintered ruin and his limbs jerking spastically as he died. His finger continued to pump the trigger and explosive rounds sprayed in a curving arc up the wall…

…and across the transparent dome of armoured glass.

Against normal solid rounds the glass might have held, but against heavy-calibre, mass-reactive shells it cratered explosively and a spiderweb of cracks snarled across its surface from the epicentre of the bolter round's impact.

Pendareva looked up, hearing the high, sharp *tink, tink, tink* of the cracking glass as it crazed wildly.

'Oh no...' he breathed. 'The glass... it's–'

The warden never got the chance to shout his warning as the armoured glass finally gave way, shattering into a thousand fragments and falling in a diamond rain of razor glass. Pendareva rolled towards the curved wall, hearing the heavy crash of the shattered dome and the screams as his men were torn apart by long, glittering daggers of glass.

The heavily armoured Space Marines were untroubled by such inconsequential missiles, but the enforcers were not so lucky. Pendareva saw de Zoysa sliced from shoulder blade to groin as a sheet of glass struck him edge on. Another enforcer was impaled by three long, glittering spears, while a blade of glass sliced down like a guillotine and sheared off another enforcer's arms.

In the wake of the glass came the acid rain. A howling gale of corrosion poured into the interrogation chambers, swirling the broken shards of glass around in a whirlwind. Pendareva cried out as he felt the acid's burning touch and desperately scrambled towards the nearest door as he saw Finn drag himself through the doorway of one of the excruciation rooms opposite.

He hooked his blistering fingers around the edge of the iron door, hearing a shout of pain from behind him. Inquisitor Lord Osorkon lay on his side, his robes smouldering and holed where the acid had eaten away at it. The inquisitor's hand reached out for him, the flesh hissing and spitting like fat on a griddle.

Pendareva wanted to help him, but knew that to head back into the maelstrom of battle, swirling acid and dancing glass was to die...

A blur of red moved past him, the thud of heavy footfalls sounding close to his head, but he ignored it and crawled onwards, pulling his battered body into the coolness of the excruciation room, rolling onto his back and gulping great gasps of air.

The clash of arms, gunshots and the shrieking hurricane of wind and acid still echoed from beyond and he pulled himself backwards on his elbows, trying to put as much distance between himself and the horror beyond the door as possible. Pendareva looked up as he heard gurgling moans of pain and the same heavy footfalls that had passed him not seconds before.

Erebus stood silhouetted in the doorway, Inquisitor Lord Osorkon gripped by the scruff of the neck in one meaty fist, with a grin of triumph splitting his tattooed features.

'The Emperor's wrath...' hissed Osorkon, just barely hanging onto consciousness.

Erebus silenced the inquisitor with a backhanded slap across the jaw, then turned his horrifying, ageless gaze on Pendareva.

'Please,' said Pendareva as the noise of battle was suddenly, horrifyingly silenced from beyond the door.

All he could hear was the roar of the wind and the hiss of bodies dissolving under the assault of the acid.

'Please what?' said Erebus. 'Don't kill you? Take you with us?'

'I don't want to die,' said Pendareva. 'Please, your... friends have rescued you, isn't that enough? I never mistreated you here. You don't need to kill me, do you?'

'Rescued me?' laughed Erebus, a harsh, humourless bark. 'Is that what you think happened here?'

'Isn't it?'

'Do you really think that one such as I would allow myself to be taken by a grubby little gaoler like you? My presence here is by design, not chance.'

'Why?' was all Pendareva could think of to say to that.

In response, Erebus lifted the supine inquisitor, holding him as easily as a man might hold a limp rag.

'This deluded corpse-worshipper has knowledge of secrets I very much desire to know – secrets I will learn as I tear his flesh and soul apart. He knows things unknown to the blind masses of ignorant humanity, ancient knowledge that has been secreted in forgotten places and the location of forbidden gateways to the Empyrean where awaits my lord and master.'

Most of Erebus's words meant nothing to Pendareva, but one thing was abundantly clear: Erebus had engineered his own capture to lure Inquisitor Osorkon to Orina Septimus, knowing that only a figure of infinite malice would draw him into the open.

Everything that had transpired this bloody day had been in service of this moment and Pendareva knew that he was a dead man.

'Good,' said Erebus. 'You see your fate.'

FINN HEARD THE solitary gunshot from the other excruciation room and pressed himself into a tight ball in the corner of the chamber. The liberation his dreams and visions had promised him had come to nothing. He prayed that these red-armoured warriors would do whatever the hell it was they were here to do and get lost.

There was still a slim chance he could come out of this with his hide intact, though he wasn't going to bet the farm on it. Finn held his breath, hearing the heavy tread of armoured warriors enter the room, and he stood, determined to face death on his feet.

Two of the daemonic warriors had entered the room, towering above him. One was without a helmet, his skull covered in twisting tattoos and Finn recognised him as the warrior who had been a prisoner earlier.

'Kill him and be done with it, Erebus,' said one of the warriors. 'We have what we came for.'

'Yeah, go ahead, Erebus,' snarled Finn, spreading his arms defiantly. 'Kill me.'

The tattooed warrior stepped towards him and leaned down, reaching towards his face. The fingers of his armoured gauntlet brushed Finn's cheek where blood from the dead enforcers had spattered him.

Finn locked his gaze with Erebus, knowing that his life was hanging in the balance.

'He is warp-touched,' said Erebus. 'I can taste it, like cold steel in my mind. This is who led you here, though he knew it not.'

'Then shall we take him too?'

Erebus shook his head and said, 'No. We will leave him and he will bring hell upon anyone who finds him.'

Without another word, Erebus turned and marched from the room, leaving Finn standing bewildered in its centre. Through the open door he saw the red warriors gather up their dead and make their way from the interrogation chambers, Erebus dragging a blue-robed figure behind him.

As they left, Finn could see the hulking bodies of Space Marines in torn silver armour littering the blood-slick ground, taking a measure of satisfaction from seeing de Zoysa's corpse amongst the dead.

He let out a long, shuddering breath and held himself upright against the doorway, unable to believe that he was still alive after such carnage. Wind from beyond the shattered dome still whipped acid squalls around the chamber, but its force was spent, the storm above moving onwards.

He reached out and hooked his fingers around the canvas strap of a shotgun and pulled it from under the body of an enforcer. Acid burns had rippled the stock, but he smiled as a quick inspection of the firing mechanism told him that it was still locked and loaded.

Finn racked the slide as he considered his situation.

He was trapped on a world bathed in corrosive acid storms in an underground prison that was rapidly filling with acid.

Erebus had said that he was going be bring hell on whoever found him...

Well, he got that right, thought Finn with a malicious grin.

THE INVITATION
Dan Abnett

BEYOND KAEROGRAD AND the fertile plains, where the northern country rises into the maw of winter, there is a place called Namgorod, which men held for a long while until the holding of it became too hard and they let it go into the wilds. Even in summer, the northern country is no friend to man: the steep, flinty hills, the ragged forests, the deep glens where streams are frozen in their beds for three-quarters of the year. In winter, the north coughs up snow upon the place, as a consumptive coughs up blood, and the region is a mortal enemy to anything warm and alive. Men knew this when they built Namgorod, knew it every winter as they tried to hold on, and when they left it to the ministry of the ice and snows, they understood that winter was its true master.

Tegget came to Namgorod on the eve of glittering winter. He could taste it in the air, like a cold stone in his mouth, and smell its sharp edge. Tegget was a catcher of men, and the northern country sheltered its fair share of outlaws, absconders and fugitives in the summer months, so he knew the trails well enough. But it was six weeks past the end of catching season, and those fugitives that did not intend to die of cold had already tried to flee across the plains: most of them into the waiting clutches of professional men like Tegget.

A catcher of men, especially one so honed and experienced as Tegget, had no business coming to the north so late in the year, but Tegget had good reasons. The bounty was one; more than he could make in three decent seasons. The loan of an expensive, self-heating bodyglove was another. Most of all, it was the nature of the request. By dint of his profession, Tegget was an outsider to the finer echelons of society in Kaerograd, tolerated as a necessary evil by the grandees and nobles of that city. For the Regent himself to make the request, well that was a wonderful thing indeed. Tegget anticipated prestige, an elevation in rank, perhaps even a royal commission. 'Lowen Tegget, Catcher of Men, by appointment to his Excellency the Regent.'

Tegget worked alone. He had explained this fact to the Regent, and it seemed to suit. The Regent, speaking somewhat indirectly to Tegget, as if a bad odour had invaded the private chambers of the Regency, had emphasised the delicate nature of the matter. It was to be kept 'close'. If rumours of it got out, Tegget would find his prize money forfeit. Other punishments were hinted at, and stipulations made.

Tegget had never been one for talking about his work. He just did what he did. He imagined that was why the Regent's people had sourced him. That, and his reputation. Though Tegget didn't talk about his work, others did, and Lowen Tegget was known for his wetwork, and the remarkable extent to which he messed people up.

Tegget rode his transport, a fat-wheeled AT-bike, to within a kilometre of Namgorod, then killed the drive and continued on foot. The bike's engine had a muteshield, which had cost him plenty on the black market, but he didn't want to push his luck. He buckled up his armoured jack, slid his hunting las from the bike's saddle boot, and threw two of his best psyber lures into the air. The metal blades of their wings opened as they ran free, and they circled the treetops with gentle beats. Both of them were small aquila-form: artificial kestrels wrought from steel and compound ceramics. Tegget pressed his left cheekbone, and the occular implant in his left eye-socket began to display, split-screen, the view from the lures.

Namgorod was quiet. Flaking black ruins, the largest a great shell of ribs open to the wind. There was a light dusting of snow on every surface. The sky was hard and dark, like smoked glass and, in the west, the first, bright winter stars had just appeared like lanterns.

'Where are you?' he whispered.

'IF I'D–' PAVLOV Curtz, Regent of Kaerograd, cleared his throat, trying to compose himself, 'If I'd had some notice of your visit, great lady, I would have prepared a rather more–'

Olga Karamanz held up her hand for silence. 'Do not exercise yourself, Regent. I require very few things of you, and a formal, ceremonial welcome is not one of them.'

Curtz shrugged. 'Forgive me, great lady, but the Cauldrus system is a backwater, most often overlooked. State visits are rare, especially from such an august personage as the Canoness of the Order of the Martyred Lady. The Ecclesiarchy will wish to schedule conference with you, to discuss matters of faith, and the–'

'This is not a state visit,' said the battle-sister standing to the left of the canoness.

'As has been specified,' added the other, waiting by the door, 'this is a private matter.'

Curtz opened his mouth to speak, then closed it again, and sat down. The minute they had arrived and been announced, he had realised something was wrong. A canoness like Olga Karamanz did not make an idle visit to a place like Cauldrus Prime. Nor did she come so secretively, hurried in through the back doors of the Regency, attended by just two sisters. There was no entourage, no massed escort. The three women were dressed in veiled black robes, which only slightly betrayed the armour beneath.

From what he could see of Canoness Karamanz's face behind the veil, she seemed surprisingly young. Her features were slim and very fair, almost adolescent in their purity. He could not guess her age, though her voice was soft and dry as if it was a thousand years old.

'You know what this concerns?' she asked.

Curtz nodded. 'The... uh, the matter of the miscreant.'

The battle-sisters attending the canoness were both considerably taller and more robustly made than the great lady herself. Faces invisible behind the veils depending from their starched black headdresses, they stood with their hands clasped in front of them. The canoness had introduced them as Sister Elias and Sister Bernadet, though the Regent had lost track of which was which.

'The miscreant,' said Elias or Bernadet.

'You saw fit to report the incidents discreetly via ecumenical channels,' said Bernadet or Elias, 'which tells us you understood the sensitivity.'

'I... yes,' said Curtz.

'Yet you are surprised to see us?'

Curtz cleared his throat again, and rose to his feet. He crossed to the sideboard and retrieved his half-drunk glass of amasec. He had been called away from the end of a trade dinner for this unexpected event. He was still wearing his formal robes and the ridiculously ostentatious badges of the guild and union offices he was patron of. He took a sip and let the sliding warmth of the liquor stiffen his resolve.

'I expected a response,' he said. 'Perhaps an envoy, perhaps even a sister ambassador. Someone to smooth things over and see that things were done properly. Not... not the canoness herself.'

He looked round at them. 'I'm so sorry, may I offer you a–?'

Olga Karamanz shook her head on behalf of all three of them.

'You are put out, Regent,' she said. 'My apologies. We were already in the vicinity at the request of the Most Holy Ordos. And, well, we want to make sure that this is handled... properly, don't we? Why don't you begin by telling me exactly what happened?'

Curtz nodded. He thought, in a sudden, uneasy flash, of Tegget, and wondered if he had done the right thing in hiring him. Throne knew, he had no wish to anger a canoness.

Nor any wish to send a man to his death.

Even a piece of scum like Tegget.

THE GREAT HALL of Namgorod loomed over him like the bones of a whale. Flakes of snow were falling, silent and soft and almost luminous, out of the night, and the wind had dropped. The air-chill was savage.

Lowen Tegget had known hardship. He was ex-Guard, ex-stormtroop elite. He'd seen some living hells, and dreamt of them still, some nights. This cold was just a trifle.

He moved in through the ruins, all the while rubbing the powercell of his hunting las with his heated glove to keep it lively. There was something here. Signs of heat residue, a cook fire, the gnawed bones of small animals. And something else: a presence, a shadow that lurked just out of reach in the silent ruin.

He knew what he was supposed to be tracking. The fact didn't scare him, but it made him particularly alert. 'The miscreant is a dissembler,' the Regent had said. 'It wants us to think it is something, and it is most certainly not that thing. God-Emperor, Tegget, I'd not send you up there if I thought there was any truth to it. This is a matter of pretence, and blasphemy.'

Blasphemy. That was a word to conjure with.

Namgorod had been the first township built by the settlers when they had reached Cauldrus Prime centuries before. They had raised it here because it was a site adjacent to their initial landing zone. The great hall he was presently creeping through had been built from ribs and girders scavenged from the wrecked colony ship that first winter. Later, the colonists had realised that other parts of the planet offered more decent and habitable conditions, but Namgorod, as the first coming place, had persisted out of respect for a long time, until it had become untenable.

Untenable. Untameable. Such was the northern country. The people of Cauldrus Prime, Tegget's ancestors, had abandoned Namgorod, because it was too wild, too inimical to human life.

Something wild was with him now. He could taste it as surely as he could taste the snow.

He checked the view from the lures. They were circling the hall, their vision boosted by cold-light and nightfibre arrays.

Tegget heard something. A tiny mouse noise in the darkness to his left. He raised the rifle, panning it slowly.

There was a blink, and his lure-sights went dead. First one, then the other. He tried to re-cue them, but the links were flat. He felt his pulse rate elevate.

Something hit him from behind so hard, so fast, that he had no time to cry out. He saw his rifle spinning in the air. He saw the world upside down as he was somersaulted away from the collision.

He saw blood in the air, jetting arterial blood, and knew it was his own.

'I STROVE, MORE than anything, to protect the reputation of the order,' Curtz said, resuming his seat. 'There were three incidents, mass-killings. The perpetrator made a great effort to suggest they were the work of a battle-sister.'

He paused, and looked at the canoness and her guards. 'A battle-sister of the Order of the Martyred lady,' he emphasised. 'A battle-sister... *corrupted*.'

The three veiled women remained silent.

'I knew this was impossible,' Curtz went on. 'Absolutely impossible. Your kind – forgive me, great lady – your kind are incorruptible. I made a careful study of the archives to reinforce my opinion. History shows us many horrors, but never a battle-sister fallen. That was when I realised it was a sham. Lunacy in fact. I suspected that it was matter of blasphemy. You are no doubt aware that the Pyrus Reach is greatly conflicted of late. Terrible times, and the poison of it, I'm glad to say, is slow to reach us. Sometimes being a backwater has its benefits. I supposed that some miscreant desired to stain the order's name by committing these crimes, to engender unrest and panic. I sent the reports to alert you to the defamation.'

He paused. Still, the three women remained silent.

'Now... now, I'm not so sure.'

'Because?' asked the canoness.

'Because you're here.'

'What did you do?' asked Elias or Bernadet.

'I hired a man. A fellow of decent reputation as a catcher of men. I hired him to hunt down the miscreant, so that the matter might be settled and the good name of the order cleared.'

The canoness rose to her feet. 'You sent a man after this... as you said... miscreant?'

'A good man. A capable man.'

'Regent,' she said. 'You have signed his death notice.'

'I made provisions,' Curtz said quickly. 'The man was no fool. Very capable, very sly. He will keep his mouth closed.'

'Forever,' said Bernadet or Elias.

'Now look–' the Regent began.

'You look, Regent,' snapped the canoness. 'I have to know where the man went, and on what clue. This must be contained.'

'Are you telling me–' Curtz began, astonished by the realisation of what they were saying.

'I am telling you nothing,' the canoness said. 'It is better that way. Throne knows, for all of us. Tell me where this man went.'

'I can do better than that,' the Regent said, his voice tiny and terrified. 'I can show you. As one of the terms of his employment, I insisted he carried a tracker.'

'Report?' whispered the canoness into her vox. The night was moonless, and flakes of falling snow stuck against the dark gauze of her veil.

'Trace is clear,' Battle-sister Elias replied.

'Advancing,' voxed Battle-sister Bernadet.

Two of the best, the canoness thought to herself. Bernadet and Elias, two of the most profoundly gifted warriors in the order. They were long since out of sight, but she could picture them. Elias with her storm bolter, Bernadet with her power sword and flamer. Two of the best.

Then again, the canoness thought, *Miriael* was the best of the best.

The canoness walked down an avenue of black trees through the falling snow, her hand upon the haft of her mace. Her gown was unheated, but the armour beneath it protected her from the hideous cold. This cold has been sent by the Emperor, she reasoned, and thus was mortifying and uplifting.

Her lander had put them down two kilometres from the place called Namgorod. The Regent had begged them to wait until morning, at which time he would have been able to summon a significant force of PDF troopers from the Interior Guard to support them.

Not appropriate. This had to remain a private matter. If anyone found out, if word spread–

Olga Karamanz stiffened in dread. This whole matter was unthinkable. Unbearable. Better it was finished now, quickly, under the silent folds of a bleak winter night. Miriael. *Miriael.*

They had found the AT-bike up on the track, and followed the tracer signal down towards the ruins. The Regent's man – Tegget – was undoubtedly hours dead, but the tracker had been a smart idea. His corpse might be cooling, but the device was still alive and signalling.

'Something–' Elias voxed.

Then, 'No, nothing. Just a dog-fox. Area's clean.'

Karamanz raised her tracker handset. The signal from the poor unfortunate's body was still clear, and stationary. Ahead, in the ruins of the great hall.

Where are you, Miriael, Karamanz wondered? That wasn't the real question. The real question was: what did they do to you?

What did the vile powers of Chaos manage to do to you when they held you in their clutches? Verdicon. That's where it happened. Miriael Sabathiel, sister superior, had been reported as missing in action during the vicious fighting against the unholy Emperor's Children.

And then this. Back from the dead. Back, but changed. Changed in ways no other Sister of Battle had *ever* been changed.

Second only to the mighty Astartes, the Sisters of Battle were the most perfect fighting mechanisms of the Imperium of Man. Unlike the Astartes, none of them had ever fallen to corruption. What a trophy for Chaos. What a twisted champion.

'Canoness?' It was Elias.

'Speak, child.'

'The outbuildings are empty. I'm coming west on your flank.'

'Close in.' Karamanz drew her mace and ignited it. It hummed blue in the snowy dark. 'Bernadet?'

'East of you, approaching.'

The canoness stepped into the great hall. Snow sifted down like flour through the bare rafters, tie-beams salvaged from a long-defunct starship. The trace was just ahead of her now. She paced forward, mace by her side, anticipating the sight of Tegget's corpse.

There was no corpse. Just a spatter of blood across the black flagstones.

A spatter of blood and small, blinking device...

Karamanz's mind turned quickly. 'Beware!' she voxed.

Her warning came too late for Sister Bernadet. Clambering over the slumped, snow-dusted rubble of the east transept, Bernadet turned and raised her weapons as she heard a whirring. The psyber lure, beak and claws to the fore, whipped down out of the night and punched through her veil, through her face, through her skull. Bernadet staggered, clutching automatically at her ruined head, her discarded sword and flamer bouncing off the loose stones around her. A half-noise burbled out of her ruptured throat.

She fell dead on her face.

Elias heard her fall and ran to her. She was ten paces away when Bernadet's fallen flamer somehow misfired all by itself. The firestorm hit Elias like a hammer, and burned off her robes, her veil, and the skin of her face. She stumbled, on fire, screaming in fury. She raised her bolter in a hand dribbling with molten fat and tissue.

A las-round, a hot-shot from a hunting weapon, burst her cranium and felled her.

Twisted and still, her corpse continued to burn.

'Elias? Bernadet? Sisters?'

Silence. The crackle of the dead-link vox. The crackle of the flames. The sigh of the winter wind.

'Miriael?'

Karamanz turned in a slow, wary circle, her mace ready.

'Was I so easy to find?' asked a voice from the dark.

'Miriael?'

'Was I so easy to find?'

'Yes!' Karamanz hissed.

'Good.'

'Miriael, please. I want to help you.'

A shadow disengaged itself from the night. Just a shadow, hunched and puppet-like, its long, shaggy hair backlit by the glow of the snowfall.

'I knew you would come looking for me,' the shadow said. 'I knew you would hunt me forever.'

'I want to help you.'

The shadow laughed.

'By the power of the Throne, and the God-Emperor–' Karamanz began.

'Shut up! I won't listen to that any more.'

'Miriael...'

'There are so many things I want to do. So many things I need to do, but all the while you are hunting for me, I can't be free. I needed this.'

'This?'

'Oh, great lady, why do you think I made it so easy for you to find me?'

Olga Karamanz froze. Her grip on the haft of her mace tightened.

'I wanted you to come, so we could be done with this.'

The shadow stepped closer. It wasn't Miriael. It was a rough-set woodsman in an armoured jack, swaying and pale, wounded. He held a hunting las across his chest, but made no attempt to raise it.

'Miriael!'

'My lord Balzaropht has plans for me,' the hidden voice said. 'But I can't accomplish them all the while you're hounding me. So I called you here, so this could be done with.'

Canoness Olga Karamanz swung around and raised her mace into the third quarter defence. The sword, its blade as bright as the snowlight, was already inside her guard. It ripped through her gown and plate armour, and opened her body to the spine.

She fell, pouring hot blood into the cold floor. Steam rose. Behind her veil, her mouth opened and closed uselessly.

'Hush,' said the voice. 'We'll speak no more about it.'

'I'M COLD,' SAID Lowen Tegget. He sat down, and hunched his head between his knees. He was tired. There was a dreadful stench of blood in the air of the great hall, like hot iron.

'Cold can be ignored,' said the shadows.

'Says you. I'm cut here. You cut me.'

Miriael Sabathiel emerged from the darkness, sword in hand, and bent down beside him. 'You'll heal. You're mine now. Daemon princes sing and my pulse quickens. Soon yours will quicken too.'

'Throne,' Tegget sighed. 'Am I cursed? Have you cursed me?'

'You were the invitation, Lowen. You helped me defeat my enemies. I'm showing my gratitude by sparing your life... and sharing with you the wonders I've seen.'

Tegget groaned.

Miriael Sabathiel straightened up and held out her arm. The two kestrel lures swooped in and perched there. One was dripping with blood.

'I like you, Lowen. I like your toys. They please me. You could serve me.'

'How, lady?'

'Oh, Lowen Tegget. By being you. You are a cunning man. A fine killer. See, tonight you did for two Sisters of Battle. There is nothing you can't do.'

Tegget smiled and shook his head sadly.

'I'm just a catcher of men, lady,' he said.

She reached out her hand and began to stroke his shaggy hair. 'You're so much more than that, Lowen,' she said. 'You're my friend, and you're an instrument now. I'd like you to walk with me and serve at my side.'

He looked up at her, his face pale and frightened. 'Is this what corruption feels like?' he asked.

She nodded, still stroking his head.

'Feels good,' he admitted. 'Where will we go?'

'Ah, now, my little hunter,' Miriael Sabathiel said. 'How are you at hunting eldar?'

A BALANCE OF FAITH

Darren-Jon Ashmore

SISTER HOSPITALLER VERINA'S chronometer told her that the sun had come up several hours earlier, as she and Colour Sergeant Allyonna Fillonova crept over the lip of their bastion's forward observation trench to survey the road up to the Dinu Pass. Not that it mattered much, however. Above, a warp-fuelled storm, conjured to keep the sky free of aircraft, shut out much of the light and only by the ruddy glow of the burning Valken Forest away to the south could the women inspect the carnage before them through their low-light field glasses.

The ground was littered with many overlapping craters and the broken bodies of the thousands of Chaos cultists who had been hurling themselves up the slope at the chain of hurriedly built fortresses each dawn for days. An attack had petered out only half an hour before and many of the corpses still smouldered, wreathing the scene in oily smog and giving off a rancid stench which even Verina's filter-veil could not quite shut out. However, it was not the ruin of the slope which she wished to examine, but the great pits at its base, just out of range of Imperial ordnance, where the beasts of Chaos had been slowly erecting siege guns of immense calibre. Ancient almost beyond reckoning, and once the property of some lost Imperial army, these great beasts of pipe and plate were still swarming with technical servitors, but even Verina could see that they were mere hours away from being ready to fire.

'My lady, look to the leftmost pit. Land Raider, or might have been once. Word Bearers.'

Verina started slightly at Allyonna's words, as if simply speaking their name would invite the dread Pain Lords among them. However, it came as no surprise to find them here. Valerius, apostle of the dread Chaplain Erebus, had landed a large contingent from the Word Bearers Legion on Hyrus Secundus a few weeks previously and it made sense that they would come, hungry for the men and women of the Guard who still waited for evacuation from the Eretov spaceport.

They might not be able to take these positions in the close assault, thanks to the automatic batteries which the Hyrusians maintained, but once those mortars had dropped a few dozen bunker busters onto the bastions they would have things their own way. She wheeled the focus of her glasses round until she could make out the corrupted transport in better detail. The blade-covered machine was clearly a close assault carrier: a 'Black Crusader'. Her worst fears were confirmed when the front ramps opened up and a Word Bearers heavy assault Marine clambered out, moving fluidly even in the enormous Terminator suit which made his already massive frame seem truly gargantuan.

Dropping back into the trench, Verina turned about and looked through the ruins of the Shrine to the Emperor Triumphant, into the valley where the remnants of the 7th and 21st Hyrusian Guards crowded around Eretov's launch pads. She counted six cargo shuttles still on their gantries and a steady stream of other vessels, from drop-ships to large private yachts, dashing back and forth to the fleet in orbit. She flinched a little to think of the Navy, whose cruisers had suspended bombarding the planet earlier that morning and, not for the first time, the enormity of the situation caused her to shiver. No bombardment could mean only the worst: the Navy had been withdrawn to picket duty along the ascent paths from evacuation points like Eretov, and Grand Marshal Helfrich had indeed conceded the planet to the Great Enemy. Still, this defence line had to be held for at least another twelve hours if enough troops were to get away.

Not wishing Sergeant Fillonova to see her concern, Verina jumped over to the rear of the observation trench to get a glimpse of the ruined Imperial iconography in the once beautiful building. When the 1st Company of the 7th Hyrusian Guard had been air-dropped to the remains of the shrine last week, Commissar Andrôz Jelinek had ordered the altar cleaned and repaired whilst Verina herself had restored a faceless statue of Saint Katherine to its place at the right hand of the Emperor. None in the company had much skill in such matters to be sure, but even so Verina had taken some heart from the work as it helped her address the conflicting feelings which had burst forth from her on the death of her master.

Before Inquisitor Lord Matanlé had taken her from the Order of our Martyred Lady, Verina had loved nothing so dearly as making devotion to the mistress of her order through the works of healing which had been her calling from childhood. She had, according to Canoness Sophitia, a gift for healing and hands that could nurture even the most broken soul back to health. Indeed, it was no lie that she was the most devout surgeon to come out of her order for generations and it was probably that which drew Lord Matanlé to the convent seeking her service, much to the disapproval of her mentor.

As her mind went back over that day, Verina recalled the bitter exchange between Sophitia and the ancient inquisitor clearly. 'I brought her up, and she is dear to me and gentle of spirit. She knows *nothing* of the world beyond these walls and is not ready for so onerous a duty'. At the time, with the arrogance that can only be found in the young, Verina actually half believed that Sophitia's words had actually been calculated to humiliate her before the inquisitor and keep her in the Convent of Saint Katherine. She had secretly been pleased when the smiling Lord Matanlé had simply waved away Sophitia's concerns and pointedly asked the canoness if the order wished to officially oppose his selection. As Verina later discovered, the lord, being possessed of the Dark Gift, not only knew of Sophitia's inherent disdain for psykers, but also that the Sisterhood would not dare oppose the Inquisition in such a matter.

And suffer Verina did, after being torn out of her world of pure faith and being ordered to put her talents to direct use in the service of the Imperium. Though not entirely unaware of the nature of the foes of mankind, Verina found herself closer to the witches, cultists and fallen of the Imperium than few ever get. Though she was regularly able to work her healing arts on the lord's retinue, her primary task was surgically examining prisoners during interrogation and over two hundred had come under her knives in the four years before arriving in the Pyrus Reach last month. 'Cutting the truth out of them,' Lord Matanlé had called it. Of course, all but a small handful had ultimately died, with the guilty being purged by fire and those judged innocent by the good inquisitor being granted the release of the Emperor's Mercy.

There lay the heart of Verina's dilemma: no matter how the avuncular Lord Matanlé had couched it to his 'fragile little Sister' in the gloomy interior of his cruiser. She had sworn the oaths of healing to Saint Katherine before being required to break them in the name of the Emperor. Either way she had turned in her mind she faced heresy; the moral sin of disobeying oaths sworn on all she held as sacred to the Golden Throne, and the mortal sin of disobeying her lawful master's, and therefore the Emperor's, orders. She had trained to save the lives of her Sisters and the Emperor's servants, yet she had been complicit in the murder of many of them and might have murdered more had not Lord Matanlé's Valkyrie been brought down as his retinue arrived in the city of Hyrograd to investigate cult risings on Hyrus Secundus.

Coming back to herself, Verina looked upon the ruined visage of Saint Katherine and felt tears on her own cheeks. She now imagined that the statue was faceless because she was shamed and could not look upon her doubting Sister. Verina had failed the test of faith on both counts. In her heart she firmly believed that she should either have had the courage to deny Lord Matanlé, and take her own life, rather than break her oaths of healing, or accept the hard duty she had been given without the doubts which now beset her. Dropping to her knees, she opened the blister on her right bracer and let the needle of the Emperor's Mercy slide quietly down, past the boom of her surgical saw, and over the back of her hand. She had used much of her supply in the piecemeal assaults which the enemy seemingly felt obliged to throw up the pass every morning. However, several full canisters remained; enough for dozens of doses and more than enough to reconcile Verina to all the questions which plagued her mind.

She imagined the drug suffusing her system, sending her into a dreamless sleep before the pyro-chemical agents in the compound set light to her flesh and reduced her sinful remains to ash.

'Hah. You still alive?'

THE VOICE BROUGHT Verina back to herself, and she turned to see who was addressing her.

She discovered that Sergeant Fillonova had moved down the trench a way. She appeared to be speaking to one of the corpses hanging from the wire. One of them, a young man in a tattered suit, had begun moaning and feebly clawing at an open laser burn on his chest. Sergeant Fillonova had taken out her laspistol and was adjusting the power setting.

'Give me a moment and I'll close that up for you.' Sergeant Fillonova gave Verina a steel-eyed smile and shot the traitor. His chest should have exploded; superheated flesh bursting from the opened wound. However, the slash simply sizzled in the low power beam and the young man writhed in agony.

'Sorry,' called the sergeant, 'but you've got to keep still. Wriggle around like that and I'll have your eye out'. She fired again and this time cut a line down the cultist's face, across his left eye, and burned a deep gash in his cheek.

'Give him one for the commissar,' shouted a Guardsman from a foxhole further up the hill. 'Make him scream for his friends down there.'

Sergeant Fillonova moved forward again, acknowledging the cheers of her comrades with a jaunty flourish of her pistol, and even Verina could see that this was getting seriously out of control. These shootings were attracting attention and not all the enemy's guns were out of range. She sprang across the trench, and hurled herself upwards to drag the sergeant down from the fire step just as a sharp crack echoed through the shrine. The back of the Guardswoman's right shoulder ballooned under her armour and she fell backwards into Verina's arms, dropping her pistol into the mud.

Verina rolled the gasping sergeant onto her side and cut away the cracked armour with her wrist saw. The entry wound was a black-edged star and, though the greatly distended shoulder had split in places, there was no clear exit point. The conclusion was obvious to Verina: a ripper. She had seen wounds caused by these tainted shards of obsidian before, designed to fragment on entry and send sorcerous splinters racing down the nerve tracks to cause decay in anyone unfortunate enough to survive the initial shot. She had only managed to save one person clipped by such a round before, and even then it had been at a properly staffed field centre, as well as at the cost of the Crusader's sword arm. Here, with few tools and no assistants, the prospects were bleak indeed. Nevertheless, Verina hoisted Fillonova onto her shoulders and began carrying her back to camp with the intent of doing whatever she could for the fallen Guardsman.

'Kill me. Please. For the love of the Emperor, just kill me.'

Verina barely registered the laser shot from the shrine which flashed over her head and silenced the young man's cries.

REACHING THE MAIN camp, Verina placed Fillonova into a cot between the ashes of Commissar Jelinek and the terribly wounded Dark Angels Librarian who had stumbled into camp at dawn and lapsed into unconsciousness without a word. The company were terrified of the Space Marine, of course. None of the

Guard here, save perhaps the late commissar, had ever met a member of the Adeptus Astartes before and to see one bearing wounds that should have killed him instantly by any sane standard, blanched even these elite 1st Company fighters.

Verina had initially thought they saw in this hooded and daemon-masked Dark Angel a reflection of Valerius's Word Bearers, who hovered on the edge of all their thoughts waiting for their moment to strike. However, she also knew that to see one of the Emperor's godlike warriors so mangled had affected them all deeply. For if the mysterious Dark Angels had been scattered, as seemed to be the case, then what hope could anyone else have?

These thoughts were unimportant at the moment, and Verina put them aside as a lifetime of training came to the fore. She tracked the course of the shards in Sergeant Fillonova's shoulder as best she could. It soon became apparent that the woman would probably not last the hour, as her wounds had already begun to exude the sickly smell of decay which would end her struggle. She dosed the area with pain killers, and restrained the sergeant when she tried to rise.

'Be still Allyonna. I will ease your suffering as best I can,' Verina said, moving her bracer into place.

'That was stupid of me, my lady,' said Fillonova in a broken whisper, stirring from her shock as the drugs took hold. 'The commissar would have skinned me alive if he'd seen it'.

Verina looked over shoulder to the remains of their former commander, mortally wounded by shell fragments the day before. 'Why did you not just kill him back there Allyonna? It is not like you to be so precipitate'

'I don't know, my lady. We've been watching those guns get closer for days and since the fleet stopped shelling we all know that we're little more than a forlorn hope. I suppose I wanted to strike back myself, and I do feel better for it.'

'How so?'

'At least I've shown them down there that we are not hiding behind our machine spirits and missiles.'

'But to die like this?'

'It is as good a death as any I can think of, and a better one than I'd feared. Though I might think differently if I could actually feel the wound.' The sergeant laughed coldly and picked up one of the empty analgesic shots with which Verina had dosed her shoulder. 'Don't let me shame myself before the company. Don't let me turn,' implored Fillonova at last, grasping at the Sister's right arm.

Verina sensed that the Guardsmen around the camp were quiet and were, whilst seemingly absorbed in many menial tasks, clearly hanging on her exchange with Sergeant Fillonova. The 1st Company respected their colour sergeant and she was speaking as much for their benefit as for any other reason. But Verina knew enough about death to know that this woman was, at the last, content with her lot and her service to the Imperial Guard. Her final act was to give her troops confidence in the one who would replace her in command and, while Verina knew that she would not long outlive the young woman, she respected Fillonova enough not to disturb her passing with the truth.

'You have given all that you can give in His name, and in His name I acknowledge that service. Allyonna Fillonova, I grant you honourable rest from your labour,' said Verina and, intoning the Litany for the Righteous, she introduced the needle on her bracer into Sergeant Fillonova's neck.

Death had visited the camp many times in the past week, but as the remains of the sergeant began to smoulder on her deathbed, it seemed to Verina that the surviving

Guardsmen were, though obviously cowed, resolved as never before. This was not the fanatical bravery Verina had seen in the Cadian Kasrkins, from whose ranks Lord Matanlé habitually drew his stormtroopers. Neither was it the righteous zeal of her order's warrior Sisters, whose battle prayers pierced the heavens. Nor was it the sure, centuries tested faith of the Emperor's own sons, for whom every act was a devotion to the Light of Man. The simple dedication of the Hyrusians shamed her own unvoiced doubts even more, and she could not bear their gaze. Once the rites had been completed, she drew herself to her feet and walked towards the restored shrine, determined to make an end of the coward which she had become.

'A moment if you please, good Sister.'

Looking round at the sound of the unfamiliar voice, Verina saw that the Dark Angel had woken. 'I sense that time is short, and not just for myself. Come closer. I would have words with you, and have not the strength to bawl across this camp at you for long.' The Librarian slowly levered himself up on his elbows, blackened blood and amber fluid oozing from rents in his abdominal armour, and beckoned Verina towards him.

Though terrified of the power which this Angel of Death, even in such a weakened state, might possess over her mind, Verina walked serenely over to the Librarian and placed her hand upon his shoulder. She pondered the possibilities and came to the conclusion that he would simply have her executed for heretical thoughts and cowardice. The Dark Angels were known to be among the most intractable of the Astartes and Verina secretly prayed for harsh judgement from this righteous warrior prince.

'My name is Crucius, Sister. What think you of our current position? What are the enemy dispositions? What is your plan?'

'We are a forlorn hope, my Lord Crucius. We are one of six such bastions and have been holding the enemy back to buy time for one of the evacuation centres at Eretov spaceport. The enemy have brought up their siege bombards and within hours we will be overrun by Word Bearers. I have no plan,' Verina said quietly.

'None save self-destruction, child?' Crucius asked. 'I sense the conflict within you and would urge reconsideration. You are in need of counsel and I am in need of your services. Therefore let us speak of what drives a devoted daughter of the Emperor to the brink of bodily heresy and we may each yet save the other.'

'I am a coward, lord,' and this was the first time Verina had confided her sins to any save her own conscience. 'I doubt all that I am and all I have trained for. I have killed hundreds and now cannot reconcile the acts with the necessity for them. How can I command these troops when I cannot command myself?'

'You are a Hospitaller of Saint Katherine are you not?'

'Yes Lord Crucius, in service as an interrogator to the late Inquisitor Lord Matanlé.'

Crucius closed his eyes for a moment and then spoke in measured tones. 'So you think that your desire to preserve life is a weakness, in that you doubt the necessity of your services to your lord?'

'Faith is purest when it is unquestioning, my lord.'

'The very words of the Canticle, but hardly helpful in this case. Why did your inquisitor call you to his service?'

Verina thought about this for a while before answering. 'Because he had heard that I was the finest healer which the order had trained in recent years. The only one in a decade to have sung the oaths of healing as a novitiate.' There was little point in lies or false modesty.

'So, he knew you to be a righteous and principled woman, dedicated to the salvation of the Emperor's servants? Anyone who so diligently trains to save life is bound to have reservations about killing, are they not?'

Verina remained quiet, reflecting upon the past, thinking about the long nights of interrogation and the things which she had done in the Emperor's name. 'He called me a Blade of Truth and would not allow anyone else help him question sensitive subjects. He must have known how I hated it, and yet he always called on me.'

'Were I in his place, I would certainly not want some over-eager butcher handling such matters. I would desire accurate results, not random violence. Who better to act in such a capacity than one whose faith is pure and who takes absolutely no joy in the act?'

'But I should not have doubted him. You speak the truth my Lord, but I should have had faith in him. My oaths to the order…'

'Cannot be cast aside,' interrupted Crucius, 'nor *should* they be so lightly discarded. You still do not see the truth before your eyes do you? Your ability to question your orders is what made your lord seek you out, of that I am certain. Doubt is an essential part of our faith and our belief in the holy Emperor's cause.'

'That is heresy.'

'Not so, though you have not lived long enough to understand the nature of such doubt as I now do. I am ancient even by the reckoning of my Chapter and might have gone to the coffins soon, had this campaign not seen the end of me. I have seen the certainties of faith twisted in ways you could not even begin to contemplate. The Word Bearers and their like for example. When they originally rose in rebellion they did so not because they doubted our lord, but because they did not doubt the right of their cause. Their hearts were so full of the certainty of their path that they were snared by their own conceit and have suffered for centuries because of it.'

Crucius looked at the storm overhead and said, more to himself than to Verina, 'And we are born out of that same rebellious stock. How can we but doubt our own strength in the face of such dreadful facts? No little Sister, the test of doubt is what keeps our faith strongest in times of crisis.'

Confused by Lord Crucius, and things which passed her understanding, Verina looked down at her hands and thought about the deaths she had perpetrated over the years. She accepted Lord Crucius's words that she had been selected from the convent because she was of a temperate nature and mindful of her oaths to her order. Yet, the universe was a savage place indeed if it could visit such contradictions on a person.

'You still think yourself poorly used?' said Crucius. 'Now *that* is verging on heresy. I know you better than you think little Sister. Your heart has not been broken by work which would have driven many mad. You are that rarest of Imperial servant, in that you stubbornly refuse to be parted from your sense of compassion. Let your doubts have their reign, but do not let them consume you as they almost have.'

Verina was strangely comforted by the Librarian's words as they peeled away her own conceits from the truth which she had evaded for so long. 'I should still die for my transgression. That is the only just punishment.'

'Maybe so, but that is not for me to decide. All our ends seem certain enough in any event and, as such, there seems little reason to hurry yours along a few minutes, for I sense that you still have employment here. Your own soul has been saved from self-destruction, but there are still others in need, and one of them lies before you.'

It took Verina a few moments to realise that Lord Crucius was referring to himself, and even then she could not bring herself to ask what it was he wished of her. 'I will help in any way I can, but even had I the proper equipment, I know little of Astartes physiology. I would likely do more harm than good.'

'That is the point though, dear little Sister. I require you to "do more harm" as you put it. My gene-seed cannot fall into the hands of the enemy, and while it is a capital crime to cut myself off from my brothers in this fashion, the greater crime here would be allowing the Ruinous Powers to seize my seed and populate their ranks with my progeny.'

Verina moved closer to the Librarian, who tilted his neck to give Verina access to his neck. Not knowing how to proceed, she fed a dose strong enough to fell over a dozen into the system of the stricken Space Marine and even then was not certain that it would be enough.

Crucius settled back onto the ground and stiffened slightly, as the Emperor's Mercy began to take effect. Struggling visibly, he took up the Reliquary from his chest, opened its doors, and removed the fragment of armour which lay within. Handing it down to Verina he closed his eyes.

'This is all we have from him, and it is the one regret I have that I will not live long enough to see him returned to us.'

Confused again, Verina could only look at the fragment of green plating and wait for Crucius to go on.

'You think me mad to wish this? There are many among your master's ranks who think our whole Chapter driven insane by our past misdeeds, but what good will his death gain for us if we cannot bring him home?'

'My lord? I do not understand.'

'Blessed is the Fallen come home to his brothers. Cleanse the penitent and strip away his spoiled flesh. Let his spirit go before the All Father. Let him be judged and castigated. Let that redeemed soul rejoice in His mercy.'

Verina could see that he was fading fast now, as the Emperor's Mercy began to attack his organs and nervous system.

'Tell me, dear little Sister. What think you now of our position? How is our foe disposed? What is your plan?' said Crucius, and his voice was barely audible.

Verina felt her soul lift as it had not done since her days in the convent. She fell to her knees in reverent awe, and even the fearful Guardsmen circled the pair in silent tribute.

'We are an Imperial Guard assault force, Lord Crucius. The enemy has ranged siege guns against us so that they can sweep away the defence of Eretov spaceport. It is my proposal to sally forth with this unit and disable those guns before they can be fully readied for action against our bastions.'

VERINA HAD NOT entirely known what to expect from the surviving Guardsmen after Crucius finally passed away. In many ways they had every right to disregard her statement of intent to the Librarian and follow their written orders to the letter. However, she was moved to tears of joy to see them quickly and professionally gathering up ammunition, poring over tactical readouts and prepping the local gun batteries to provide cover. One of them had obviously communicated the idea down the line however, and Verina soon found herself with a vox set in hand discussing her scheme with the other base commanders in the chain.

The decisions were taken in moments and the batteries primed in minutes, and very soon the cannons and rocket turrets began firing, throwing up great gouts of mud and rock into a sight screen just beyond the defensive wire.

'Follow the barrage closely,' shouted Verina to the assembled troops. 'Those with charges know where to go, and what to do. Disregard all but your targets and you will prevail'.

'Difficult to ignore fifty Word Bearers coming at you, my lady,' called one of the women at the back of the group, who carried Sergeant Fillonova's standard, unfurled and ready for the advance.

'Unless you've got Sister Verina snapping at your heels,' replied one of the veterans at the front, which drew a murmur of amused assent from many.

This was good, thought Verina as she allowed a smile to play on her young face. They were frightened and obviously knew they were marked for death, but they believed in her and that would be enough to see them through.

Hefting the ornate chainsword, once the property of Andrôz Jelinek, Verina considered what it meant. She had never wielded so mighty a blade before and knew she had not the skill for it, but this ancient device spoke more of her final understanding of the nature of her oaths and what they actually meant to her. Thus, readied for her final act of devotion, Verina mounted the fire step and looked upon the remains of the young cultist who Alyonna had tormented. She offered a silent prayer to the Golden Throne that his desire for redemption had been heartfelt, then stepped up onto no-man's-land and began following the creeping cannon and missile barrage down the hill.

A light screen though it might have been, it covered the Guardsmen well enough and much of the fire which came their way fell short, went wide or flew over the company's heads. However, all too soon the curtain dropped and Verina's attack groups found themselves only yards away from the enemy, who were attempting to brace themselves for an assault.

The technical servitors, as numerous as they were, melted away before the fire coming from the sixty or so

Guardsmen, and there were no Word Bearers to be found in the gun pits as the Hyrusians dropped into them to place their thermo-explosive packs. Verina knew that these small engineering charges would not destroy the guns, but she also knew that this was not necessary. Melting the elevation gears, the traverses and the breach locks would delay the enemy by at least a day and by the time the guns could be repaired, Eretov would be a burned out, and very empty place indeed. She counted off the dull *crumps* one by one until, with her own team at the end, all six bombards were blazing away, bathed in a blue-white glow.

The incoming fire to the rear was intensifying now and her troops were finally coming to grips with hardened foes. Verina could also hear the chilling mechanical wails of enraged Word Bearers Marines amid the tumult and prayed that her soldiers made the end they deserved.

Casting her gaze back up the hill one last time Verina's heart leapt to behold a break in the storm above the pass. For an instant, the briefest of moments, a shaft of brilliant light played across the ruins of the Shrine to the Emperor Triumphant and, even after it had been put out by the swirling clouds, a soft glow seemed to emanate from that sacred hilltop. Commending her soul to Saint Katherine, a joyful Sister Hospitaller Verina turned to face the towering, dead-eyed monsters that advanced upon her group with great shimmering claws attached to their befouled Terminator armour. Stepping slightly forward of the firing line she raised the commissar's chainsword above her head and called out to her force. 'In the name of the Emperor, sell yourselves dearly, and show these things how Guardsmen can fight.'

GATE OF SOULS
Mike Lee

DIRGE WAS A cursed world.

It was a planet of bleak stone and black rock, and it didn't belong in the Hammurat system, of that much the Imperial surveyors were certain. It was a rogue world, one orphaned from its home star countless millions of years in the past, and it had wandered through the darkness of space for millions of years more before being trapped in the grip of Hammurat's three blazing suns. Where Dirge had come from – and what strange vistas it had crossed over the aeons – the surveyors didn't care to know. Its surface was a wasteland of deep craters and jagged peaks, shrouded in thick, poisonous air that howled and raged under the cosmic lash of Hammurat's suns.

What mattered was that Dirge was rich: a virtual treasure trove for the ever-hungry forge worlds of the Pyrus Reach subsector. The planet's crust was thick with valuable metals, radioactives and minerals, and the cometary impacts that had shattered Dirge's surface had brought with them even more exotic elements in amounts never before catalogued. When news of the discovery reached the subsector capital it touched off a frantic rush of prospectors and mining expeditions, eager to cash in on the new world's untapped riches. Within the space of a year, almost two million prospectors, miners, murderers and thieves had come to Dirge to feast upon its riches.

Little more than a year later three-quarters of them were dead.

Seething electrical storms burned out equipment and raging winds tossed fully-loaded ore haulers around like toys. Seismic activity collapsed tunnels or trapped gases exploded under the touch of plasma torches. Men were carved up in backroom brawls over claims too hazardous to mine. The outnumbered proctors mostly looked the other way, pocketing bribes equal to a year's salary on more settled worlds and counting the days until their transfers came through.

Sometimes prospectors would return to the crater-cities from the crags or the deep tunnels, bearing artifacts of polished stone inscribed with strange inscriptions. When the rotgut was flowing in grimy taverns all over Dirge, men would sometimes go quiet and whisper of things they'd seen out in the storms: strange, corroded spires and dark menhirs covered in symbols that made their blood run cold. No one paid the stories any heed. Prospectors loved to tell tales, and what difference did some strange stones make when there was money to be made?

And so the crater-cities grew, spreading like scabs across the deep impact wounds the comets left behind. Men died by the thousands every day, killed by storms, earthquakes, carelessness or greed. Still more lost their minds from metal poisoning, mounting debt, or simply snapped from the stress of constant danger and merciless quotas from corporate masters dozens of light-years away. They blinded themselves with homemade liquor or wasted away in the grip of drugs like black lethe and somna. Some sought comfort in the words of itinerant priests, putting their salvation in the hands of holy men who took their tithes and sent them back to their dormitories with empty prayers and benedictions.

In the end, nothing made a difference. Until a prospector named Hubert Lohr came down from the crags one day, sold off all his possessions and began preaching a new faith in the bars and back alleys of the crater-cities. Lohr accepted no tithes; instead he offered people the secrets of Dirge. He spoke to broken-down miners, diseased prostitutes and petty thieves and told them of the Lost Princes, who still wandered the void in search of their wayward world. The Lost Princes possessed powers greater than men – greater even than the God-Emperor, who offered nothing but mouldy catechisms and cruel exhortations for the men who lived and died beneath His gaze. Lohr told the fevered crowds that if they made an offering large enough it would shine like a beacon across the void and lead the Princes back to Dirge. And when they returned they would reward the faithful with gifts beyond their comprehension.

By the time the agents of the Ecclesiarchy and the planetary governor realised the peril in their midst it was already too late.

THE BATTERED AQUILA lander had barely touched the plasteel tarmac before Alabel Santos was out of her seat and striding for the landing ramp. Even without the grim badge of the Inquisitorial rosette gleaming upon her breast she cut a fearsome figure in her ornate power armour. One hand rested on the butt of her inferno pistol and a sheathed power knife hung in a scabbard on her other hip. 'Get the gun servitors ready,' she snapped at the portly, middle-aged man struggling with his own restraints while fumbling for his respirator mask. 'I don't plan on being here long.' Her man Balid bleated something in reply but she paid little heed, her armour's respirator system whining with strain as she headed swiftly out into the howling wind.

Purple lightning flared overhead, etching the bustling airstrip in sharp relief. Tech adepts swarmed over a long line of parked Vulture gunships, tending fuel lines and reloading rocket pods for another fire support mission over Baalbek City. On the other side of the plasteel tarmac sat a cluster of Valkyrie Air Assault craft, red tags fluttering from the Hellstrike missiles loaded on their stubby wings. A platoon of armoured stormtroopers, part of the Guard regiment's mobile reserve, huddled near their parked transports, cursing the wind and waiting to be called into action.

Santos spotted the permacrete bunkers of the regimental field headquarters just a few hundred metres from the airstrip, the pale colour of the new structures standing out sharply from the dark grey terrain. The guards on duty raised their weapons at her approach, but hurriedly stepped aside when they saw what badge she wore. She cycled through the atmosphere lock then pushed past bewildered and tired staff officers before marching stiffly up to a broad planning table set with an old-fashioned paper map of Baalbek City. Grainy aerial reconnaissance picts were spread across the table, highlighting different city districts. Studying them was a short, broad-chested officer in the uniform of the Terassian Dragoons, surrounded by a pair of staffers and a tall, forbidding woman whose cold eyes glittered beneath the rim of her peaked commissar's cap.

The colonel glanced up at Santos's approach, a curt order on his lips, but his exhausted face went pale at the sight of the gleaming rosette. His gaze continued upwards. The inquisitor's head was held stiffly erect in a frame of brass, lending her stunning features the severe cast of a martyred saint. 'Colonel Ravin, I presume?' she said without preamble. Red light flashed balefully from her augmetic eye. 'I am Inquisitor Alabel Santos of the Ordo Hereticus. What is your situation?'

To his credit, the colonel didn't skip a beat, as though having an Imperial inquisitor arrive unannounced at his headquarters was all in a day's work. 'Two months ago dissident elements among the mining population engineered a planet-wide revolt, overwhelming the local proctors and PDF contingents–'

'I know why you're here, colonel,' Santos snapped. 'I've been reading your despatches since you arrived on Dirge.' She studied the picts scattered across the table and plucked one from the pile, sliding it over to the colonel. The aerial image showed a mob of citizens surrounding a bleached pillar of bone, their gloved hands raised in supplication before the blasphemous sigil at its peak.

'You aren't dealing with dissidents,' Santos replied coldly. 'They are something altogether worse.'

Colonel Ravin and the commissar eyed one another. 'They call themselves the Cult of the Black Stone,' the commissar said. 'That's all we've been able to learn so far.'

'Then I shall educate you further,' Santos said, leaning across the table. 'This is the symbol of the Word Bearers, colonel.' The inquisitor rapped the pict sharply with her knuckle for emphasis, causing the staff officers to jump. 'The Ruinous Powers have taken an active interest in Dirge, and I have reason to believe that one of their greatest champions is at work in Baalbek City. I've come halfway across the subsector to find out why.' And to stop him once and for all, Emperor willing, Santos thought grimly. You have much to answer for, Erebus.

Colonel Ravin's pallor deepened. 'But that's... that's incredible,' he stammered. 'Traitor Marines? *Here?* How do you know this?'

'Because it is the Inquisition's business to know such things,' Santos snapped, turning back to the picts. Out of the corner of her eye she saw the colonel stiffen, then with an effort she reined in her temper. You have enough enemies without needing to make more, she reminded herself.

'It's all in the reports, colonel,' she explained. 'I've been studying every status report, Administratum log and Ecclesiarchal dictum filed from Dirge for the last six months.' Santos picked up one of the picts: it showed the planetary governor's palace in Baalbek City. Like all city structures, it was low, broad and windowless, built to withstand the frequent cyclones that swept over the crater wall from the wastelands. The resolution of the pict was good enough that she could recognise the impaled figure of the planetary governor, suspended on a girder among an iron forest set on the palace roof. The inquisitor set the pict aside and reached for another.

'Four months before the uprising, merchant ships were reporting strange surveyor readings in the vicinity of the system's far asteroid belt,' Santos continued. 'The local port authority dismissed the reports as pirate activity, but curiously, there was a dramatic drop in pirate attacks in the system over the same time period. Shortly afterward, orbital traffic control detected a number of unidentified flights into and out of Dirge's atmosphere. Again, these reports were passed off as smuggling activity, but I have another theory – a Chaos warship entered the system and is likely still here, hiding in one of the system's asteroid fields.'

Santos studied an image of cultists dragging bloody corpses from a burning dormitory towards the base of one of the cult's sacrificial pillars. She set it aside with a frown of contempt. 'Then there are arrest reports from the local Arbites headquarters. In the days leading up to the uprising several cult figures were arrested and when put to the question they described their leaders as armoured giants – the "Lost Princes", according to one of the prisoners. The cultist described the greatest of these princes as a god among men, who wore the skins of his foes as testament to his power and bore a mighty talisman of his gods' favour.'

'The Chaos champion you spoke of,' the commissar declared. 'Who is he?'

But Santos shook her head. 'I dare not speak his name. I've placed your souls in peril just telling you this much.'

One pict after another showed cultists at work around hab units and municipal buildings across the city, carting out truckloads of debris and hauling them away. After the fourth such image she began to line them up on the map table in chronological order.

'If the prisoner was to be believed, there were no less than five Word Bearers present on Dirge, including the Chaos lord. That's an astonishing number for such a minor world.'

'Minor?' Ravin said. 'Dirge supplies more than half of the industrial materials used by forge worlds across the subsector.'

'The Word Bearers don't make war according to the Tactica Imperium,' Santos declared. 'They don't think in terms of lines of supply or resource interdiction. They fight for souls, spreading terror and debasement from world to world like a cancer. Dirge, however, is both isolated and sparsely populated. From their standpoint, it's a poor target.' The inquisitor studied the line of images and her frown deepened. 'Colonel, why did you order these images taken?'

Ravin looked over the picts and waved dismissively. 'We were trying to gauge the extent and composition of the enemy fortifications based on how much material they were excavating. Those work teams have been at it day and night since before we got here.'

Santos straightened. 'Excavations.' The inquisitor felt her blood run cold. 'These cultists aren't using floor panels and wall board to build fortifications, colonel. They're hollowing these buildings out to dig for something. That's why the Word Bearers are here. Why *he* is here. The rebellion was just a diversion so they could search the planet without interference.' Her hand was trembling slightly as she snatched up the last pict in the line. The time code in the corner indicated that the last excavation had begun almost three days ago. No new excavations since, she realised. They must think they've found what they're after.

'Colonel, I require the use of your mobile reserve and a flight of Vultures,' Santos declared in a steely voice. 'I'll brief the platoon leader en route.'

THE BUILDING HAD formerly housed the local tithe assessor's office. Only three storeys tall, square, windowless and slab-sided, the structure was built like a treasure vault, which wasn't far from the truth. A small army of servitors and stooped scribes had toiled night and day within its cold, gloomy cells, recording the profits of the mining cartels and the independent prospectors and assessing the Emperor's due.

Now the square outside the building was piled with the guts of the Imperial tax collection machine. Large, ornate cogitators stood in drunken ranks, their wooden cabinets splintered and their brass gauges tarnishing in the corrosive air. Drifts of torn cables and mounds of flooring and wall board were plucked and pushed by the restless wind, and a pall of glittering dust swirled endlessly in the harsh construction lamps erected by the work crews outside the building.

Glass crunched like brittle bones beneath Erebus's armoured boots as he stepped through the narrow doorway. Just beyond the threshold a tiled floor extended for less than a metre before ending in a jagged cliff of permacrete and steel.

The miners of Dirge knew their trade well. Working day and night, they'd completely torn out the first two floors and the building's two sub-levels. Tangles of shorn wiring, crumpled metal ducting and shreds of wallboard hung like man-made stalactites from the gutted ceiling, painted white with a layer of grit that sparkled in the harsh light of the construction lamps.

All work had stopped in the pit below. More than two dozen men set aside their tools and prostrated themselves on the rocky ground at the Chaos Lord's arrival. Erebus looked out over the fruit of their labours and was pleased.

Once the sub-levels had been removed the miners had dug another three metres into the grey, ashy soil before they'd found the first of the black stones. It had taken another day of careful work under difficult conditions to lift away millions of years of rock-hard encrustations that had covered the strange symbols carved into their surface. The work had gone slowly because the delicate sonic brushes would run out of power after only a few minutes in proximity to the rocks, and because the workers' brains disintegrated from prolonged exposure to the symbols themselves. Even from where Erebus stood he could feel the power of the warp rising like black frost from the surface of the accursed objects.

On the orders of Magos Algol, the tallest of the stones had been pulled upright again. It rose five metres into the air, casting a long, misshapen shadow across the excavation site. The surface of the object looked crude and rough-hewn, but the symbols carved into the rounded surface were sharp and precise. They climbed the stone in a kind of spiral, following the rules of a language that had died out before the birth of mankind. At the top of the stone the symbols ended at the base of a perfect sphere, haloed by an arch of stone wrought in the shape of twining tentacles.

Erebus smiled, revealing pointed teeth and the fearful demeanour of a cruel and vengeful god. The Chaos lord was clad neck to foot in the imposing armour of a Space Marine – but where its ancient engravings once extolled the might of the Emperor of Man, it now preached an altogether different faith. Blasphemous runes and symbols of ruin pulsed sickly from the Traitor Marine's breastplate and the edges of his pauldrons, and the skulls of defiled Imperial priests hung from a brass chain around Erebus's neck. Psalms of vengeance and depravity were scribed in blood upon the tanned hides of fallen Space Marine heroes and stretched between barbed spikes across the Chaos lord's pauldrons and from hooks at his waist. In his right hand Erebus held aloft a talisman of fearsome power – the dark crozius, symbol of his faith in the Chaos Gods.

A broad ramp, wide enough for two men to walk abreast, had been built from the ground floor to the base of the excavation. Its steel supports quivered slightly as Erebus descended slowly into the pit. His black gaze was fixed on the standing stone and the orb at its summit.

Erebus stepped unflinchingly into the stone's twisted shadow. The darkness that fell upon him was unnaturally cold, sinking effortlessly through the bulk of his daemonic armour. The Chaos lord felt his shrivelled insides writhe at the icy echo of the warp, and Erebus welcomed it, spreading his massive arms wide. His mind filled with visions of the Seething Gulf, the ocean of mad wonder that the servants of the false Emperor called the *Occularis Terriblus*. It was the font of godhood, the birthplace of universes. Amid the roiling sea of unfettered power, Erebus beheld a swollen red orb that glittered like a drop of congealing blood. He heard the cries of multitudes, the chorus of supplication sung at the feet of his unholy master, and he longed to join his voice to the song. *Lorgar!* His mind called into the void. *The time draws nigh, unholy one. Soon the gate will swing wide!*

Erebus chuckled to himself, the sound echoing in the cavernous space and causing the cultists to tremble in fear. He turned to the assembled multitude, his eyes alighting on two figures kneeling apart from the storm-suited labourers. One was a hulking giant in red armour similar to Erebus's own; the frail, elderly man hunched next to the Word Bearer looked as slight as a children's puppet, all slender sticks and grimy rags, too fragile to touch.

The Chaos Lord favoured his servants with another dreadful smile. 'Arise, Phael Dubel,' he commanded gravely. 'And you, Magos Algol. Blessed are you in the eyes of the Gods Who Wait.'

The magos rose to his feet with an agility that belied his frail and aged appearance. His skin had the grey pallor of a corpse, his thin, wrinkled lips pulling back from gleaming steel teeth in an avaricious grin. His dark robes, once decorated with the fur mantle and chains of a *Magos Archaeologis*, now bore lines of depraved script that spoke of his allegiance to the Ruinous Powers. Algol's eyes glittered like black marbles in the shadows of his sunken eye sockets, bright with forbidden knowledge and reptilian cunning.

Dubel, one of the Chaos lord's chosen lieutenants, bowed deeply to his master and stepped to one side, turning so that he could keep the assembled workers and the open doorway in view at all times. One hand rested on the butt of his holstered bolt pistol. The other, clad in a fearsome, outsized gauntlet called a power fist, opened and closed in an unconscious reflex, as though the weapon hungered for a victim to crush in its grip.

Magos Algol walked a careful path around the sharp edges of the stone's shadow, looking up at Erebus with a calculating smile.

'You see, great one? It is just as the *Book of the Stone* described,' Algol's voice was harsh and quavering, like the sharp note of a plucked wire. 'I told you we would find it here.'

Erebus regarded the towering stone greedily. 'Have you deciphered the runes yet, magos? Does it tell us where the Orb of Shadows lies?'

'In time, in time,' the magos said, raising a wrinkled hand. 'The runes require careful study, great one. Their meanings, if interpreted without proper care, could be… explosive. But,' Algol added quickly, 'it does indeed speak of the orb. You will have the answer you seek.'

'Then do not let me keep you from your work, blessed magos,' Erebus said to the man. 'Inform me the instant that you have deciphered the text.'

The magos bowed to the Chaos lord and approached the stone, his hands fluttering eagerly as he began to contemplate the inscriptions. Erebus joined his lieutenant. 'Send word to the *Throne of Pain*,' he said quietly, referring to the cruiser hiding in Dirge's outer asteroid field. 'We will return to Ebok as soon as Algol has uncovered the location of the orb. Then our work will well and truly begin.'

Dubel looked back at the looming stone, his black eyes lingering on the sphere. 'Once we have the orb, what then?'

'Then we seek the Temple of Ascendancy,' Erebus replied. 'I believe it to be on Fariin, in the Elysiun System, but the orb will tell us for certain.'

The Traitor Marine stiffened, fixing his master with a suspicious stare. 'Ascendancy? You seek to follow the same path as Lorgar?'

Erebus returned his lieutenant's stare. 'I? No, Dubel. I am but a humble servant,' he said enigmatically. 'Perhaps I seek to blaze a path for Lorgar to follow *me*.'

Dubel's eyes widened in shock. Before he could reply, however, the ground shook beneath a drumbeat of thunderous explosions as Imperial rockets slammed into the side of the hollowed-out building.

ONE HAND GRIPPING a support strut just inside the Valkyrie's open hatchway, Alabel Santos leaned out into the assault craft's howling slipstream and watched the Vulture gunships streak over the flat roof of the target building. Fires were burning from rocket strikes in the debris-choked square and tendrils of smoke rose from craters blasted into the building's thick permacrete wall. The landing zone looked clear.

The three Valkyries of the mobile reserve platoon – plus an extra support craft carrying Balid and his gun servitors – were howling along at roof height down one of the city's narrow streets, right on the heels of the gunships. She could already feel the Valkyries start to slow as they dropped toward the deck, preparing to flare their engines for tactical deployment.

Santos swung back into the passenger compartment and addressed the platoon commander. 'Once we hit the ground we're going to have to move fast. Have two of your squads form a perimeter around the Valkyries and I'll have my gun servitors provide support. You and the assault team go in with me. Once we're inside, don't hesitate. Don't think. Just kill everything that moves.'

The stormtrooper lieutenant nodded at Santos, his face hidden behind a full-face tactical respirator that gave him the look of an automaton. His vox unit crackled. 'We're with you, inquisitor,' he said curtly. 'The Emperor protects.'

Santos drew her pistol just as the Valkyrie plummeted like a stone and then stopped less than a metre over the rubbish-strewn square with its engines shrieking. There was a stuttering roar as the door gunner let off a burst with his heavy bolter at some distant target. 'Go, go, go!' she shouted, leaping from the assault craft and heading for the building at a run. Behind her the stormtrooper assault team deployed with speed and precision, hellguns covering the building's entrance. The lieutenant followed right behind Santos, a plasma pistol in one hand and a crackling power sword in the other.

The inquisitor pulled her power knife free from its scabbard and thumbed its activation rune. She rarely carried it; the knife was an heirloom weapon, given as a gift from her mentor Inquisitor Grazlen when she attained the rank of inquisitor.

Santos held the weapon in a white-knuckled grip as she charged into the building's narrow doorway. She was going to bury that burning blade in the Chaos lord's eye or die trying.

Chunks of broken permacrete and twisted plasteel continued to rain down from the gutted ceiling among Erebus and the cultists as turbofans shrieked and heavy weapons fire hammered outside. The Chaos Lord looked for Magos Algol and found the corrupted scholar on his knees, coughing wetly amid falling drifts of dust. 'Finish your translation, magos!' Erebus thundered, then raised his accursed crozius before the huddled cultists and spoke in a piercing voice. 'Rise up, warriors of the faith! The servants of the false Emperor are upon us! The eyes of the gods are upon you – go forth and win their favour!'

With a lusty howl the cultists staggered to their feet and brandished the tools of their trade: heavy sonic drills, power mattocks and arc hammers. They knew from bitter experience what those tools could do to soft flesh and brittle bone.

Dubel drew his bolt pistol. There was a searing crackle as he ignited his power fist's disruption field. 'Death to the servants of the false Emperor!' he roared, and the cultists surged forward, racing up the ramp to the doorway just as the first of the attackers stepped into view.

An inquisitor, Erebus thought, catching sight of a woman in ornate power armour leading the charge. Her alabaster face was distorted in a snarl of almost feral rage, and she fixed him with such a black look of hate that he could not help but think they'd met somewhere before.

Erebus bared his teeth in challenge and spread his arms in welcome, words of blasphemous power hissing off his tongue.

There! The shock of seeing the Chaos lord again sent a bolt of pure, righteous fury through Alabel Santos. Erebus was mocking her, grinning like a devil, his arms open wide. I'll give you something to smile about, she thought, raising her inferno pistol. Just as she drew a bead on Erebus, another armoured shape rushed in front of the Apostle, bolt pistol raised. The mass-reactive rounds smashed into her shoulder and chest before her ears registered the flat boom of the pistol's report. The impacts spun her around, the servos in her power suit whining dangerously as they sought to compensate for the blows.

Footsteps thundered up the ramp towards Santos as a dozen cultists charged forwards, weapons ready. The lieutenant appeared beside the inquisitor, levelling his pistol and firing two quick shots into the oncoming mob. Bolts of superheated plasma blew the lead cultists apart. 'Flamer to the front!' the platoon leader ordered over his vox.

Armoured stormtroopers fanned out on the narrow lip of permacrete to either side of the doorway, firing red bolts of las-fire into the charging cultists. Then a soldier stepped to the top of the ramp and fired a hissing stream of burning promethium point-blank at the charging miners. The cultists shrieked and fell back from the tongue of searing flame, setting the ramp alight with their tumbling, thrashing bodies.

Two stormtroopers to Santos's right were blown off their feet by bolt pistol rounds, their carapace armour no match for the Traitor Marine's deadly fire. The inquisitor dropped to one knee, trying to peer through the thickening black smoke and strobing las-fire for another glimpse of the Chaos lord. She couldn't see him, but she could hear him, his deep, sonorous voice chanting terrible words that sent a shiver down her artificial spine. The Chaos lord's voice rose to a terrifying crescendo – and for a moment it felt as though the very air in the room was receding, drawing back from the battle as if in horror.

The screams of the burning cultists went silent all at once. Then Santos felt the fabric of reality come unravelled. She heard a chorus of screeching howls and tasted hot brass on her tongue, and before she could draw breath to shout a warning the daemons were upon them, charging straight through the fire.

They had faces like skinned wolves and their powerfully-muscled bodies gleamed with freshly-spilled blood. Their eyes, their fangs and their twisted horns were pure brass, bright from the forge, as well as the razor edges of their two-handed axes. Upon their sloped brows was carved the mark of the Blood God, and they had come for a bounty of skulls to lay at the foot of his throne.

Men screamed. The stormtrooper carrying the flamer fell to one knee and toppled onto Santos, splashing the inquisitor with blood. Roaring an oath to the Divine Emperor, she pushed the corpse aside just as a blood-spattered figure loomed above her.

She didn't feel the blow. There was a hot wind against her face, and then there was the strange sensation of warm blood soaking through the bodyglove around her shoulder. Her left arm locked in place and Santos felt the sting of needles as the suit's medicae unit attempted to keep her from lapsing into shock. All she could think was *thank the Emperor it missed my head*, then she put her pistol against the daemon's midsection and pulled the trigger. A bolt of pure cyan, powerful enough to pierce the armour of a Land Raider, tore the daemon apart and then detonated with a thunderclap against the ceiling. The bloodletter dissolved in tatters of stinking, oily smoke.

Santos fell backwards, landing against the marble verge. As though in slow motion, she could see another daemon rushing at her, axe raised to strike. There were screams and the clash of steel somewhere nearby – and then, out of the corner of her eye, she saw the smoke shift and reveal the red-armoured form of the Dark Prophet, standing before a monolith of twisted stone.

Death approached on cloven feet. Santos could feel her strength fading, and between one heartbeat and the next she made her choice. Taking her eyes from the daemon, she steadied her pistol against the marble tiles. With a tic of her cheek, she activated her augmetic eye's laser sight. The needle-thin beam glittered in the smoke, tracing a merciless line across the open space and painting a bloody dot on the Chaos lord's forehead.

'This is for Krendan Hive,' she whispered, and pulled the trigger.

The bloodletter howled above her – and then staggered as a bolt of plasma smashed into its head. The daemon staggered, then the blade of a power sword sank into its chest. The lieutenant leapt over Santos's body as the daemon's form dissolved. 'Get the inquisitor to safety!' he ordered, taking aim on another daemon and shooting it in the face. 'The Emperor protects!' he bellowed, taking another step down the burning ramp.

Santos felt hands grab the collar of her armour. Darkness crowded at the edge of her vision. The thunderclap of her shot rang through the open space and she tried to catch a glimpse of Erebus again, but all she could see was the lieutenant advancing coolly into the face of the onrushing daemons and firing shot after shot from his plasma pistol. The weapon's discharge vents were glowing white-hot, and his armoured gauntlet was melting from the heat.

'The Emperor protects!' she heard him say as another daemon loomed before him. The lieutenant fired his pistol again – and this time the overheated power core exploded, consuming him and his foe in a ball of incandescent light.

Santos felt herself dragged across the stone floor and passed out in a fiery wave of pain.

EREBUS SAW THE bright flare of the inferno pistol and for the briefest instant he feared that the dark gods had deserted him. His vision deserted him in a blaze of cyan, and a clap of terrible thunder dashed him to his knees.

By the time he regained his senses the battle was over.

The ramp was gone. Indeed, the entire front of the building had collapsed, sealing the doorway with tons of broken permacrete. A bare handful of flickering work lights still cast a fitful glow over the site.

After a moment, Erebus started to laugh. He raised his crozius and offered his thanks to the Ruinous Powers for their dark gifts. Nothing in this universe would keep him from reaching the Damnation Gate.

Still laughing, the Chaos lord turned to look for Magos Algol, and saw that the Dark Gods had been fickle with their blessings.

The inquisitor's bolt had missed Erebus and struck the monolith instead. Its dark surface had exploded, erasing the engravings in a storm of razor-edged shrapnel. Algol lay on his back at the foot of the ancient stone, his frail body shredded and a look of surprise etched on his bony face.

Erebus knelt by the body of the dead magos. Nearby, he heard a shifting of fallen rock, and glanced over to see Dubel picking himself up from the rubble. The Traitor Marine saw what had happened to Algol and hissed a vicious curse. 'We'll go back to Ebok empty-handed now,' the Traitor Marine spat.

The Chaos lord studied Algol's shocked face. 'I think not,' he said, taking the magos's head in his left hand. The man's thin neck snapped with an expert twist of his wrist; vertebrae popped in dry succession, and then Erebus held Algol's head up to the flickering light.

'The monolith is gone, but the eyes that beheld it still remain,' Erebus said. 'The eyes are the gateway to the soul, Dubel. And gates, once opened, will give up everything they contain.'

Erebus looked into Algol's eyes and laughed, seeing his future.

FATE'S MASTERS, DESTINY'S SERVANTS

Matt Keefe

THE ROOM WAS silent apart from the fizzing static of the communications array and even that was so slight in volume that Captain Elogos found himself stifling the noise of his own breathing just to hear it.

His hasty summons to the bridge of *Guilliman's Hand* had come while he had been at prayer. So, he wore ceremonial white robes, and not the blue power armour of his chapter, the Ultramarines.

Elogos's uncustomary appearance provoked no reaction from the assembled trio. They were all captains, and this was a matter of great importance. Between them, they commanded four full companies, four hundred Space Marines in all, yet no more than a few dozen of those were present on the huge battle-barge their captains now occupied. The kilometres-long ship required just a handful of Space Marines for its operation, being otherwise crewed by thousands of loyal Chapter serfs and machine-minded servitors.

The remainder of this huge force was dispersed across the two further battle-barges and countless strike cruisers and rapid-strike vessels that made up Fleet Camidius. Periodically, one of these craft would drift into view in front of the vast observation window, which filled the front wall of the elevated bridge.

Brother-Captains Junius and Aulus nodded silently as Elogos approached them. Only Omneus made no reaction. He was the only one who wore a helmet and the communications array ran low for his benefit. A purer signal at a lower volume was relayed through the superior sensors of Omneus's helmet in the hope of capturing some of its badly degraded content. For the others, the faint crackle offered few clues as they waited patiently. Omneus stood near motionless over the ship's console, the rapid movements of his gauntleted right hand over the side of his helmet the only sign of activity.

Seven or eight minutes passed before Omneus conceded defeat with a swift shake of his head, removing his helmet as he did so.

'Nothing?' said Elogos.

'Nothing I would repeat for fear of a lie,' said Omneus. 'I could make a thousand words from what I have heard, but they would be little better than the thousand faces I could see staring at the clouds above Ultramar.'

Aulus smiled a little at the memory of beloved Ultramar and pressed his armoured palm to Omneus's shoulder by way of thanks for his efforts.

'Then where the machine fails,' said Aulus, 'the man must surely succeed.' His voice rose to a confident boom as he spoke and his free hand motioned to two figures huddled in the doorway. Alerted by his voice and summoned by his hand, two astropaths shuffled slowly across the room towards the four Astartes. The awkward, bald-headed pair were in obvious contrast to the towering Ultramarines.

The crude machine-audio of the communications array was useless to the psykers and they instead funnelled the laser, by which means this unfathomable signal had first reached their ears, through an ancient crystal spectrum hoping to make clear with their minds what the ear simply couldn't discern. That the communication had been sent in this crude, material fashion in the first place hinted at a remote source, a place where no astropath could be found to transmit it by the intangible, otherworldly means upon which such communication most commonly relied. Some trace of the psychic, however, clearly remained.

The astropaths' sightless eyes rolled back and they started to shuffle about. They began a slow intonation. One astropath's voice rose sharply higher than the other's, yet the result was uniform nonetheless, their finely pitched tone and measured pace forming a single, unearthly voice.

'Alpha-alpha-alpha,' it rang out, emanating from nowhere at all it seemed, an effect that would be startling, if not horrifying to ordinary men, but was unremarkable to the assembled Space Marine captains.

'Alpha-alpha-alpha,' it came again.

'A distress signal,' said Omneus, though the meaning was clear to all.

'Alpha-alpha-alpha, omega-san-omega,' it went on. 'Alpha-Alpha-alpha, omega-dox-omega.'

Elogos gasped – it was an Ultramarine distress signal.

'Omega-san-omega, respond, omega-dox-omega,' said Junius hunched over the console, barking at it as his fingers skimmed over the operation runes inset into its surface.

'It's phased and relayed,' said Omneus who had earlier so closely scrutinised the signal. 'There's no way of sending a reply.'

Junius rose to his full height and turned to the others, a troubled grimace playing across his features.

'Alpha-alpha-alpha.' The intoned message still resounded across the room, though it had long since faded into nothing more than repetition. Omneus drew closer to the console, though it was an altogether different frame of runes over which his fingers now danced.

'Do you have its source?' said Elogos.

'Yes,' said Omneus.

'Good,' said Elogos. 'Then give it to me, and there I will go.'

'Elysium.'

The words droned out of the metal pipe that served as the servitor's mouth as the ship shuddered in the backwash of its translation back into real space. They had barely strayed more than a day into warp space, for which Elogos was thankful.

The ship shuddered as its impulse engines returned to life, igniting once more to propel the ship through the cold vacuum of space after its motionless, spectral voyage through the warp. Space offered no resistance, the jarring was not turbulence, but time in the warp invariably affected the alignment of the ship's impulse engines and their great thrusts at first fought against one another.

Elogos and his company had broken off from the main fleet, taking a strike cruiser to investigate the curious distress signal. Though it was a large vessel in its own right, the cruiser, *Shield of Vigilance*, was dwarfed by the immense battle-barge where they had first detected the signal's origin. *Guilliman's Hand* was now many miles away, with the rest of Fleet Camidius.

The shuddering soon faded as, far below, the serfs properly calibrated the engines for the return to real space under Brother Caius's watchful gaze. While it might be Caius's wisdom that instructed them, it was the serfs' dutiful labours that brought such swift results. These serfs were responsible for all such labours across the ship, sparing their Space Marine superiors for the more important tasks of command and defence. The serfs themselves were humans, recruited from the Ultramarines' homeworld of Macragge, and their knowledge made them skilled and useful servants. Hundreds of them, garbed in their customary blue and white robes, scurried throughout the *Shield of Vigilance*'s endless corridors.

'Have you determined the source?' asked Elogos. From the distant *Guilliman's Hand*, Omneus had been able to do no more than trace the signal to this particular star system. Now that they drew nearer, Elogos demanded more accuracy of his crew.

'The northern continent of Elysium,' came the reply, though its source was of some surprise. Cyriacus, the Librarian stood in the doorway, his hands pressed to the low arch which divided bridge fore from bridge rear. Elogos had insisted upon Cyriacus's presence but was unaccustomed to the venerable psyker involving himself so readily, and on such a vast ship it was rare that Elogos would find himself accompanied on the bridge by anyone but the servitors and Chapter-serfs.

'The serfs have set a course already,' said Cyriacus, his prescient anticipation of the question probably little more than that. Elogos nodded and sank into his seat.

'Elysium,' said Elogos as the last of his battle-brothers emerged into the hangar bay. The planet and its moons turned slowly beneath them, the thinnest wedge of its surface visible beyond the invisible field of energy which divided their otherwise open hangar from the void of space beyond.

Sergeants Nerion, Auralius and their men clustered around the lowered ramps of the Thunderhawks they had each dutifully occupied throughout the voyage, ready, if need be, to man the gunships in case of attack. Sergeant Estarion's men, having returned separately from their myriad stations across the length and breadth of the strike cruiser, formed a loose circle around Elogos and Cyriacus.

'Auralius, Estarion,' said Elogos. 'Your squads will accompany me to the planet's surface. One Thunderhawk per squad. Estarion with me. Auralius, Brother-Librarian Cyriacus will accompany you. Nerion, remain here and await further instruction.'

'Aye, my captain,' came the only verbal reply, from Nerion. Both Auralius and Estarion nodded dutifully in response. Nerion's men moved away from the ramp of the foremost Thunderhawk and Elogos quickly ascended, followed by Estarion and his squad. Behind them, Auralius led his own men back in to the second Thunderhawk, the venerable Cyriacus following close behind. A third such craft remained unmanned at the right-hand side of the hangar and Nerion's men made for it as the other two craft prepared to launch. It would be their deaths if they remained in the hangar when the Thunderhawk's engines ignited.

Elogos settled himself in one of the many transport seats towards the rear of the Thunderhawk. He had little desire to interfere in Estarion's well-drilled routines simply for sake of rank and deferred the cockpit seat to his brother-sergeant. Two Marines accompanied Estarion to the front of the vessel as the remaining seven men of the squad settled quickly into the transport seats around Elogos, their positions, even in this largely empty Thunderhawk, carefully rehearsed to allow a swift, and if need be, fighting, deployment.

'Vigilus-Di, ready for launch.' The sound of Sergeant Auralius's voice crackled over the comm-link.

'Vigilus-Prime, ready for launch,' replied Estarion from his seat in the cockpit, the engines of the Thunderhawk roaring to life at the same time. Another moment's pause and the comm-link crackled into life again.

'*Shield of Vigilance*, ready for launch,' said Nerion, he and his men obviously well clear of the hangar. 'Emperor guide you,' he said.

Vigilus-Di rose up first, its slowly retracting legs passing across Estarion's vision as it crossed the hangar and entered the launch bay proper. Vigilus-Prime followed, rising more swiftly than its mate to glide over the motionless Vigilus-Ter below. The Thunderhawk turned sharply as it drifted towards the launch bay, sharp enough to bring it to a position out to the rear-left of the leading Vigilus-Di. The two craft remained in this formation as they straightened up and entered the long launch corridor at the very front of the bay. Stepping their engines up to full power, the craft raced out of the launch bay and into the starry-black gulf beyond.

As the craft sailed out into space, the sturdy adamantium blast door slid into place between the cockpit and transport compartment, depriving Elogos of any view of the Thunderhawk's exterior whatsoever. At that, he removed his helmet from where it was clipped to the top of his thigh, and secured it firmly on his head.

'Transmission source located,' came a voice from the comm-link mounted inside Elogos's helmet. It was Estarion, from the cockpit.

'Follow it in, sergeant,' said Elogos.

'Yes, my captain.'

The comm-link fell silent and Elogos dipped his head in quiet meditation. The calm persisted for little more than ten or fifteen minutes before the Thunderhawk was rocked and buffeted violently from outside – a sure sign of atmospheric approach. The noise of the engines rose immeasurably and the roar of afterburners and stabiliser jets was added to the relatively meagre output needed to guide the gunship through space.

'Contour scan gives us safe touchdown point-five kilometres from signal source, captain. Approach?' The voice rang out inside Elogos's helmet once more.

'Yes. Approach and land at once,' said Elogos.

The Thunderhawk lurched and Elogos felt his weight slide against the broad metal harness which covered his chest. A moment later and he found himself pressed hard back in his seat as the gunship banked and then began its rapid descent. At the last moment, the Thunderhawk levelled out and dropped vertically to the ground, landing with a just noticeable thump.

No sooner had the gunship landed and the rear exit ramps descended to the ground than the Space Marines around Elogos were up, out of their seat-harnesses and moving down the sloping metal ramps in well-practiced covering formations.

A signal crackled over the comm-link and the cockpit's blast door rose swiftly. Estarion and his two brother Space Marines emerged and the three, accompanied by Elogos, descended the ramp while the rest of the squad formed careful guard around it on the ground below.

The Ultramarines had arrived at the edge of a large plain, covered in tall grass that bowed in the strong wind that raced over the ground. Beyond this, close by the landed Thunderhawks, a forest rose up, ringing the edge of the plain. The forest masked higher ground, and the treeline visibly rose and fell in a series of undulating crests.

Beside Elogos, Auralius's squad emerged from the second Thunderhawk, Cyriacus with them. Two of the

Marines configured auspexes, searching for the signal's exact source, only to have their search cut short as Cyriacus raised his staff and pointed towards the heavily forested ground away to the south-west. The Librarian's mind was keener than any machine.

Following his lead, Elogos led his men in the direction indicated by Cyriacus. Five Space Marines surrounded Elogos as he marched while four more remained with Estarion, taking up position some way behind. Between these two groups, Cyriacus, accompanied by four of Auralius's men, followed suit, while Auralius himself led the remaining men out on a wider route, guarding the flanks of their brothers, ever mindful of attack.

There was no need for such concern, and the brief march proceeded unhindered. The group crossed the flat plain quickly, arriving at the edge of the forested area beyond. From its edge, the forest appeared deep and dense, but upon entering it the Space Marines found it quickly dropped away, forming a forest carpet over a series of deep ravines beyond. Their path fell away into the first of these ravines as they advanced and brought the horizon up short in front of them. Elogos paused before allowing himself to descend the ravine.

Cyriacus came up close on his shoulder and nodded ahead, towards where a second rising bank of trees covered the opposite slope of the ravine. Elogos sent two of his men forwards and down into the ravine to search out a viable crossing, though he himself waited a moment longer, allowing Estarion and his men at the rear to catch up. By the time Estarion arrived, another opportunity had presented itself.

'There is a crossing to the north.' Auralius's voice came over the comm-link. Auralius and his men, ranging wider out across the landscape had reached the ravine some distance from Elogos's own position, a fact which had clearly proved fortunate. Elogos recalled the two Space Marines from the ravine below and, now accompanied by all bar Auralius's own men, picked his way along the ravine's edge, heading north to the promised crossing.

Here and there, the ravine's edge fell away so sharply that the marching group was forced back into the woodland in order to find a safe path, and their view of the chasm beside them was greatly obstructed. A great rocky spur jutted out halfway across the ravine, covered in a thick mass of vegetation, and this, combined with a sharp turn in the ravine's course, blocked out any view of what lay beyond.

It was thus almost by surprise that they emerged from the heavy vegetation to find Auralius and his men perched atop a flat, rocky promontory that extended some several metres out over the ravine.

Beyond this ran a high, gradually arching bridge, though it was not rock and its colour did not at all match the surrounding landscape. It was the colour of bone, and its surface, while not quite smooth, boasted a form quite unlike the craggy spars of rock that pock-marked the ravine's edges. Its shape too was more deliberate than could have come from the simple ageing of rock by the ravages of wind and rain. The bridge's underside bore smaller arches, their sides forming regular fans or wings which strafed down towards the narrow valley at the ravine's base. The bridge looked like no product of nature, but by whose hand it had been made, there was no clue.

No matter its origin, its nature was plain enough. It was a bridge, and it would get them across the ravine. As Elogos and the others emerged from the wooded edge, Auralius strode out beyond the promontory and onto the bridge itself. It was not especially broad, but offered no real danger as the Ultramarines moved across it in single file.

Nearing the bridge's centre, its very highest point, Elogos gazed down into the valley below. A trail of broken rock, buried amidst a raft of smaller shale and pebbles, littered the floor. No water now ran there, but the winding course of the debris made clear it had been carried there by some long-gone river, the same river which had surely cut the ravine itself in an age gone by.

Focusing his sight, Elogos could make out a handful of solid shapes. Some of those sections of crumbled rock beneath him stood out as brighter than the surrounding stones, though still considerably tarnished, and their shape gave hints of the same architecture as that of the bridge beneath him. The remains of other such artificial crossings, he thought, fallen to the river below. Much more than just this solitary bridge had once stood here, Elogos thought to himself as he reached the far side of the ravine.

The edge here was higher and steeper, and the Space Marines remained in single file as they snaked up this farther, equally forested, slope. Its crest was the highest of all the surrounding hills, and as Elogos ascended it, the source of the mysterious signal that had brought them here became immediately apparent.

Beneath them, a second ravine opened up, shallower, and divided by a fork in its dry river bed. On the island of rock formed between these parting, now long-dead, streams stood a fort of kinds, a thing of stone and steel with a look to it so aged and worn that it appeared almost derelict. Yet its surface was adorned with a very familiar insignia: the brilliant white omega symbol of the Ultramarines.

'Then we are not alone,' said Cyriacus wryly as he joined Elogos on that high vantage point.

'How can this be?' said Elogos as he received the final report from Estarion, on his reconnoitre of the fort. It had taken almost an hour to complete a thorough search of the building, but it had been clear from the beginning that few answers would be found and Elogos felt himself merely waiting for the inevitable.

The fort's construction had proven to be surprisingly primitive, formed of a mass of roughly hewn stone and metal that was really no better than scrap. Yet for all this, the place bore all the marks of the Astartes, providing for their most basic needs.

This was exactly as Estarion's men found it. The fort was bereft of so much as a single brother Ultramarine.

'Nothing?' said Elogos in reply to Estarion's shaking head. 'Nothing at all?'

'Not nothing,' said Estarion. 'A dozen serfs, but mutes all of them.'

Elogos's face wrinkled up into a quizzical frown.

'Mutes?' said Elogos.

'Yes, captain,' said Estarion.

'Show them to me.'

Elogos entered the dingy chamber, the lowest room in the entire building, a cave within the rock itself, its entrance covered by the fort's structure. A dozen serfs stood lined up against the far wall. They were a sorry bunch, almost all bearing extensive modifications, their bodies greatly damaged by the additions. Some appeared more like servitors than true serfs. Whoever created these sorry specimens would have been in desperate need to use serfs in such a way, thought Elogos as he approached the first creature in line.

The serf's eyes blinked with a speed seemingly impossible for any living thing. They flickered and flashed, open and shut, several times every second, sometimes independently of one another as though the blinks somehow mimicked the clicks, beeps and flashes that raced through the creature's machine mind.

Elogos drew back from the serf, able to decipher nothing from this frenetic blinking. He had seen serfs muted before, but it was not a practice he had ever witnessed amongst his own Chapter except where function demanded it, and it puzzled him greatly now to see these dozen subjects, the monastery's only inhabitants, mute to a man. One or two bore augmentations that could perhaps have caused their speechlessness but the others seemed silenced for reasons of custom alone and Elogos could not fathom the meaning of such a practice.

These frantic blinks might perhaps be the substitute for their lost tongues but if communications they were, they meant nothing to Elogos or the assembled Space Marines. The mutes seemed possessed of no other form of communication for they remained unresponsive to the gestures Brother Longinus traced in the air with his hands.

As Elogos passed down the line, even the Librarian, Cyriacus, conceded defeat with a growl, the serf's mind too machine in nature to be easily probed by one such as he. The stylus offered by Caius to another serf remained unused, unnoticed in fact, and it was clear to Elogos that these serfs would indeed be keeping whatever secrets they held.

Elogos motioned for Cyriacus to join him as he moved towards the door.

'I am confounded, Brother Cyriacus,' said Elogos.

'It is, I agree, most strange,' said Cyriacus. 'Though this is without a doubt a place of our great Chapter's making. Its relics are real enough, its every design is as Codex demands and its spirit is as pure as the heart of Macragge. I cannot doubt its origin, but I cannot explain it.'

'And none have ever set foot here before us? You are quite certain?' said Elogos.

'Quite certain,' said Cyriacus. 'The Fleet Camidius alone has heretofore entered the Pyrus Reach at all, and this distant Elysium, well, we are the first sons of Guilliman to touch its soil by any account I can find. I have yet to receive final word from my brothers but I am sure they will confirm that this world is a place to which no Ultramarine has ever before been.'

'Not one Ultramarine, and yet a whole fortress for their occupation,' said Elogos.

'Indeed,' said Cyriacus. 'I shall consider it. Though, I have little hope of finding answers soon.'

'I will pray on it,' said Elogos, moving towards the far end of the corridor, away from the venerable Librarian. 'Yes, I will pray on it.'

ELOGOS KNELT SILENTLY in prayer, his lips framing the words of an Ultramarines' catechism as he reached deep within himself for answers to what whim of destiny had brought him to Elysium and what fate now awaited him.

Though comforting, his prayers had yielded few answers. He rose from his genuflection and paced across the stone floor of the chapel, his armoured boots giving off resounding clangs as they struck the cold surface.

Elogos reached the far end of the chapel, where a large banner, hung like a mural, occupied fully two-thirds of the wall. He stopped at the foot of this relic and knelt in reverie. As he did so, the last of the day's light fell upon him through gaps in the fort's stone wall.

The banner's design was typical enough. In its centre stood the almighty Emperor, presenting his side to the observer, his stride carrying him from one side to the other and his face turned away as if looking beyond. Behind him rose a landscape dominated by a vast mountain, a symbol, perhaps, of his might, while his head was crowned with a halo of six stars shining brilliantly in the night sky above. He touched the top of his left arm with the hand of his right and where his fingers parted, blood ran. Upon his right cheek there was a single tear. Elogos was sure that this place was truly of Astartes manufacture. Such humanity as this grim portrait cast upon the Immortal Emperor was a thing known only to the Space Marines; there was no mere man who would know so truly the face of their saviour.

Elogos rose and walked slowly towards the high arch of the chapel's only doorway. Before he even reached it, Caius appeared, greeting his captain with a meaningful stare. Elogos knew his meaning at once but thought better than to break his silence while within the chapel's walls and allowed himself to pass through the door before addressing his brother Marine.

'You have some news, Caius?' said Elogos as he passed from the chapel into the dimly lit corridor.

'Brother-Librarian Cyriacus requests your presence, my captain,' said Caius.

'Very good,' said Elogos. 'Show me the way.'

'THIS WAS THE transmitter they used,' said Cyriacus. He stood at the head of a large, wooden table at the centre of this, the building's largest chamber, serving apparently as its great hall As well as the stone walls common throughout the fort, this larger room boasted a great many metal struts running from floor to ceiling. The ceiling itself bore a covering of metal plates, making it armoured, after a fashion.

'This is it?' said Elogos. Cyriacus nodded.

'Paleus has confirmed it.' At the far side of the room, Paleus nodded. Such matters were well within his expertise and Elogos trusted his judgement without hesitation. On the table between Elogos and Cyriacus sat a transmitter, its shell stripped away and its contents connected to a vast array of auspexes, sensory arrays and receivers used by the cunning Paleus to uncover the little box's secrets.

'Then what more does it tell us, Cyriacus?' said Elogos.

'There was more to the transmission, captain. There were messages sent that we did not receive.'

'And what did they say?'

'Chaos attack, captain. They said Chaos attack.' Cyriacus fell silent and Elogos frowned.

He turned away from the table and gestured for Estarion to follow him. The pair paced out of the room side by side, before moving through the building's dimly lit corridors. The external walls of the fort lacked windows, and instead light flooded in through blank spaces in the wall where stones had been omitted to provide ad hoc, glassless windows.

'I will take ten men and discover what I can,' said Elogos. 'You may inform Sergeant Nerion that this place is safe and he and his men may join us on the planet surface. Wait here until they arrive, then take ten men and begin a search elsewhere. Nerion will protect the fort.'

'Yes, captain,' said Estarion, nodding and stepping aside as the pair reached the door. Elogos stepped through it, out onto the broad steps at the building's front. Behind him, Elogos gestured to the Marines following a discreet distance behind and several hurriedly made to catch up with Elogos while others halted their advance and stood dutifully beside the fort's doors.

'Captain?' said Sergeant Auralius, as he emerged into the fading daylight. 'Where do you wish us to go?'

Elogos paused, stepping down three of the broad stone steps so that the building's edge no longer blocked his view as he surveyed the landscape.

He pondered for a moment before his eye caught an oddly familiar sight. He pointed. 'There. We will go there,' he said, pointing at the great mountain that rose up on the distant horizon. It looked just like the one in the chapel's mural.

Elogos marched on and, as the sun set behind him, his suspicions were proved correct. The coming night revealed a half-circle of six brilliantly white stars piercing the not-yet-black sky above the mountain's peak. If the mountain's likeness had not been enough, these brilliant beacons made Elogos certain that he was headed towards the very same landscape he had earlier seen depicted so vividly in the banner on the chapel wall.

Their journey in the Thunderhawk had narrowed the distance considerably, but with the broken terrain at the mountain's base offering precious little hope of a suitable landing spot, it was still a trek of an hour or more before Elogos and the eight men who followed him at last reached the foothills of the mountain proper. Two more battle-brothers remained in the Thunderhawk some way distant and Elogos would periodically hear Brother-Marine Longinus's comm-link crackle to life as the Thunderhawk's remaining crew tracked their party's position.

Like the ravines amongst which the mysterious fort nestled, these foothills were heavily forested and surveying the landscape for a great distance in any direction was remarkably difficult. Elogos cast his gaze over the tree tops and was at last rewarded with a promising sign – smoke rising from a spot some distance ahead.

The group moved swiftly through the trees and as they drew near they could hear the crackling noise of a fire and the sound of voices. Bolters were raised and the Ultramarines moved apart from one another, forming an encircling chain as they closed in on the source of the smoke and the fire.

Elogos burst from the cover of the trees into a broad, oval shaped clearing. Beyond him, the blue-armoured figures of his brothers also lurked, bolters raised. In the clearing, a dozen or more savage-looking men and women danced and whooped around a huge pyre in the clearing's centre. At the sight of Elogos, one of the wild men turned from his revelry and launched himself at the captain, a huge bloody bone in his hand, wielded like a club. He struck at Elogos, the bone shattering harmlessly against his shoulder pad before Elogos voiced his bolter and silenced the wailing savage.

The other Space Marines stepped from the trees, ready to cut down the rest of the primitive group, but Elogos raised his hand and bade them hold their fire. His first display of power would be more than enough to quell any fight these primitive wretches had in them. Elogos lifted the man's corpse from where it lay at his feet and hurled it effortlessly across the clearing. It flew several metres before crashing to the ground amongst the other savages beside the flaming pyre.

Two of the women fell to their knees over the body, wailing in a series of screams and howls that could have been either rage or grief. Three small children cowered behind two more women while half a dozen of the men fell to their knees, clasping their hands together and uttering indecipherable grunts in an apparent plea for mercy.

Elogos lowered his bolter and stepped forwards whilst the remaining Ultramarines closed in, forming a tight circle around the clearing and its primitive occupants.

The savages scurried away from Elogos as he approached, but the ring of armoured men prevented them from fleeing. They shuffled nervously back around the pyre, trying to keep the flames between themselves and the hulking Space Marine captain. As they parted, the pyre's purpose, and the cause of the savages' celebrations, became apparent.

A huge armoured corpse, its surface blackened by the flame but its substance hardly touched, lay atop the pyre. Elogos reached into the fire with his armoured first and, grabbing at what he could find, hauled the corpse to the ground.

The thing smouldered as it lay at his feet but the heat bothered Elogos little as he stooped and cracked away the charred top layer of the corpse's power armour. A great sheet of blackened armour came away in his hand. Beneath it, a second layer of armour was revealed, entirely untouched. Untouched by the flames, that was, but bedevilled with craven symbols.

'Emperor damn all you have ever done,' said Elogos as the Chaos Space Marine's armour became apparent, cleared of its blackened exterior. Elogos tore the heretic's plated armour from his shoulder. He smacked the butt of his other hand against the sooty, charred covering, bashing away the flakes of scorched metal to reveal the dread insignia beneath. Word Bearers.

Elogos threw the armoured piece to the ground and made for the nearest savage. He snatched the scrawny, wild-haired man up by the rags he wore around his shoulders and lifted him clear from the ground.

'What happened here?' said Elogos as the terrified man writhed in his grip. He pitied the wretches for what they had surely seen, and in some ways felt a great sense of pride in seeing their obvious joy at the demise of the traitor, but he desperately needed to know what had transpired in this place and he had no time for kind treatment. He could not for a moment believe that they themselves had killed the monstrous Chaos Space Marine.

'Y... y... you kill them.' The man stuttered as he spoke, never once daring to look Elogos in the eye.

'Yes, I am going to kill them,' said Elogos. 'But tell me what has happened here. Tell me!'

'He means,' said Cyriacus, grabbing Elogos's attention, 'that you have *killed* them. Not that you are going to.'

Elogos turned his head to see Cyriacus close by the pyre, his hand on the shoulder of one of the frightened women, though unlike the struggling man in Elogos's grip this woman seemed frozen by her terror and did not so much as flinch from where she stood beside the Librarian.

Cyriacus took his hand from her shoulder and the woman fell to the floor, her mind reeling from the Librarian's inescapable grasp.

'They have seen others like us and mistook us for them,' said Cyriacus. 'Ultramarines killed this traitor, and more like him. The girl has seen battle raging, close by here I think. You surprised the first man, made a cornered beast of him and he attacked you, but these people do not think us an enemy. They are harmless enough, and they are loyal in their own way.'

Elogos thought on that a moment, then said, 'Very well, set them free. But destroy the traitor's body and get these wretches away from here. I do not wish them to look upon it a second longer.'

At the far side of the circle, Caius stepped aside, giving the frightened savages an escape route. They clustered together, one woman picking up the other from where she lay at Cyriacus's feet and the whole crowd shuffled slowly towards the edge of the clearing, not yet sure of their fate.

Elogos released his grip, pushing the man towards his companions as he did so. The force of it sent the man into a run and this was enough to send the savages fleeing, diving for trees through the gap left by Caius. In an instant the clearing was empty but for the Ultramarines, their grisly find and the fire that raged between them.

Longinus stepped forward, taking a grenade from his pocket before hauling the corpse upright against the edge of the pyre. He thrust the grenade into the traitor's breastplate and withdrew swiftly. A moment later the corpse erupted into an incandescent mass, the melta-bomb's fiery charge first engulfing then utterly consuming the wretched thing's every tissue.

A sheet of ash lay where the heretic had been a moment before, and even this was but a passing shadow as the licking flames of the fire caught up the ash from the air, or else cast a hot breeze with which to disperse the gruesome silhouette painted on the ground. Elogos paused just long enough to see that no trace remained before turning and leading his Ultramarines once more into the line of densely packed trees at the clearing's edge.

'THIS IS THE way,' said Cyriacus, opting for the higher of two paths where the forest's floor offered one route towards the mountain's peak and one towards its base. Elogos nodded in agreement and the group adopted single file as they marched quickly behind Cyriacus, the Librarian apparently familiar with sights his eyes had never before witnessed.

The tree cover quickly thinned and a broad, low spur of the mountain rose up from the forest. Cyriacus stared at this for a moment, cementing the image in his mind and checking his bearings, before leading the others forwards once more.

The ground quickly became open and rocky, bare in places where it was exposed to the wind and blown clean of any covering of sand or rocky debris. Turning around the spur, the mountain path became entirely exposed and the distance which they had covered now became apparent to all. The wind blew hard about them at this great height and, as they reached a small plateau topping the spur, they found the enemies they had been looking for, and with them the friends they had yet to meet.

They were all dead. A dozen proud Ultramarine warriors and twice that in heretics lay strewn across the plateau, the signs of their struggle readily apparent. Elogos knelt beside the body of the nearest Ultramarine and carefully prised the helmet from his head, taking great care not to besmirch his brother in death. The face that greeted him was that of a stranger, and yet eerily familiar. The figure was aged, a swathe of grey hair covering his head and Elogos found himself greatly unsettled staring into the dead eyes of a brother whose name he thought he should know but could not quite bring to mind.

The others moved out amongst the carnage and inspected the other bodies. Though all were plainly Ultramarines, the personal insignia and monographs of their armour did nothing to reveal their identity. Most curious of all, they were every single one as aged as the proud slain warrior Elogos had first knelt over.

Beneath the knee, their armour bore a curious marking, a campaign badge displaying a halo of seven stars. Elogos took it at first to be a marking taken from the banner he had seen on the chapel's wall before close attention revealed the extra star. Whether the badge was meant to match the window or not, neither symbol matched any campaign in their Chapter's long, proud history.

These were the certainly bodies of Ultramarines, but they had no place in any company which Elogos or any of the others could bring to mind.

The near total darkness of night fell as Elogos and his brothers made proper the bodies of their strange brethren. Their gene-seed was taken, their bodies made pure and committed to the earth. The traitors were destroyed just as before, every sign of their treachery scorched from existence. And still no answers. Elogos muttered a prayer as he puzzled this continuing enigma.

THE BRILLIANT ORANGE sun was just beginning to rise as the Ultramarines' long march brought them close to the mysterious mountain's peak, where Cyriacus and Elogos were both sure answers must be found.

The rising sun brought with it a revelation. The first fronds of orange light to cross the horizon illuminated the silhouette of an ancient monolith perched atop the mountain's peak, just thirty metres above them. The shape of its two delicate, yet impossibly high arms, had been masked from sight lower down the mountain by the cunning angle and elevation of their construction. It was only from their position on the high ridge leading to the peak proper that the monolith was made apparent to Elogos and his men. They made for it at once, but stopped suddenly as a terrible sight greeted them.

The Word Bearers were encamped around the monolith, twenty or more of the traitors engaged in some vile ritual with the monolith as their focus.

Elogos, Cyriacus and the others sank to their knees, or pressed their bodies close to the mountain's slope, keeping themselves out of sight as they readied themselves to attack. They suffered from a position below the Word Bearers and would have to be cunning if they were to defeat an enemy on higher ground.

Elogos gazed around and saw a high ridge running parallel to the plateau at the mountain's peak. The ridge offered a spot just two or three metres lower than the peak itself, and Elogos gestured for two of his battle-brothers to follow him as he moved stealthily towards it. He paused by Auralius as he went, and with several swift hand gestures indicated his plan to him. Auralius nodded and began his own ascent up the steeper path in front of him, accompanied by Cyriacus and followed by the remainder of his squad.

Elogos headed around the mountain rather than up it, moving behind the ridge and leading the other two men up the slope, behind the ridge, safely out of sight of the traitors. Reaching the crest of the ridge, Elogos paused for a moment until the two by his side gestured their readiness and all three sprung up over the ridge, unleashing a withering volley of bolter fire at the Word Bearers. Attacked from such an angle, the Chaos Marines sorely lacked for cover in their exposed position and were instantly driven back towards the monolith. Three of the heretics fell to this first volley, two more before they reached the safety of the monolith.

With the Word Bearers driven back from the edge of the plateau, Auralius, with Cyriacus and his men, took their opportunity to dash the short distance up the mountain's slope. They reached its peak quickly and hauled themselves up on to the high plateau. A moment later the sound of their bolters joined those of Elogos's men and the Word Bearers were trapped in a deadly crossfire. The Word Bearers shuffled backwards once more, returning fire as they turned back to back in a desperate attempt to prevent their complete encirclement.

Elogos quickly led his men forward along the ridge, heading for the plateau. The semi-circular shape of it allowed them to move round the monument, bringing the retreating Word Bearers into sight once more. The Ultramarines opened fire, driving the Word Bearers further round the monolith. As the Word Bearers regrouped behind the monolith, Elogos and his men dashed for the edge of the plateau.

Auralius split those Ultramarines at his command into two smaller groups, one of which was led by the Librarian. They surged towards the monolith from both sides, one group circling it clockwise, the other anticlockwise, trapping the traitors between them and creating a crossfire that pinned the Word Bearers to the ground, slaying several more in the exchange.

Encircled and increasingly desperate, the Word Bearers responded with a brutal counter-assault. They concentrated their fire forwards, towards the group led by Auralius and rushed towards them, ignoring the other Ultramarines entirely.

Caius fell to the heretics' fire as they retaliated. Longinus drew his body to the safety of a shallow dip beneath the monument's base, but he couldn't raise his fallen brother and relayed to Elogos that the first Ultramarine blood of the day had been spilled.

With Caius dead and Longinus momentarily out of the fight, the Word Bearers rushed Auralius and the lone Space Marine who remained by his side. Two of the traitors at the fore of the pack raised their chainswords and made to engage Auralius at close quarters. Auralius counter-charged, ducking beneath the first swinging chainsword blow and unleashing his bolt pistol at point blank range into his enemy's armoured stomach. A second clumsy swipe followed before the Word Bearer toppled backwards, dead. The blow was a pathetic last strike and the chainsword's teeth skidded ineffectually across Auralius's vambrace, but the force of the blow was still enough to send him reeling. As he tumbled, he caught sight of fellow brother Tyrus beside him, overwhelmed by three more Word Bearers and finally succumbing to their blows. There was no sign of Cyriacus.

The second Word Bearer drew nearer and raised his chainsword as Auralius struggled to regain his footing. The traitor grasped the chainsword in both hands, ready to plunge it straight down into Auralius's back before a hail of bolter fire rang out and sent the traitor's bullet-riddled body tumbling to the floor.

Elogos and Auralius's second battle squad had rounded the monument and come up on the Word Bearers from behind, saving Auralius at the last moment. One of the traitors, their apparent leader, caught sight of the encircling groups and led the others away from the monolith. Their headlong rush had overwhelmed Auralius and allowed the Word Bearers an opportunity to escape their encirclement. Any more delay and they would be surrounded once more, so the traitors hastily retreated towards the plateau's edge, leaving a fortunate Auralius to haul himself to his feet.

The Word Bearers were far from defeated, however. Sonarius, one of Auralius's men who had led the second group around the monolith, tried to pursue the traitors, but moving away from the sturdy structure and into the open only served to hand the Word Bearers a swift victory. Sonarius, Psalitus and Gregorius fell as the Word Bearers covered their retreat with a hail of fire. With their pursuers slain or repulsed, the Word Bearers threatened to reach the cover of the forest which lay just beneath the plateau on the opposite slope.

Their threatened escape ended explosively a moment later as Vigilus-Di hovered into view above the mountain. Auralius's men, left with the Thunderhawk and summoned at a moment's notice, unleashed the full fury of the gunship's considerable weaponry and the startled crowd of traitors was consumed by the hail of bolter fire and the barrage of battle cannon as the Thunderhawk roared overhead. Elogos and Auralius halted their own pursuit as they saw it made needless by the gunship's timely intervention.

Lacking a place to land, the Thunderhawk disappeared from view as quickly as it had arrived, a swift message of thanks over the comm-link the only signal its pilots needed that the battle was over. As its engines roared off into the distance, the survivors gathered around Elogos, Cyriacus emerging from the treeline. There was, again, much that had to be done. The Ultramarines' dead had to be laid to rest and the traitors cleansed. Two battle-brothers, under Longinus's watchful eye, were quickly set to it. Elogos, his mind on the aged Ultramarines they'd found before the battle, wasted no time in investigating the colossal monolith, Cyriacus in tow. Auralius followed close by the captain and Librarian as they scrambled over the series of circular plinths, which led up to the artefact. It was immense, though curiously delicate in appearance. It was immediately apparent that it was constructed from the same curious, bone-white material as the bridge which had earlier offered such an expedient crossing. Its makers and the monolith's were one and the same.

Those makers, it seemed, were not the Word Bearers themselves, for Elogos saw now that they had done their best to defile the thing, daubing it with bloody symbols of their own craven gods. Auralius called up Brother Teleus, who at once unleashed the cleansing fire of his flamer over the heathen symbols in an attempt to obliterate them, but this was not at all the result it brought.

As the flames licked over the reaching arms of the monolith, their fiery, orange glow was at first sucked upwards, as though carried by some unseen force, and then repelled utterly, hurled back from the monolith in a cloud that threatened to engulf Teleus and the others. Teleus quickly cut off the gout of his weapon and plunged to the floor. Elogos, Cyriacus and Auralius escaped harm likewise before all four rose to their feet and stared in amazement at the monolith.

Between the high span of the monolith's arms, an opaque purple light now throbbed, crackling and swirling with the fury of lightning, yet racing and spiralling towards the sky like smoke escaping a fire. The beam of light burst upwards, piercing the sky and shooting towards space. Elogos gazed up, following the light's course and gaped in astonishment at what he saw above him.

The rising sun had not yet blotted out the stars, and in the dim grey sky, something moved. Its shape was unclear at such a distance, but even then Elogos was certain that something vast was suddenly awake amongst the stars above him.

THE THUNDERHAWKS ROARED into the launch bay, side by side, their pilots setting them down with little thought to their location, such was the urgency with which Elogos now ordered their return to the *Shield of Vigilance*. The planet below still held many secrets to be uncovered, the mysterious fortress certainly warranted further investigation, but there was clearly one matter in priority greater than either of these.

Elogos dashed down the Thunderhawk's ramp and swiftly crossed the hangar. All around him the other Marines raced back to their stations.

A minute later and Elogos arrived on the bridge, where Nerion patiently waited in his place.

'Greetings, Elogos,' said Nerion. 'And tell me, what is this you have conjured up for us?' Nerion gestured towards the forward observation window and Elogos cast his gaze out into space – straight at a second, colossal monolith. The thing was vast, its arms reached out to such a width that a ship could easily pass between them, yet apart from its size it was all but identical to the smaller monolith on the planet below.

'Approach it,' said Elogos. 'Slowly.'

'Aye,' came the reply and the strike cruiser moved slowly forward. Its progress was interrupted as the ship suddenly rocked with a force sufficient to fling

Elogos to the ground and leave Nerion desperately clutching the seat beside him in order to keep his feet.

'We're under attack!' roared Nerion into the comm-link, instantly alerting all stations.

A dizzying blur of motion raced past the view screen and two brilliant streaks of light shot forth before the blast hatch came down and obscured the view. Elogos waited for the inevitable impact but instead felt only the mild judder of shields receiving fire. Auralius, it seemed, had got just a little more out of the *Shield of Vigilance*. Elogos gazed down at his console as he hauled himself to his feet; a dizzying array of sensory readings and energy signatures across it.

'Eldar,' said Elogos, cursing as he hammered the console with his fist. Nerion braced himself at a console behind his captain, as they readied for a counter-attack. Only an eldar ship could have come upon them so utterly unseen, and moved with the disconcerting ease that Elogos had witnessed moments before through the view screen.

'What are they doing here?' said Nerion. His console comm-link sparked and died before him as he spoke.

'I do not know why the accursed alien wretches do any of the things they do. If I did, I would be their master, nay, their destroyer and this matter would be done,' snarled Elogos, his temper building as, one by one, the rest of the bridge's delicate systems began to fade into powerlessness, or spark violently as energy coursed through their damaged circuits.

'Brother Longinus,' Elogos said through the comm-link, raising his voice to be heard over the sound of the warning claxons that rang throughout the whole ship. 'Order the serfs to fire at will.'

'Aye, my cap–' came the disjointed reply. The ship rocked furiously again and for a moment all lights dipped out. A moment of black silence fell on the bridge before the ship's emergency lighting came to life and bathed everything in its dull red glow.

'Weapons down!' came the frantic reply from Longinus in his post in the gun-batteries far beneath the bridge.

Elogos roared in annoyance but waited no more than a moment before forming a new plan of action.

'Brother Auralius, do we have warp engines?' said Elogos.

'No, captain, our warp engines are crippled, but we have impulse power,' said Auralius, his voice faint over the comm-link, now running on low power. The situation was grim.

'Make for the gate,' said Nerion, his voice lacking conviction.

'What?' said Elogos.

'That gate out there, head for it. We can escape.'

Elogos frowned, but he had little other option. Nerion was right. The monolith was clearly some kind of astral gate. It was a massive risk, entering into the unknown; they could be ripped apart by the ravages of the warp or be thrust into some hellish daemon dimension. To do nothing meant certain destruction. The choice was not a good one, but it was the only choice Elogos had. Reluctantly, he gave the order.

'Brother Auralius. Make a course for the monolith, pass between its arms and go through the gate, do you understand?'

'Yes, captain.'

Elogos punched at his console and the small screen in front of him rolled over to a view of space beyond the ship. Sure enough, its approach summoned the monolith into life and the same hazing purple energy that Elogos had seen on the planet played in a swirling whirlpool at its midst. A moment later, and the *Shield of Vigilance* passed into this curious maelstrom.

They were in it for barely a moment before Elogos's screen showed them emerging out into space once more.

'Nerion,' yelled Elogos. 'Confirm position.'

'Position reading is...' Nerion paused. 'No readings, Captain Elogos, we are not yet clear of the gate.' A tense wait ensued before Nerion spoke again.

'Position is... Captain, we are still over the planet Elysium, our position is just beyond the gate.'

'Curse the aliens!' roared Elogos, his hopes of escape dashed.

'We don't appear to be under attack, captain,' said Nerion, 'but the hull is badly damaged and we are unable to hold our course.'

Elogos leaned forwards to consult his console but halted as he felt a dread sensation run through him. All around him the ship seemed to twist and turn, slowly at first, then speeding up into a spiral motion. Such a sensation was impossible in space and Elogos knew instantly that his ship had lost all power and been cast into the well of Elysium's gravity.

'All power to engines,' roared Elogos. For a moment, the ship was gripped by inertia as the engines fought back against the planet's deathly grasp, but it was hopeless and a minute later the engines fell silent, burned out and made useless in their futile struggle to escape the force of gravity.

Trapped in the gravity well, the *Shield of Vigilance* was doomed, and its crew with it, unless Elogos acted swiftly. There was no escaping such a plunge, and Elogos cursed as he gave what might very well prove to be his last order.

'All crew to drop-pods! Abandon ship!'

NERION RELEASED THE hatch and crawled out onto the damp ground outside, followed by Elogos. They now stood side by side on Elysium's surface gazing up at the sky to see if any more of their brethren had managed to escape.

They stared at the sky for what seemed like hours looking for signs to tell them they were not the sole survivors. When first they saw something, it was not a sign of hope.

Two blazing white streaks appeared in the sky, hurtling earthward at a terrifying speed. As they fell, their shape became clear – it was the *Shield of Vigilance*, its hull severed in two by the eldar's attack and now falling through the atmosphere in a dazzling blaze of light. The shooting streaks of light vanished from sight over the horizon and a moment of calm reigned until a huge explosion sounded through the air and a cloud of smoke, flame and debris rose up in distance.

The noise deafened Elogos and it was with utter surprise that he looked up once more to see a second group of white streaks tearing through the sky. They were smaller, but far more numerous, perhaps a dozen in number. Drop-pods. A moment later and Nerion's auspex came to life. Inbuilt beacons broadcast their positions and a dozen white dots flashed up on his screen. Elogos and Nerion didn't waste a second in heading for the nearest one.

It was several hours before Elogos reached Cyriacus and located all the survivors, moving one by one to the location of their drop-pods, guided to each by the invaluable auspex. In time, their little group numbered a dozen brother Space Marines and perhaps four times that number in serfs and servitors. These were all that now remained. They were, however, without so much as a Thunderhawk. They were stranded, and only one thing now offered them hope of survival.

* * *

'THIS IS IT, all the auspexes say so. It was right here,' said Auralius, clearly finding it hard to believe his own words.

'It can't be, it simply cannot be. It can't have just disappeared.' Elogos was disbelieving. For all the auspex's readings, he simply could not believe the spot they were now standing on was that which the stone fort had occupied, earlier. He fought against his doubt, but as he gazed out in every direction, the rise and fall of the ravines, the splitting of some ancient river's course and the gentle slope of the high crest above him made him more and more certain this was indeed the place they had been less than a day before. But there was simply no fort in sight, or even any evidence of its existence.

'How can this be?' said Elogos, though none could offer him an answer.

He cast his gaze out towards the mountain now so familiar and, as dusk began to settle over it, he counted the stars over its peak. One, two, three, four, five, six, *seven*. Seven of them! To the right of those he had seen before, a seventh star now burned, though much dimmer than the rest, as though weak, dying. His surprise must have been audible.

'What is it?' said Auralius, drawing near.

'This *is* the place,' said Elogos.

'What do you mean?' said Cyriacus, standing and moving away from the fire.

'There will be a fort here soon enough,' said Elogos. 'And before it is finished, that star will have burned out. The chapel of that fort will house a banner, bearing an image of six stars, but from this day our armour, will bear seven stars, there, beneath the knee. This will be our badge henceforth.'

A look of surprised realisation spread over Cyriacus's face. 'It seems we have come a long way indeed,' he said.

'What do you mean?' said Auralius.

'The gate,' said Elogos. 'It has taken us little distance, but carried us far. We are cast adrift, flung to a time I cannot place and stranded here until destiny comes to meet us. Then, I think, we shall find ourselves here all over again. It is the Emperor we serve but I think it is destiny that commands us now.'

'Destiny?' said Cyriacus. 'I would not be so sure it is destiny that leaves us here. And for what end?'

'To be sure that this place never falls to Chaos,' said Elogos, strong and confident in his belief of a destiny waiting for him and all his brother Astartes. He looked at Auralius, worn and tired after their frantic escape from the strike cruiser, and in that haggard face he saw an older version of the same man. It was this aged Auralius whose body he had discovered the day before, whose helmet he had removed and whose face he had not then been able to place. Elogos was sure that to wait in this place, to be ready to fight the traitors when they came and set the chain of events in motion once again was the duty for which he and his men were now destined.

'The Emperor began our march, and guides it still, but it is destiny that wills the universe to mankind. It is destiny that gives us a part in that now. We will do as it asks of us: we will keep this place and all its ancient secrets safe, and for our efforts, the universe will one day be mankind's, just as the Emperor told us it would be.'

'Nerion,' said Elogos, turning to his sergeant. 'Draw together the serfs. Mute them all, every last one. It will not serve to have those who come after us too well prepared – they must find themselves unwitting, as we have been, or they will have too little reason to follow in our steps.

'Once that is done, take the serfs and find the wreckage of the *Shield*. Salvage from it all that you can. Her hull will provide a fine starting point.'

'A starting point for what?' said Nerion.

'For a fort, a fort of stone and metal,' said Elogos. 'We are going to build a bastion of the Ultramarines here, right where I stand, and we will be ready when Chaos comes. Or, at least, some of our number will be ready, though we may not live to see it.

'That is why we have been brought here, that is what destiny demands of us – to guard this place, to be ready and to fight and die in this place. This is how it must be, for we are destiny's servants.'

'It is as it should be,' said the old farseer, the elegance of his race less apparent on his aged figure, his shuffling gait carrying little of the lithe grace so characteristic of his kind as he moved slowly towards the seat that awaited him beside his predecessors in the Dome of Crystal Seers now that his work was complete.

'*All* is as it should be?' said the young acolyte.

'Yes, all is as it should be, the gate will remain open for us, I have made sure it will be so,' said the farseer. 'For we are fate's masters.'

TEARS OF BLOOD

CS Goto

'She was little more than a child when the end had come. It had wrapped her up like the arms of her long-dead mother, embracing her as though it were a haven or a new beginning. But she could see the true nature of things – she was the ehveline. She could see the deceptions and the illusions pouring out of the future, smothering her sight and striving to leave her swaddling in the present. She was so much more than a child when the end had come, and she had seen it for what it was: the end of days.'

– The Tears of Blood:
The Chronicles of Ela'Ashbel, vol.2
by Deoch Epona, Craftworld Kaelor

THE AIR SWIRLED with burning dust, riddling the heavy darkness of the once glorious court with infinitesimal dying stars. It was as though the air itself smouldered with the scent of entropy, and the solitary little girl breathed it in. She stood in the midst of the ruins, with the devastation reflected in the moist sheen of her sapphire eyes. The tiny flares of sulphur and wraithbone that danced around her fluttered brilliantly like short-lived insects, and then singed her pale, grubby skin, extinguishing themselves in silence. As she swept her gaze across the rubble and through the flames, a single almost imperceptible tear trickled through the grime on her cheek, leaving a glistening trail of pure white in its wake. The tear was a crystal prism, glinting with the memories of the battle that had brought ruin to Kaelor. As it fell, dropping onto the blood-tinged and broken ground, the whole of the once magnificent court seemed to fall with it.

A soft, old voice wafted across the battlefield, like a pocket of twilight in a cloudy sky.

'Ela.'

In response, the little girl turned her head slightly, as though cocking her slender ears to the sound. The movement made her resemble a prey-animal, wary of predators but accustomed to their presence; predators are only dangerous on their own terms.

'Ela, come out of the rain.'

It was Ahearn, the ancient and decrepit Rivalin farseer. His stooped form shuffled towards her through the fire-flies and smoke-haze. Leaving her ears cocked for a moment longer, Ela realised that she could hear the metallic strike of his staff as he used it to balance his increasingly unsteady walk.

'It is hardly rain, caradoc,' she replied, holding out her palms like a child collecting water from the sky. Leaning back, she looked up into the eddying constellations of embers and smouldering dust, watching them dance and whirl like an incredible shoal of fish. Her eyes stung and watered as the fires fell into them.

Turning at last, Ela looked up into the old face of the once-great farseer. For an eldar, his face was ugly and wrinkled. He had lived for longer than even the eldest of Kaelor could remember. And he had lived through such times: first the Great House Wars that had seen the ruination of the Ansgar, and then the terrible Prophecy Conflict that had brought the Teirtu and all of Kaelor to its knees. Through it all, this hunched and gnarled old farseer had maintained the Court of Rivalin in unblemished glory. Only now, with the court in tatters and flames before him, was the ancient House of Rivalin finally humbled. Yet, beneath the heavy folds of his dark hood, Ela could see a youthful sparkle in the old eldar's eyes.

Cracks of warpfire suddenly flashed and arced like lightning through the wraithbone structure of the invisibly distant ceiling. The entire craftworld teetered perilously close to the raging Maelstrom outside.

'Like the planet-bound rain, this weather will pass, my little morna.' The faintest traces of a smile creased Ahearn's wrinkled and leathery features.

For a moment, the two of them stood together amongst the flaming debris of the court, Kaelor's past and future side by side, standing alone at the end of days. They surveyed the ruination and the despair of the scene. Here and there the broken forms of burning bodies flared amongst the rubble.

'Come, my morna, my child. There is nothing more to be done here.' As he spoke, Ahearn reached out his hand. 'Let us take some shelter from this storm.'

Ela looked up at him and saw the fiery destruction reflected in the old farseer's glinting eyes. For a moment, it seemed to her that she was looking back in time, as though she could see the battle unfolding once again in the purpling depths of his pupils. A terrified and agonised face screamed out of the reflection, but faded instantly, replaced by the dancing reflections of myriad fireflies.

'Come.' He smiled and turned his hand palm upwards, as though beckoning or beseeching the child protégé.

Ela nodded slowly, as though deciding that the old eldar was right: there was so much to be done, if anything was yet to be salvaged. She reached out her small, white but dirty hand and placed it into Ahearn's. The wrinkled farseer's eyes gleamed from under his hood and, as he smiled, Ela thought that she caught a glimpse of his tongue moistening his lips.

THE COMMAND DECKS of the *Relentless Wrath* were shrouded in darkness as the strike cruiser skirted the lashes of the roiling warp storm. In the faint, green glow that emanated from the chattering monitors and terminals, Master Kalidian Axryus cast a brooding and heavy shadow into the dimly lit chamber. He stood implacably before the swirling and oily images of fire and warp torment that swirled and stirred across the main viewscreen. His battle-scarred and age-gnarled face was hidden under the folds of his coarse hood, his long flowing robes hanging heavily over his deep green power armour. A starburst of red shone out from where his right eye should have been, the eye having been replaced decades before by a bionic implant.

'A likely place, indeed.' Kalidian's voice was like gravel. He rubbed his left hand over his unshaven jaw and let his index finger touch the corner of his ocular implant. Despite the long years since it had been fitted, he had never become accustomed to it. The angular and cold touch of metal on his face made sure that he could not forget the vengeance owed to the renegade Space Marine who had gouged out his eye; there was no crime more heinous than to turn against one's own. Kalidian would never even breathe that forsaken warrior's name.

'The report was inconclusive, Kalidian.' The Interrogator Chaplain was standing in the deepest shadows at the back of the control room, away from even the faintest hints of light shed by the monitors and viewscreens. He was leaning against the wall, his features hidden completely by the dark and his cloak, and he spoke in tones that were barely more than whispers.

'They always are, Lexius.' The master of the Dark Angels Fourth Company did not turn away from the screen, but he permitted himself a wry smile at his Chaplain's scepticism. There was not a single Astartes aboard the *Relentless Wrath* with more passion for the pursuit of vengeance and righteousness than Lexius Truidan. The devoted Interrogator Chaplain would chase even the vaguest of rumours if he thought that there was any chance of an element of truth lurking in their hidden depths. He, more than any other, would see the sense in this diversion to the edge of the great Maelstrom.

'You place such faith in the mention of his name, master. Yet his name is not mentioned in the report.'

'There are few who would recognise his name, Lexius, and fewer still who would recognise him for who he really is. We are both fortunate and unfortunate to be amongst those few, old friend. There is enough here to warrant an investigation. The report mentions ancient, black power armour and a magnificent sword that remained always sheathed. Moreover, it lingers on the details of a stranger claiming to personify the voice of the Emperor himself. This is a stronger lead than many of those we have rushed to pursue before this day.'

At last, Kalidian turned from the gyring and curdling warpmire of the Maelstrom, looked over the heads of the mind-wiped serfs who were busying themselves at the various terminals on the bridge, and smiled faintly at the obscured Chaplain, his bionic eye easily picking Lexius out of the darkness. 'This is our fate, brother. Prosecute repentance today, for tomorrow we may each come face-to-face with the Lion or the Emperor.'

'We answer for our own sins, and those of our brothers,' whispered Lexius, his face hidden in the darkness.

'Yes, brother Chaplain. We must take no chances with the souls of Dark Angels.' Kalidian turned back to the viewscreen. 'Verify the integrity of the warp shields and lay in a course for the Tyrine system, just inside the fury of the Maelstrom.'

'IT SHOULD BECOME *known as the Scouring of Tyrine, but the scribes and apostles of the terrible warriors that descended on us are already hard at work, producing the documents and justifications that called it a ritual purification. For the benefit of posterity and for the use of seekers of truth, I make this last report in sincerity and with despair in my heart. I have no hope that this report will reach the eyes of any who can help, since we are already beyond the help of all but the Emperor himself. But in my soul there lies a tiny vestige of faith that tells me to set this message free into the void.*

When it began, the sky burned and roiled with richly coloured clouds. Rivers of blood evaporated into the water cycle and stained everything touched by the hellish precipitation. The touch of death left its mark on all things. Huge, towering cathedrals dominated the tops of the mountains, and streams of blood poured down their spires and cascaded out from their foundations, as though they wept.

The once verdant and fecund world of Tyrine had teetered on the cusp of the Maelstrom for many centuries, like a village perched precariously on the top of an eroding sea-cliff. It had only been a matter of time before the cliff would crumble and the planet would fall. And when it fell, a strange and god-like warrior, calling himself an apostle of the law, had been poised ready to catch it.

Long ago, the people of Tyrine had placed their faith in the Emperor of Man, devoting our desperate energies to acts of penitence and worship. We had laboured with the last breaths of oxygen granted to us by our doomed world before it fell. We had dragged massive stones up to the mountaintops, pulling them by hand in chaingangs to demonstrate our piety, and then erecting them into magnificent cathedrals that aspired into the stratosphere.

Tyrine had been a monument of devotion and Imperial glory.

Despite its impending doom, Tyrine became renowned as a shrine world and drew pilgrims from across the system. Arcoflagellants flocked to the planet, spilling their own blood onto the streets, which each led up one of the many mountains to one of the many cathedrals – so it was that the first blood soaked into the forsaken soil of Tyrine, eventually to mingle with that of the tortured and violated dead.

But the Emperor never answered our prayers.

At first, as our planet finally succumbed to the lascivious tendrils of the warp, spinning into the fringes of the Maelstrom like a whipping-top, the devoted Imperial subjects of Tyrine had collapsed into despair. As the skies had boiled and the mountains had begun to twist in agonies of contortion, our pleas and prayers to the Emperor became yells and screams of accusation and hatred: our god had forsaken us. In amongst the swirling mire of psychic panic, disgust and pain, whispered voices started to call out to other powers, seeking refuge from the storm from anyone who could promise it.

This time, there was somebody who heard these calls.

The god-warrior had descended through the roiling, warp-drenched clouds in a blaze of radiance, letting his light echo around the planet like the silvered voice of the Emperor himself. He had held his cruiser in a low orbit for seven days, letting it shine like a star in the diminished and desperate heavens. And then, when the people of Tyrine had fixed their attention on his star like a beacon of new hope, defacing their monuments with impromptu tributes to the only point of steady and fixed light in their dark and warp-mired world, he had pulled the Word of Truth *out of orbit and let its light blink out of the skies of Tyrine, plunging the doomed world into hopelessness.*

For another seven days, he watched the spires of the great cathedrals fall. It is said that he smiled as we defaced the old images of the Emperor, over-etching them with the symbols of the gods who listened to our prayers. Cults arose all across the planet, and cultists started to reconstruct the once-glorious cathedrals, forcing their broken spires back into the skies with their sweat and blood, filling the cracks and ruins with the bones and skulls of the dead. Millions of souls cried out for a power, any power that could bring them salvation or direction.

Then, when he could see that the planet was ripe with fear, desperation and a clawing desire for a saviour, the Keeper of the Faith dropped back into orbit, returning a brilliant and pristine star of hope for the forsaken Tyrinites. He had rained his Space Marines down through the atmosphere in drop-pods that had burned like meteors, riddling the curdling darkness with signs from the gods: he brought hope and order to the betrayed, the desperate, the lost and the confused. And we hailed his coming as we might have once hailed the Emperor himself, had he ever bothered to come.

So it was that the Keeper of the Faith had walked amongst us like a god, making manifest the true voice of the Emperor, giving new direction and purpose to our devotions.

Tyrine is still a shrine-world; its pious and devoted people laboured to rebuild the magnificent monuments and temples that had once been dedicated to the cult of the Emperor of Man. But now they have been resurrected in grotesque splendour, punctuated with icons and symbols of the Great Betrayal – blood runs from mutilated images of the false Golden Throne. On the altars and in other places of honour, the regalia of the Imperium has been replaced crudely by the iconography of other powers, reflecting the directions of the voice of the true Emperor.

Where the air is thickest with fecund decay and where the people are most heady, cults of Slaanesh have seduced many others, and some of the Tyrinites began to delight in the perverse pleasures of their own suffering. Pain, suffering and death quickly became synonymous with artistry for these people. Torture and mutilation replaced prayer and sacrifice. Rather than moving against these cults, the Great Apostle embraced them as his own: the apparent voice of the Emperor calls on us to bathe in the blood of the slain and the innocent.

Our world was saved from despair by the Great Apostle, and now our sickly cries of joy reach out beyond the lashes of the Maelstrom, like a giant beacon to lure fellow pleasure seekers to the orgiastic grotesqueries that have engulfed our world.

Be aware, dear reader, that Tyrine is no longer a world for the sane or the pious. I do not dare to hope that you will come to rescue us, but I do trust to hope that you will never sully your soul by approaching our atmosphere. Stay away.'

– Unencrypted, repeated signal. Originator: Slefus Pious III. Source suspected to be the Tyrine system. Intercepted by Exiel Queril, hierosavant of Dark Angels strike cruiser, *Relentless Wrath*. 364.M38.

THERE IS NOTHING *but blood. It runs like rivers, as though the gods themselves are weeping.* Ela's lips moved as though she were giving voice to her silent thoughts, but she made no sound. Her words diffused the psychic ambiance with an unusual gravity tinged with a quizzical childishness. Her startling sapphire eyes sparkled with crystal tears as they gazed into an invisible distance.

The courtiers of the once-glorious Rivalin Court observed the infant seer with mixed emotions.

'This abomination knows nothing of blood,' hissed Maeveh of the Hidden Joy, pledged seer of the ancient House of Yuthran. She was herself a youthful protégé, having passed through the Ritual of Tuireann only twelve years before, but she was still more than three times the age of little Ela. Her own youthful features were twisted into an ugly snarl that pulled a matrix of scars into an intricate web over her face. Yet something smiled within her, giving her expression a faint hint of nausea. 'She cannot know what she sees. And in not knowing, she is also not seeing.'

The other courtiers murmured in response. Some of them in agreement, but others in trepidation: they had heard Ela's prophesies before and knew better than to take them lightly. She was no ordinary child bothered by nightmares or daydreams. Maeveh's relationship with the infant seer was fierce and adversarial for reasons that not everyone could properly understand.

'Exactly what did you see, young Ela of Ashbel?' Uisnech Anyon's tone was calm and deep as he pushed himself back into his seat in the crumbling remains of the Rivalin farseer's throne chamber. Although his voice seemed gentle and coaxing, it was edged with fatigue and cynicism. He was one of the oldest eldar in the court, having sat in attendance since before the House Wars. He had been one of the first of the High Eldar of Kaelor to see through to the vulgarity of Iden Teirtu and his Warrior House when they had been awarded a place of honour in the venerable court. He had watched the way that the refined high culture of the Rivalin legacy had been diluted and sullied by the lesser minds of crude eldar Houses from beyond the Styhxlin Perimeter. After centuries of change, he had learnt to be sceptical of the new and the youthful, but even he could see the unusual power that resided in the mind of this infant.

Standing in the middle of the Circle of Court, surrounded on all sides by the ancient and the prestigious of Kaelor, each seated in the crumbling remains of their family's status, little Ela simply shook her head. She grimaced slightly, as though a flash of pain had suddenly flickered through her head. 'You do not want to hear my visions. You want my silence.'

'Perhaps you suggest that some members of this council wish you ill, little morna? Is that what you see?' The farseer himself leaned forward out of his throne, propping his weight on his gnarled and twisted staff. He pushed his hooded face towards his protégé and smiled encouragingly, patronising her.

'She is confused, Ahearn of Rivalin. She merely senses that we desire her mind to be at peace, and that we each seek a future in which this furore is replaced by quiet.' Maeveh's voice hissed as though her tongue were split or forked.

Ela looked around the circle again, feeling a sudden chill wisp around her like a whirling breeze. She looked again, concentrating on each of the faces of the honourable court: Maeveh, Uisnech, Bricriu of the Sloane, Celyddon of Ossian and Ahearn himself – her own avuncular caradoc. For a moment, she felt as though they were drawing in around her, contracting the circle of power and enveloping her. It was as though they were reaching for her innermost thoughts, teasing her and playing with her intent.

She blinked and looked again, and the eldar of the court were each in their proper places, each gazing at her odd behaviour with quizzical concern written across their unaccustomedly dirty faces.

'I see rivers of blood cascading down the walls of cathedrals. I see monuments to the Great Enemy towering into a roiling, blood-red sky. I see a mon'keigh sorcerer communing with daemonic forces that fill my soul with terror. I see...' She trailed off, as though there was worse to come – things for which she could or would not find the words. 'I see the end of days. It is a Fall.'

'Look around you!' scoffed Maeveh, rising from her ruined seat and gesticulating dramatically with her arms. 'What is this if it is not the end of days? The court of Rivalin is in ruins, hundreds of Kaelor eldar lie in pools of their own blood under piles of rubble, with the blades of their own kin riddling their bodies in the animosity of false consciousness. This... this abominable infant does not see the future, she merely sees echoes of the present; she is yet too young to know the difference. It is fear that we should see in her words, not wisdom. We need not waste our time and meagre resources policing the fairy-tales of children. There are more pressing tasks at hand.'

As she finished her speech, the Yuthran seer let her flaming eyes meet those of Ela, as the infant stood in the middle of the circle of office. Maeveh's eyes flickered with deeply rooted emotions, like windows into her soul, and Ela recoiled slightly from what she saw. As she stepped back, instinctively trying to keep distance between them, she nudged back into a figure behind her.

'Come, my little morna, my child. Let us leave this place – there is no need for you to be part of this.'

Ela turned her head to see Ahearn gazing down at her. He was stooped over her, with the hood of his cloak concealing most of his features, even at this intimate range. Whilst one hand gripped his gnarled staff, supporting his age, the other rested affectionately on Ela's shoulder. In the shadows under his cloak, Ela thought that she could see the glint of his well-polished teeth, and a syrupy trickle of blood seeped over his lower lip. Instinctively, she shrugged her shoulder free of his hand.

THE CAVERNOUS INTERIOR of the great Basilica of the Rapture of Tyrine echoed with the voices of thousands raised in adoration. A deep, resonant chant thundered through the massive flagstones and masonry, making the monstrous building tremble as though it were alive.

The basilica was the glory of Tyrine; it towered out of the peak of Tyrinitobia, the highest mountain in the habitable realms. It had been constructed in the most majestic traditions of High Gothic architecture: a long, triple-aisled axis reached from the main gates through a high-vaulted nave to the altar, nestled in front of the grand apse. There was space for thirty thousand worshippers in that cavernous hall, and it was full from dawn till dusk, and then again from dusk till dawn. A constant stream of devotees poured in through the gates, forcing others out into the transepts and then out through the side gates into the city beyond.

The famous transepts themselves crossed the nave in front of the altar, and at that point of intersection a magnificent sweeping dome rose out of the distant ceiling. It was made entirely of red-stained glass, and this Blood Dome filled the basilica with a deep, ruddy light, illuminating the altar with the blood of the Emperor himself, or so it was said. From the sky, the plan of the great cathedral had inspired the devotions of millions of pilgrims as their shuttles dropped towards the spaceports in the valleys: rather than being conventional rectangles crossing the main axis, the transepts had been skilfully rendered into huge wings, as though the basilica itself echoed the shape of the Imperial aquila.

'From the fires of betrayal unto the blood of vengeance, we bring the voice of truth to your neglected and misremembered ears.' The deep, resonant voice of the orator boomed around the cavernous space, echoing between the thick stone columns and rolling over the tens of thousands of up-turned faces. 'For I am the Master of the Faith, first son of the great iconoclast – the bearer of the true word and the favoured son of the gods themselves.'

As he spoke, the dark-armoured giant pounded his gauntlets against the font, splintering its structure and sending chips of stone scattering into the congregation. His magnificent sword hung in silence from a harness on his leg. The people gazed up at the massive figure in awe and wondrous incomprehension, soaking in his words like desiccated, desert-weary men soaking in water. They had waited millennia for the coming of the Emperor and then, after it seemed that he had failed them utterly, this magnificent warrior had descended from the heavens in streams of fire. He told them that their devotion was welcome and proper, but that they erred in the focus of their devotions: their Emperor was false and deceitful – he called on them for obedience and obeisance, but then he ignored them. He was a false idol, and this newcomer was the voice of truth – the voice of iconoclasm and true devotion – the master of the faith.

When the congregation had first assembled in the basilica, the mysterious warrior-god had stridden to the altar and lifted the giant aquila in his own hands – a feat that could not have been accomplished by twenty men of Tyrine. With a defiant yell, he had flipped it upside down and crunched it back onto the altar, violated and ruined; an icon of its own perversion. At that moment, he had set the fires of revolution on Tyrine.

'I ask for nothing that you have not already given to another: your faith and undying devotion. You have lost these already, and I take them as my burden. You need pay them no more mind, since they are already in the nature of your souls.

'I ask only that this devotion be turned towards its proper target – turn it towards truth. Turn you devotion and your prayers to those who will hear you... to those who will listen to you.

'You cried out at the falling of your world, and who came to your aid? Who was it that brought light back into your skies and passion back into your hearts? Who was it that brought life and blood and fury back to Tyrine?

'Did your Emperor do this?'

A tremendous roar erupted from thirty thousand voices as they hurled their rage and discontent into a cacophonous rapture. The crowd teetered on the point of frenzy.

'No!' boomed the master orator, letting his voice fill the cathedral as though it were the very word of god himself. 'It was me!' He smashed his fist against the font and obliterated it. 'I brought your world back to life with the voice of truth and the word of the gods of Chaos!'

Another roar blasted out of the congregation, like a volcano of ecstasy, as the people of Tyrine opened their souls to the master of the faith.

'All praise be given unto them – the gods that touch our lives with their wills and their graces – the gods that reward our devotions with their divine favours! We offer our praise to those who listen, that they might turn their gaze our way and lift us with the boon of pain, to turn the galaxy red with blood and feed the hunger of the gods!'

THE WARP SPIDERS of Kaelor moved without moving, dipping in and out of reality like the tiny crystalline creatures of the webway from which they originally drew their name. The powerful, compact jump-generators on their backs meant that they could rip momentary holes in the materium and weave through the warp, surfacing and resurfacing in reality like threads of continuity through an impossibly black cloth.

As the squad of garnet and gold Spiders lurched into being on the edge of the crumbling sector that encompassed the farseer's court, Adsulata raised her hand to draw them to a halt and then dropped down into cover. She had been into the precincts of the court before, and she knew the dangers. Despite the devastation that had been wrought upon it by the Prophecy Wars, the court was still well defended. There were many powerful seer and warlocks in the service of the farseer, and the farseer himself was more than capable of seeing the approach of a clumsy Warp Spider squad; the ability to slide out of material reality meant little when sentries and security systems could see so clearly into the immaterium as well.

The Temple of the Warp Spiders, hidden out in the forested regions near the Styhxlin perimeter, had also suffered during the recent wars. Its position on Kaelor was now uncertain, and many of those who had remained unquestioningly loyal to the Rivalin farseer would still consider the Warp Spiders to be enemies of the craftworld. Uisnech of Anyon was one who would not hesitate to execute a Spider on sight – his own forces had suffered greatly at the hands of the Great Exarch, when he had led the Warp Spiders into battle against the court. Thankfully, reflected Adsulata, not many of the farseer's surviving courtly supporters had any backbone for battle.

Even from the outskirts of the court sector, Adsulata could see the damage that had been inflicted on the area. The once immaculate and beautiful buildings were cracked and their perfection was shattered. Flames still flickered here and there, where jet-bikes or Falcons had been left to burn out in the streets. It would probably not take long for an industrious and conscientious farseer to arrange the reconstruction of this area – after all, the court had been largely rebuilt after the House Wars, not so long ago. However, Adsulata was not convinced that Ahearn Rivalin would see this done. His priorities appeared to lie elsewhere.

The future of Kaelor lay in the hands of little Ela; Adsulata was as convinced now as she had ever been.

As she surveyed the scene, the Warp Spider arachnir – the squad leader – saw the faint flickering of warp-disturbance crackle through the wraithbone structure of the ceiling. Despite all the aesthetic and practical advantages of building with wraithbone – a substance drawn out of the warp itself and then fashioned into a material substance with rare and particular conductive qualities – Adsulata knew that the structure of Kaelor worked to its disadvantage when it sailed so close to a powerful warpstorm like the Maelstrom. She knew that the visible crackling of warp energy through the structure of the craftworld meant that it was drifting too close, that the tendrils of the warp were reaching for Kaelor and trying to draw it in, thirsting after the psychic glory of the children of Isha, which was only amplified and made manifest by the wraithbone itself.

The crackling in the sky was an ominous portent for the future.

The farseer's tower rose like a needle of light out of the flame-shadowed ruins. It had been the most heavily defended building of the entire war, and it bore few scars from the vicious battles that had raged around it. Adsulata had heard the rumours that its foundations hid a labyrinth in which lurked a pleasure cult of the kind that had not been seen since The Fall of the eldar all those millennia before, when the Sons of Asuryan had been forced to flee from their home worlds to escape the lascivious clutches of Slaanesh, the Great Enemy, set adrift into the darkest reaches of the galaxy in these monstrously large craftworlds. The ancient poems tell of how it was the very decadence of the eldar themselves that called Slaanesh into being, and how it had hunted them ever since, like an affection-starved child.

The craftworld eldar had adopted a disciplined and austere lifestyle in an attempt to keep the lusting fingers of Slaanesh at bay. But a pleasure coven on this ancient model would act like a brilliant beacon for the Great Enemy, luring it towards Kaelor, or dragging Kaelor towards it. Perhaps the farseer himself was blind to this terrible evil; it is not unwise to hide beneath the nose of your foes.

And all the time, the massive craftworld seemed to drift closer and closer to the roiling warp energies of the Maelstrom. Only the little seer, Ela'Ashbel, sister of the Great Exarch himself, had seen glimpses of the terrors that lay in wait for the children of Isha in the lashes of the warp storm. She had seen a mon'keigh sorcerer-daemon on the planet of Tyrine, summoning Kaelor to him in a grand gesture of sacrifice and obedience to the Great Enemy. And now, one of the humans' space cruisers had been sighted entering the Maelstrom. And yet the farseer and his court did nothing. Yet again it fell to the Warp Spiders to preserve the once magnificent and honourable spirit of Kaelor. If the court would not act on the wisdom of the Ashbel, Adsulata would.

The arachnir turned to check the readiness of her squad, nodded a brief but unambiguous signal, and then blinked out of existence. One by one, her Warp Spiders vanished in pursuit of their leader, heading for the farseer's tower, where they knew the infant seer was being kept.

THE SCENE THAT greeted Kalidian and his Dark Angels as they strode down the landing-ramp of their Thunderhawk filled their souls with nausea. Their gunship had crunched down onto what must once have been a bustling plaza in the centre of a white-stoned city, nestled elegantly into the side of a Tyrinian valley-basin. Tall, angular mountains aspired into the heavens on one side while the valley dropped away into a wide, meandering river on the other, and the city showed every sign of having been affluent at some point in its history.

In the centre of the plaza, just beyond the nose of the gunship, was a fountain; it was a statue surrounded by a pool of liquid. Even from the ramp of the Thunderhawk, Kalidian could see that the figure had once been a representation of the Emperor. It had never been beautiful or even competent, but its purpose and the motive of the primitive artisan who had produced it could not have been questioned. But now its form was quite changed. It was daubed in bright colours, and strange symbols had been etched into it; script had been scrawled across its base and hacked out of its surface with blunted blades. A long, broad sword had been hammered through the figure's chest, clearly rupturing the mechanism of the fountain and causing the water to stream out of the wound as blood. Some kind of amplification system had been riveted to the side of the figure's head, and a howl of hideous noise oscillated out of it, filling the atmosphere of the plaza with the scream of ecstatic souls.

Looking more closely, Kalidian realised that the liquid in the fountain was blood. In fact, blood slicked the flagstones of the entire plaza. The city streets were running with it, as streams of bloody water flowed down the mountainsides from the cathedrals on the peaks towards the ruddy river below.

Without saying a word, Chaplain Lexius vaulted down out of the Thunderhawk, levelled his bolter and blew the fountain apart, sending bloody shards of masonry raining into the side streets and silencing the daemonic noise.

'Suffer not the aberration,' he muttered, as though explaining his action. The other Dark Angels passed no comment as they swept their gaze around the perimeter of the gaudily coloured plaza, securing it in their minds.

There was a suggestion of movement in a couple of side streets and the Space Marines responded instantly, bracing their weapons and levelling them ready for combat.

'Hold,' said Kalidian firmly.

As they watched, a few tentative people started to emerge from the buildings and streets around the edges of the plaza. They were ragged, ritually scarred and blood-drenched, and their eyes shone with a dull, lunar light. Their movements had no urgency, as though they were intoxicated, and they appeared to be utterly unconcerned about the presence of the two-metre high, cloaked and power armoured warriors standing before them with braced bolters.

The tentative few gradually became a tentative group and then a crowd. It seemed that people were pressing into the plaza from all over the city. They all looked stunned, as though teetering on a state of rapture – their eyes were wide and their pupils dilated. Kalidian realised that this was more than merely shellshock or trauma. The atmosphere in the plaza was shifting towards hysteria, and the crowd seemed to view the Astartes with hunger and anticipation. They had been drawn to the plaza by the blaze of fire that came down with the Thunderhawk, and, after a matter of seconds, the plaza was teeming with people; the Dark Angels were surrounded.

'Do you bring the Voice of the Emperor?' The sound was almost a chant, arising from many mouths at the same time, as though practiced or drilled into them. There was little music, but the voices seemed to rejoice in their spontaneous harmony.

'We bring vengeance and justice,' growled Lexius, restraining his trigger-finger until Kalidian had taken the lead.

'Are you the Keepers of the True Faith?'

Kalidian watched the crowd for a moment, weighing up its mood and its movements. 'Yes we are,' he said finally. He singled out one of the men at the front of the throng, whose face was lined with self-inflicted scars and whose chest carried the carved, blood-crusted sign of Slaanesh. 'You have seen others like us?'

'The Voice of the True Faith has passed amongst us,' answered the man, his eyes widening in a mixture of fear, awe and excitement.

'This "Voice" has instructed you in how to behave with proper piety and devotion?' said Kalidian.

'Yes, Lords of the Word. We have been graced by the presence of the Keeper of Faith. He remains amongst us always.'

'He is like us?'

'Yes, Lords of the Word.'

'You will take us to him.' Kalidian turned from the bloodied Tyrinite and saw the venom burning in the eyes of Lexius – the Chaplain burned to annihilate these repulsive offences to the Emperor's sight. 'Wait, Lexius – righteous purification can come later. For now, there is a chance of vengeance. Perhaps we have found him after all?'

THE MASTER ORATOR'S eyes flashed with daemonic fire as he watched the rapture grip the hearts of the already twisted and desperate people of Tyrine. The basilica roared and rumbled with frenzies of impassioned dedication. He had seen it on countless worlds before, and it had happened every day since he had landed there; the planet was ripe with fear and loathing. The souls of the people were crying out for his words, they had dragged him from deep within the Maelstrom like a burning beacon. Millions of souls ripe for the plucking – such a powerful offering for the gods!

But there was a more subtle plan at work behind his machinations on Tyrine. This was no mere blood sacrifice for the pleasure of Khorne, for the Master of Faith did not answer to any one single god. He had heard whispers of more refined prizes, muttered into his ears by the most seductive of temptresses. An ancient and once-glittering eldar craftworld was straying deliciously close to the fringes of the Maelstrom. If he could turn Tyrine into a rapturous shrine-world for Slaanesh, the daemon would give him the power to lure the eldar into the Maelstrom and gift him legions of daemonettes to do battle with the craftworld, which was already falling slowly into Slaanesh's hands. In return for the souls of thousands of eldar, which would be enough to bring Slaanesh out of the warp and into the soupy space of the materium itself, the master of the faith would be granted the favours and talents of Slaanesh.

The temptation was simply too great, even for him.

Looking up through the glorious, blood-red glass of the Blood Dome above him, the once-loyal Space Marine thought that he could already see the glint of a new star in the firmament: the eldar craftworld could not be far away now.

'All praise be given unto the gods that reward our devotions with their divine favours!' he yelled, listening to the way that the congregation anticipated and chanted his words in unison. 'We offer our praise to those who listen, that they might turn their gaze our way and lift us with the boon of pain,' he continued, letting a smile crack across his face: they were his now. 'To turn the galaxy red with blood and feed the hunger of the gods!'

AT THE TOP of the farseer's tower, hidden in a circular room in the heart of the shining structure, away from the light, commotion and the temptations of the craftworld below, Ela'Ashbel sat in silence. Her legs were folded beneath her and her eyes were closed in the darkness as she mouthed the soundless words of a mantra, drawing her mind back in on itself and trying to push it out the other side into the timelessness of the immaterium beyond.

She did not understand why the farseer's manner towards her was so uneven. He swung from being her doting caradoc to being hostile and patronising. He told her that he believed in her powers and her abilities, but then he reprimanded her for speaking out in the Circular Council, telling her that it was not the place for a child to speak so disrespectfully to her elders.

There was no doubt in her mind about the authenticity of her vision, and the mire of warp energy that lashed and cracked through the wraithbone structure of Kaelor seemed to support her theory with every flash. The vast craftworld was pitching into the fringes of the Maelstrom, drawn in by the power of a mon'keigh sorcerer who worked in league with the Great Enemy itself – Slaanesh was calling its creators home at last. She just couldn't understand why Ahearn could not see this – he was the farseer!

In the distant and mythical past, Ela reflected, the powerful psykers of the hoamelyngs – the planetary eldar of before the Great Fall – had failed to see the conjuring of the Great Enemy. They were lost in the concerns of their own decadence, and blind to the swirling maelstrom of daemonic lust that had been birthed into the immaterium.

At that moment, the image of Ahearn reaching out his hand for her in the smouldering ruins of the old court flickered through her mind. There had been something wrong with that scene, but she had hardly noticed it at the time, and she couldn't quite identify it now. And then there was the way that he had ushered her from the Circle of Court itself. There was something about the curl of his wrinkled old lips and the dark glint of his teeth. She remembered the cold touch of his hand on her shoulder, and shivered inwardly at the thought.

A series of explosions of light flickered around her chamber, making her eyes snap open suddenly, but she did not move from her posture of meditation. As soon as the bursts of light appeared, she knew what was happening.

'Adsulata,' she said, closing her eyes again as though completely unconcerned. 'It has been a long time.' She did not need her eyes to see the actions of those she knew well. She sometimes wondered whether she needed her eyes at all. Who other than the Warp Spiders could breach the security of the tower so easily, and appear like sudden stars in her secret meditation chamber?

There was no reply, but, in her mind's eye, Ela could see the arachnir and her squad of Warp Spiders bowing deeply in an ancient ceremonial greeting, usually reserved for the farseer himself.

'Farseer Ashbel,' said Adsulata eventually. 'We come to liberate you from this prison.'

'You are mistaken, Arachnir Adsulata. I am not the farseer, and I am in no prison.'

'As you wish, farseer,' bowed Adsulata, her voice betraying no capitulation on either point. 'Nonetheless, we are here to free you from this place. Kaelor is in peril. You have seen the mon'keigh vessel entering the Maelstrom?'

'Yes, Warp Spider, I have seen it. And I have seen other things besides – bloody things. The future is perilous and bleak, Adsulata.'

'And yet the Rivalin court does nothing?'

'I have told them what I have seen.'

'And they locked you in here?'

'For my protection and peace of mind,' said Ela, realising that she was unconvinced by her own words.

'It was not that long ago that the Warp Spiders stood behind you in the Prophecy Wars, Ela of Ashbel. We will stand with you now. Instruct us, and your will shall be done. Tell us, farseer, what was in your vision.'

'I am *not* your farseer, Arachnir Adsulata.' The Warp Spider's adamance about the title was disconcerting and annoying.

'I saw cascades of blood rushing down the walls of great cathedrals, and sacrificial pyres to the Great Enemy burning into a roiling, blood-red sky. I saw a human psyker communing with daemonic forces that filled my soul with terror. I saw the Fall of Kaelor, Adsulata – I saw the end of days.'

'You saw Tyrine, farseer? The mon'keigh planet that floats in peril in the lashes of the terrible warp storm? If the false farseer's court will not act on this, the Warp

Spiders will act – we will escort you to Tyrine, and we will see to it that your visions of the future are not permitted to crash back into the present. If it is your will, it shall be done.'

For a long moment, little Ela'Ashbel said nothing. She sat with her eyes closed and pondered the various futures that lay before her, weighing up the consequences of her decision. She had known Adsulata for a long time, and knew her to be an honourable and devoted Aspect Warrior of the Great Exarch of the Spider Temple, and a loyal subject of Kaelor. Her intentions were beyond reproach and her instincts were reliable. On the other hand there was Ahearn – the farseer, her caradoc. Glimmering images of his face as he reached his hand for hers swam through her mind unbidden. Why could he not see all this?

Another possibility entered Ela's head for the first time: perhaps the farseer could see what was happening, but was choosing not to act on it. The thought was full of horror. Had the court really fallen so far?

'It is my will.'

THE CIRCLE OF Rivalin was broken but it was not destroyed. The grand ring of wraithbone thrones that had stood untarnished for millennia was cracked and crumbling, but they were not all empty; a number of the courtiers had survived the turmoil of the Prophecy Wars. They had watched as their ancient and glorious ancestral homeland – the great craftworld of Kaelor – had collapsed into despair around them. One or two had rejoined their own Great Houses and taken up arms in the struggle, but most had remained hidden in the confines of the High Court itself, holding themselves above the petty violence of their degenerating people. Of the fighters, only the wizened and cynical Uisnech of Anyon had returned to reclaim his ornate, rune-encrusted seat of office. House Anyon had been battered and devastated by the wars, but it had seen them through to the end, fighting proudly in the name of the farseer.

Some of the most exclusive and secret areas of the massive court complex had remained almost untouched by the fury of the unrest, and a number of the councillors had been able to continue to live their lives in the privileged and courtly manner to which they had grown accustomed. The Yuthran Seer, Maeveh, had been one of those who had remained ensconced in the haven and, now that Kaelor seemed to be burning into ruins around her, she felt that her disdain for the violence of her brethren had been entirely justified.

'I cannot believe that the old knavir agreed to permit that sleehr-child a voice in this court.' Maeveh sneered as the ancient tongue of heresy slipped into her speech. Her eyes flashed like those of a serpent. Since the farseer had left the chamber to escort the little abomination to her tower, Maeveh had been reclined into her seat with such confidence that it may have seemed to an outsider to be her own court.

The others laughed with a mixture of pleasure, anxiety and fear, nervously enjoying her irreverence.

'You will not use such language in this chamber, Maeveh of Yuthran. It does not become this court to speak so ill of the farseer, nor of his choices. The infant seer may yet have a role to play in all this. In the absence of certainty, some prudence would suit you better.' Uisnech rose to his feet. He was invariably the only one to stand up to the Yuthran wytch, but his solitary opposition was usually enough to silence the others. 'Besides,' he added, 'it seems that the mon'keigh have indeed been sighted on the fringes of the sector: it appears to be a strike cruiser of some kind, perhaps of the Adeptus Astartes. Ela'Ashbel's vision may not be completely fabricated, Seer Maeveh.'

'Yes, the appearance of the mon'keigh at this time should not be ignored.' Maeveh smiled in a superior manner, without rising to Uisnech's challenge. She shared a glance with the youthful and dark-skinned Celyddon Ossian, whose golden eyes were accentuated by his luxurious and richly coloured robes, immaculate and untainted by the tempest of destruction that had been raging through Kaelor. Only the damp stain of blood around the hem of his extravagant cloak betrayed the mark of the times on his appearance.

'I agree,' nodded Celyddon, his smirk masking myriad emotions.

Uisnech looked from Maeveh to Celyddon, shaking his head in undisguised exasperation. It was bad enough that these two youngsters were on the council in the first place – they were only there because the senior heads of their Houses had perished prematurely, in unforeseen and dramatic events before their times, in the early stages of the Prophecy Conflagration. It had never been the custom of the Court of Rivalin to grant senior office to such inexperienced eldar, even to the eldar of the exalted Houses of Yuthran and Ossian; the power, the affluence and the lifestyle of the farseer's court had a tendency to *change* the impressionable mind. And these two were certainly enjoying the privileges of their rank, despite the turmoil of the day.

Uisnech was sick of their pretension and their snide little secrets. They never *did* anything; they just talked and jibed about things. When the forces of the farseer had stood on the brink of annihilation and Uisnech had marched proudly into the flames in the place of Ahearn himself, Maeveh and Celyddon had been drinking Edreacian ale and watching a performance of *The Birth of the Great Enemy* by a troupe of travelling Harlequins.

'So, you both agree that this should not be ignored. What form do you agree that "not ignoring" the mon'keigh should take *in practice*?' he snarled, letting his cynicism overflow into hostility.

'Why don't you ask little Ela'Ashbel, Uisnech?' Maeveh turned the senior councillor's anger into a joke, and then she laughed, finding her own act of ridicule amusing.

The apparently careless words of the Yuthran seer contained complicated and cutting connotations. On one hand she was patronising him, implying an equivalence between him and the ageing farseer himself, suggesting that his only possible functional relationship with Ela'Ashbel was as her caradoc. As he realised this, Uisnech's mind made an even more cynical leap: did Maeveh mean to imply that the farseer himself needed to be patronised in this way? Was this a veiled heresy?

On the other hand, Maeveh seemed to be telling him that his scepticism about youth was old-fashioned and anachronistic – her allusion to the farseer serving to demonstrate that even Ahearn Rivalin seemed to have embraced the presence of the child-like Ela on the council.

If the farseer was willing to open his soul to the abominable infant, surely Uisnech could accept the presence of Maeveh and Celyddon. Of course, the real political importance of these implications was that, despite their ostensibly similar ages and the length of their shared histories, it was Uisnech, not the young upstarts, who was the outsider in the court. Maeveh seemed to share a new appreciation of youth with the farseer that isolated Uisnech and suddenly made him feel like an impostor in a private club. The unpleasant chain of thought sparked another cynical question in Uisnech's subtle mind: if Ahearn and Maeveh were more alike than he had previously considered, did this mean that he should reconsider the whereabouts of the farseer when he, Uisnech, had stood at the head of the Rivalin armies in Ahearn's place at the culmination of the Prophecy Wars?

Had Ahearn really been here with Maeveh and the Harlequins?

The implications of these questions opened up routes for heretical conclusions of the kind that Uisnech would never want to reach. Instead, he contented himself with cursing the infinitely subtle complexities of eldar politics and the enigmatically devious mind of the Yuthran seer. For all of their primitive and clumsy stupidity, the mon'keigh at least had the virtue of being intellectually incapable of the kinds of multi-layered meanings and intrigues that so beset his own kind. Not for the first time in his long and eventful life, Uisnech wondered what it would be like to lead the short, direct and simple life of a human being.

'You ARE NOT the first to fall victim to the arbitrary whims of this false god,' said the orator, leaning forward over the shattered font at the front of the basilica of the Rapture of Tyrine, as though imparting a secret. Responding to the change in his tone, the congregation fell into a hushed silence.

'You are not alone in this, although you may feel the isolation deep within your souls.'

Murmurs of affirmation whisked around the nave, like a breeze being pushed ahead of a great storm.

'I too have laboured under the false promises of this self-interested *Emperor of Man*. I once drove his light across the galaxy in the righteous fury of the Great Crusade. I knelt at his feet, exposing my very soul to his words, bowing my head to await the touch from his golden hand. But, like you, I waited in vain. The touch of his duplicitous fingers was never bestowed on me, nor on any of his most devoted servants. Instead of honour and salvation, he rewarded us with ridicule and insult – calling our labours faulty and misguided.

'And even then, like you, we did not lose our faith. Instead, we sank into despair, struggling to comprehend what grave offences we must have enacted on our god for him to treat us in this way. "It must be our fault! We must have failed in our devotions! The Emperor is just and would not treat us thus without just cause!" We fell into prayer for weeks without end.'

Muttered voices rippled around the basilica as the people of Tyrine recognised their own plight and reactions in the orator's grand story. A few yelled their agreement, breaking the wash of noise like crested waves.

'But,' continued the orator, before pausing dramatically, letting the power of silence descend over the congregation, making every face in the basilica strain to catch his next words.

'But the fault was not with us,' he whispered, watching the eagerness of the Tyrinites before him as they strained to hear him.

'The fault was not with us!' he shouted, letting his voice boom and resonate around the cathedral. 'It was the Emperor himself that erred. He did not listen to us. He did not care for us. He did not raise a finger to grant us even the smallest favour. He left us adrift and alone with our faith!

'But *you* are not alone!'

The congregation exploded into rapture.

'We stand here together, united in our realisation of truth! We give our devotion to those who will hear us – to those worthy of our blood and toil.'

A rhythmic chanting struck up out of the assembly, calling out the name of the great orator, even as they stamped their feet in devotion, making the basilica rock with their passion.

'We offer our praise to those who listen, that they might turn their gaze our way and lift us with the boon of pain,' said the orator, turning the frenzy of the congregation towards the litany, and smiling as he heard every voice in the cavernous cathedral take up his call. As a single, mighty voice, they finished the lines: 'To turn the galaxy red with blood and feed the hunger of the gods!'

LEAVING THE CRUMBLING and lost grandeur of the Circle of Court in the wake of her billowing cloak, Maeveh of Yuthran swept through the atrophied corridors of the Farseer's Palace with the train of her robes dragging through the dust and debris, sweeping a meandering trail behind her. She turned through a series of damaged corridors and passed along a number of subsiding passages, moving deeper and deeper into the ancient complex.

After a few minutes, she paused in the middle of a rubble-strewn aisle. Looking furtively in both directions to check that nobody was watching, she reached out and pressed her soft, velvet-gloved fingers against the pursed lips of an elegant wraithbone figurine. A faint electric green crackled around the outline of the statue, then it clicked gently and slid back away, revealing a hidden passageway beyond. Checking the main corridor one last time, Maeveh ducked quickly inside and the statue moved smoothly back into place.

The narrow, dark corridor beyond the statue might have been part of an entirely different world, or from a different, more elevated period of Kaelor's past. Its shimmering wraithbone walls were alive with myriad points of light, as though they were windows into impossibly distant star systems. The scene was immaculate, untainted and utterly unscarred by the turmoil of war.

As she stepped into the glittering space, Maeveh paused for a moment and sighed. It was as though she could feel the pollution and dirt of the corridor outside dropping off her. A wave of relaxation rippled through her body, and she set off down the beautiful passageway.

About halfway down the corridor, she could already hear raised voices and the clatter of feasting. The sound echoed up the passageway towards her, flickering through the flashes of light and shadow that betrayed the movements of the eldar that had congregated secretly into the cavern up ahead.

By the time she emerged into the wide, low chamber, the scene was a riot for her senses. A long, ornately sculpted, glimmering wraithbone table stretched out across the room, strewn from one end to the other with expensive and ostentatious foodstuffs, carafes of whyne, and glistening decorative statuettes. There was even a jug of Eldreacian ale. Around the table, sunk into lusciously embroidered, throne-like chairs, reclined over a dozen eldar, each bedecked in glorious colours and sumptuous robes. They picked casually at the feast before them, laughing and lost in conversation and debate. It was a scene that might have been depicted in a fresco from the grand days of the height of the Rivalin dynasty. Despite its intimate scale, it made Maeveh wonder about the glories of eldar life before the Fall.

As Maeveh stepped into the chamber, bathing in the warmth, the light, and the overflowing decadence of the atmosphere, a number of the feasters turned and lifted their glasses in greeting. She nodded mirthfully in return and then watched as a pair of semi-circular double-doors on the far side of the room cracked open and the entertainment was wheeled in.

Strapped to a complicated, antique rig on the jade-coloured, metallic cart was the figure of a mammalian primate. Most of its clothing had been stripped away, exposing its ugly, pallid flesh to the intrigued and amused gazes of the assembled eldar. Maeveh had seen that particular mon'keigh before – she had captured it as it attempted to flee from the Maelstrom in a pathetic, primitive space vessel. It had been broadcasting some form of distress call, which had intrigued Maeveh sufficiently to attract her attention. Indeed, sculpting and resculpting the content of the distress call had proven to be quite a distraction from the mundane and filthy business of Kaelor recently.

'Ah,' she said, letting the sound gasp lightly out of her mouth, as though it gave her physical pleasure to utter it. 'The alien that calls itself... what was it? Ah yes: Slefus Pious III. How delightful that it is still alive for our pleasure.'

'There are more important affairs than this creature, Maeveh of the Hidden Joy.' The voice seemed to have no origin, but the rustle of faint discomfort in the room drew Maeveh's attention to a hooded figure sitting at the foot of the great table.

'Of the not-so-hidden joy, I should say.'

A wave of mirth and chuckled agreement flittered around the room, as though each of those present knew of the joys of Maeveh. Meanwhile, the sinister, hooded figure reached across the table with his gnarled staff and hooked the tankard of Edreacian ale, dragging it back towards him as though too weak or intoxicated to stand and grasp it with his hand.

Maeveh tilted her head and inspected the wizened and hunched old figure. His hood and cloak were dark beyond blackness, of a colour and fabric that spoke of incredible, unimaginable affluence. His staff was unmistakable, and his manner betrayed him instantly.

'Ahearn,' whispered Maeveh, projecting her aspirated words across the room. 'How wonderful to see you here again. I confess that I had begun to wonder whether you had abandoned us for that hideous stickler, Uisnech of Anyon. He seems so earnest, dear farseer, and I am sure that he would not approve of our little pleasure dome, here.'

The farseer looked up from his tankard, with a froth of drink lining his wrinkled lips, and he smiled. 'You were always my favourite, Maeveh, but you should not belittle the Anyon. He is loyal to me, and he has his uses; how else could we sustain this... this level of civilisation amidst the violent atrophy of our times if it were not for the industry and earnestness of our friend Uisnech. He fought in my place at the head of my armies! Without him, none of this,' continued Ahearn, swirling his staff in a dramatic gesticulation that toppled his tankard and sent a sheen of liquor flooding over the already food-thick table. 'None of this would remain possible.'

Maeveh nodded and dropped herself into the seat at the head of the table, facing the farseer from a long distance. The eldar nearest to her hastened to provide her with a glass and to shuffle the table arrangement so that the seer's favourite dishes would be within her reach.

Letting her eyes flick over the face of the servile eldar, she realised with satisfaction that it was actually Bricriu of the Sloane. How delicious, she thought, to have one of the Circular Council pouring her drink; only here in her hidden world of pleasure could this happen. It was a testament to the appeal of her secret coven that even eldar of that stature were willing to humble themselves to gain entry – this life spoke to something essential in the soul of every eldar, whether they were willing to admit it or not.

Only a few years before, this chamber had been nothing more than the frustrated and lusty dream of Maeveh and a few of the more visionary seers of House Yuthran. Now it was a veritable cabal of bliss, exclusive and hidden like a glistening pearl in an ocean of ugly and primitive destruction.

'You are right, of course.' She smiled. In all honesty, none of the politics of the Circle of Court really interested her at all. She only sat on that sober and boring council because the status associated with it opened a great many doors on Kaelor, not least the secret doors into this very chamber. Since the start of the Prophecy Conflagration, things had only become worse on the rest of the vast craftworld and the earnest Uisnech had only increased his influence at the steadily crumbling court. At the end of the day, however, she didn't really care what Uisnech did, as long as he didn't prevent her from enjoying the finer and more developed aspects of eldar life. From time to time, however, she had to admit that she took some pleasure from coaxing and teasing the head of House Anyon – he always responded with such delightful violence.

'At least the old warrior has not yet come to appreciate the… special qualities of our little Ela,' said Maeveh, toying with the food on her crystalline plate. 'He finds the little abomination to be too young and beautiful, it seems.'

'He is a wise old fool, Maeveh. None of us can see the future of that infant seer. It is clouded even from me.'

'Perhaps it is time for us to bring her here, Ahearn?' The idea tantalised her, and her expression thrilled as though pulsing with physical pleasure. She felt as though she had given voice to something forbidden. 'Perhaps she would be… receptive.'

'Do not think that I have not thought of this. But her visions suggest that her concerns lay beyond those of this delirious chamber. She is… distracted from these truths about the eldar soul. She sees blood always behind her eye-lids; whenever she sits into meditation or lies down to rest, blood cascades into her mind.'

'We are not strangers to blood here,' toyed Maeveh, her eyes slipping over towards the bound shape of the mon'keigh, who was caught in between raptures of bliss and agony, held in the clutches of a group of sensuous eldar.

'She may yet be our enemy, Maeveh. Do not presume that the innocence of her youth will make her pliant in your hands... delightful as that thought may be.'

The Yuthran seer said nothing; her attention was transfixed for a moment by the enthralling performance of Slefus Pious III. In her mind's eye, she imagined that the squirming mon'keigh was the little abomination of Ashbel.

'She has left Kaelor. Were you aware of this? The infinity circuit has been deprived of her presence: Kaelor has felt her departure. The Warp Spiders have escorted her to Tyrine, the nearest planet on the cusp of the warp storm. She seeks to prevent the fall of Kaelor into the Maelstrom, Maeveh. She believes that we are being drawn in by the powers of a mon'keigh sorcerer in league with the *Great Enemy.*' Ahearn mouthed the last words with theatrical emphasis. 'She believes that this is the only possible explanation for our craftworld's trajectory.'

'Then we may yet be able to rely on the innocence of her youth, farseer.' The rhetorical flourish pleased Maeveh, and she smiled broadly. 'Besides, it seems as though her dear *caradoc* has already earned the trust of his little *morna*.' Her words dripped with theatrical sarcasm as she imitated Ela's and then Ahearn's voice in turn.

'As for her activities on Tyrine, you may rest assured that I have already arranged for a little extra company for her.' As she spoke, she cast her eyes back over to the bloodied and broken figure of Slefus, who had finally slumped into motionlessness. 'The Adeptus Astartes themselves are going to offer their assistance, thanks to our recently deceased friend there. These mon'keigh are such simple-minded, primitive creatures – they have no self-discipline: dangle a temptation before them and they run to it.'

'And temptation is something that you understand better than most.'

A SWIRLING VORTEX of warpfire erupted spontaneously in the sky, hanging low over the ruins of a once-ornate and grand stone plaza. It spun with an eerie, deep purple whirl of flame, pulling in the clouds from the darkened sky and rippling against the blood-stained, colour-daubed buildings. As though in dramatic sympathy, smaller eddies of dust started to swirl into miniature tornadoes around the plaza, sparking and crackling with warp energy.

Jagged lances of lightning flashed into the whirling portal, transforming its vaporous circle into a shimmering pool of reflective energy. After a few seconds, the pool ruptured and a group of slender figures dropped out of it into the plaza below, their garnet and gold armour glinting in the dull light of Tyrine. Amongst them, as they landed lightly on blood-slicked flagstones, was a small, hooded figure that might have been a child.

As soon as their feet hit the ground, the Warp Spiders deployed into a ring around the little, ruby-robed Ela, guarding her from the unknown. They were anticipating a hostile reception; a group of glittering eldar souls dropping into the mire of a world in the grip of temptation by Slaanesh would be sure to attract attention.

Even as the Warp Spiders swept the scene with their death spinners, checking the terrain for signs of daemonic infestation, the cyclones around the edges of the plaza whirled into solidity. They drew in air and energy, spinning them into sleek, humanoid forms. After a few seconds, the once-secure and deserted plaza was punctuated with the elegant and pale forms of Slaaneshi daemonettes. It was as though the Great Enemy could smell the presence of the children of Isha.

At the same time, mutilated and blood-streaked mon'keigh started to seep into the plaza from the side streets. They came clutching tools and bladed weapons, whips and primitive projectiles. Covered in vividly coloured paints where clothing should have been, the mammals chanted and sang in a hideous cacophony of noise that assailed the sensitive senses of the eldar.

As the daemonettes started to move towards the eldar, slipping through the unfamiliarly dense caresses of material space, slicing casually through the gathering throng of humans, thrilling as they slid and danced in breathtakingly lethal displays, the Warp Spiders lurched into action. Ela had foreseen the presence of daemonic forces on Tyrine, and they were not unprepared.

Without a word, Adsulata blinked out of existence, reappearing abruptly on the far side of the square, surprising a group of mon'keigh from behind. Her death spinner spluttered and spun like a gatling-gun, mowing down a swathe of the mammals before they even had a chance to turn. The nearest daemonette was faster, ducking and spinning in a nauseatingly graceful turn, before springing into a slow flip that brought it to rest only a couple of meters from the arachnir.

Adsulata did not pause or hesitate, but left her weapon spinning with fire, strafing it through the crowd towards the lithe and exquisite shape of the daemonette. But the maid-servant of Slaanesh moved as quickly as the ballistic spray, hopping, turning and springing around the fire until the range was closed to nothing. At which point, the daemonette swatted the death spinner from Adsulata's hands and lashed out with a viciously curving blade.

Letting her gun fall, Adsulata met the daemonette's strike with the powerblades that ran along the backs of her forearms.

Meanwhile, the rest of the Warp Spider squad had followed their arachnir's lead, warp-jumping to strategic positions around the combat zone from where they could outflank the massing foe and ensure that the daemonettes could not co-ordinate an assault on the infant seer.

Three Aspect Warriors remained positioned around Ela, cutting down any of the mon'keigh that were pressed towards them by the weight of the crowd, and spraying out fire in support of their brethren who were engaging the daemonettes.

Ela herself stood in the eye of the storm, feeling the sickly fury swirling around the plaza like a maelstrom of blood lust. For a moment, her mind flashed back to the ruination that had engulfed the once-glorious Kaelor – something in the air on Tyrine shared the same nauseating taste as that terrible event. Looking up the mountainside, past the fury of combat that raged around her, she saw the towering shape of a majestic basilica rising into the clouds. Its sides ran slick with blood, just as in her vision, and she knew that the sorcerer was there, waiting for her.

Fate waited for nobody.

Muttering a few words of power, the infant seer pushed her arms out from her cloak and summoned a corona of crackling energy from her hands, sending streams and arcs of lightning jousting out from her fingers, as she conjured the Storm of Eldritch into the plaza.

THE DARK ANGELS paused at the end of one of the long boulevards that opened up into the wide courtyard before the gates of the towering basilica dominating the mountaintop. The squad stopped to survey the lay of the land before entering the open space, their suspicions having been raised by the atmosphere of the city itself. They stood, magnificent and colossal, amidst the crowd of

Tyrinites that had followed them through the streets, chanting and howling with delight at the second coming of the Voice of the True God.

'I do not like this,' said Lexius, staring up at the awesome edifice before them.

Even with the massive gates closed, and even from the other side of the wide courtyard, the Dark Angels could hear the chanting of heretical prayers and sonorous cacophony that echoed around the interior of the cavernous building.

'...lift us with the boon of pain, to turn the galaxy red with blood and feed the hunger of the gods!' The muffled words wafted across the square.

The journey through the streets of the sprawling city had been long and enlightening. The buildings were beginning to crumble through a combination of neglect and violence; they had been transformed from the simple, pious dwellings of pilgrims and penitents into gaudily coloured and decadently arrayed abodes for hedonists and pleasure-seekers. Images of the Emperor had been desecrated or torn down and left in pieces in the dirt. Crude statues of unspeakable things had been hastily erected to replace them. And everywhere was the relentless howl of ungodly noise, piped through amplification systems, tumbling out of the cracked windows of the gaudy abodes, or simply yelled out of the lungs of the people that staggered through the streets. The effect was a barrage on the senses.

'I cannot believe that he is here,' snarled Kalidian, looking back down the boulevard along which they had just travelled. The red light of his bionic eye shone constantly, as though always in focus. He lowered his voice even further, until it was barely audible: 'Surely there are depths to which even a fallen angel will not fall.'

Lexius made no reply, as though he were considering the question. He had followed up dozens of leads over the last couple of decades, chasing across the galaxy in pursuit of the merest murmur or the smallest hint in a report. As a result, he had become extremely sceptical about his chances of fulfilling his vocation. But, despite his scepticism, he had to admit that the report from Tyrine had been the most promising in years. It was a virtual plea for them to investigate the planet.

For a moment, the thought crossed his mind that the perfect, cryptic certainties of the report might imply that someone was trying to lure them into a trap, but then his senses returned to him: who could possibly know of the shame of the Dark Angels. Who could have set a trap such as this? The logical answer sent a thrill through his augmented and reinforced spine: only Cypher himself could do this. So perhaps he was here, after all? More likely that it was an act of misdirection – luring the Dark Angels to Tyrine while he vanished off in the Belt of Ophorine.

'So close,' growled Lexius eventually. 'We should purge this place, Master Axyrus. Its existence is an aberration and an offence to the light of the Emperor.' But then his thought lurched in a new and unexpected direction: if anyone ever discovered their hidden shame, they would be able to use hints like this to lead them all over the galaxy, rendering the Interrogator Chaplains into little more than puppets. As a simmering rage of resentment started to boil in the Chaplain's soul, his mind raced through the various possible manipulators.

'Eldar!' The cry came from behind him as the Tactical Marines started to move in response to the sighting. A line of heavily armoured, red and gold eldar warriors had appeared abruptly in the plaza before the cathedral gates. Looking closely, Lexius realised that there also seemed to be some kind of child with them, shepherded along in the middle of the formation, as though for protection. For a few moments, they appeared unconcerned or unaware of the presence of the Dark Angels. Instead, they were busying themselves planting charges around the frame of the gates.

'Lion damn them!' whispered Lexius as he spun his crozius arcanum ready for battle. He could only hope that their presence on Tyrine was a coincidence – anything else was far too appalling to contemplate. Whatever the case, his patience for the terrible afflictions of this fallen planet was already exhausted, and the appearance of these vile, xenos creatures only made Tyrine more disgusting. He would see it burn. All of it.

'Repent!' yelled Kalidian, sharing his Chaplain's thoughts, with his bolt pistol aloft in one hand and his chainsword brandished in the other. 'For today you die!'

With that, the Dark Angels broke into a charge across the plaza.

THE BOLTER SHELLS punched into the gates of the basilica, behind the Warp Spiders, chipping out shards of shrapnel and making the Aspect Warriors spin. The impacts shook the gates and sent booming sounds echoing into the nave beyond – so much for the advantage of surprise.

Adsulata slid instinctively in front of Ela, shielding her from the sudden barrage from the other side of the plaza. A squad of cloaked, power armoured Space Marines were storming towards them, with their weapons blazing. Looking around her warriors, Adsulata saw that the Warp Spiders were springing away from the gates, abandoning the thermal mines that they had been planting as they braced their weapons ready for the fight.

She scanned the surroundings, but could find nothing that would afford them any cover: they were completely exposed, standing before the gates of the basilica like red and gold targets for the mon'keigh warriors. Her immediate instincts were to get her Aspect Warriors clear of the site – they could blink through a series of warp jumps over to the side of the plaza and then take the fight to the Space Marines from a better position. But then there was little Ela – she could not make the jumps, and Adsulata would not leave her alone.

There was nothing for it but simply to exchange fire.

As though sharing the same thought processes, the rest of the Warp Spiders suddenly opened up with their death spinners, sending sprays of tiny, explosive projectiles screaming across the plaza. They had formed into a line in front of Ela'Ashbel, shielding her from the fray.

The Space Marines simply charged at them, ignoring the volleys of fire as though they were impervious to the weapons of the eldar. The death spinners' projectiles just seemed to bounce off their deep green armour. They were yelling battle cries in the crude, ugly tongue of their species, and behind them Adsulata could see a pressing crowd of bloodied and gaudy Tyrinites, squealing with pleasure at the violence that was unravelling before them.

A shriek of pain made Adsulata turn. At the end of the Warp Spider firing line, one of the Aspect Warriors dropped to his knees, clutching at his throat. Blood bubbled and jetted from the open artery, spraying over the white flagstones before the figure slumped forward into his own blood.

As the Warp Spider fell, Adsulata realised that its wound must have been caused by a blade, not by a bullet. She scanned the flanks quickly and saw that they had more to worry about than the charging Space Marines. Out to both sides of the gates, she could see spinning cyclones of daemonettes whirling into the materium. Already, there were three lithe and nauseatingly graceful figures working their way towards the eldar position. One of them had paused at the end of the line of Warp Spiders to lick the blood of the fallen off her poisoned blades. At least four more cyclones spoke of worse to come.

Two more Warp Spiders shrieked as hails of bolter fire punched through their slim bodies, throwing them back against the gates of the basilica and leaving them crumpled, shredded and ruined in heaps on the ground.

Adsulata checked behind her and saw Ela standing calmly and unmoved. Her sapphire eyes glistened with ineffable, distant fires, and her smooth face betrayed no signs of emotion, even as her honour guard was slaughtered around her. The arachnir could not believe the composure of the infant.

At that moment, the great gates of the basilica burst open and hails of bolter shells lashed out of the yawning space within, accompanied by the roar of tens of thousands of raised voices. The sound wave was like a tsunami crashing over the Warp Spiders and throwing them off balance. In the distance, the pressing crowds in the street behind the dark green Space Marines returned the rapturous noise as though it were a sign from the gods themselves. Adsulata could hear them flooding into the plaza in their thousands, raising their voices and their weapons in tune with the grotesque noise that crashed out of the basilica.

As the blast of sound and air threw her off her feet, Adsulata just had time to turn and see a rampage of red and black Space Marines emerging from the shadows of the cathedral, their weapons blazing. Without knowing who they were, the arachnir realised instinctively that these were different creatures from the Astartes that had charged through the plaza.

The great gates crashed back against the massive stone walls, crushing the thermal mines that the Warp Spiders had set into the hinges, triggering a huge detonation that blew the immense doors into the air amidst an inferno of radiation and flame.

Rolling back up onto her feet, Adsulata saw that the eldar force was spent. Her Warp Spiders lay shredded and dead on the white flagstones, bathed in the fires of their own thermal charges. Mon'keigh warriors stormed towards them from in front and behind, trapping them in a lethal crossfire of bolter shells. To either side danced the sinister and deadly forms of daemonettes of Slaanesh, and all around were tens of thousands of mammalian cultists, all of them baying for blood.

In the very heart of it all stood little Ela. She seemed tiny and innocent amidst the fury and brutality of unrestrained battle. The corpses of her brethren were strewn around her feet, and their blood was gradually soaking into the hem of her long cloak. Yet somehow she remained untouched by the sullied reality of the combat. Bolter shells, projectiles and blades just seemed to slide past her, as though they could not find purchase in the pure form of an infant. She stood unmoving, with her brilliant blue eyes shining like distant stars.

Adsulata nodded a sorrowful farewell to her charge just as volleys of shells punctured her abdomen from both sides at once. The impacts seemed to balance each other, leaving her standing upright before the gates. But then a daemonette slid past and swept her blade through the arachnir's knees, severing her legs and sending her crashing to the ground. Howling with pleasure, the daemonette sprang onwards, landing down onto the corpse of another fallen eldar and ripping at its flesh in search of its soul.

Lying in amongst the corpses of her Warp Spiders, with the last of her long life bleeding out onto the once-white flagstones of a forsaken world, Adsulata lifted her face to see Ela one last time. *I have failed you, my farseer.*

No, came the gentle reply as Ela walked calmly through the furious battle that raged around her. *You have brought me safely to this place. Your duty is done, and your soul will be returned to the infinity circuit of Kaelor to join its ancestors. My destiny lies within this basilica – you can take me no further.*

With that, Ela reached down and took Adsulata's waystone from its place of safety in the chestplates of her armour. Then she turned and walked slowly towards the yawning entrance into the cathedral. Thousands of stinking mon'keigh were rushing past her, pouring out into the plaza to join the fray. But they paid her no attention at all. She moved through them like a little fish swimming up-stream, heading up the main aisle towards the orator in the apse.

For a brief moment, Ela realised that the coincidence of forces in the plaza implied the machinations of a great intelligence. She could not believe that all those various warriors, daemons and cultists had converged on that point at that time by accident. It had been *arranged* in order to thwart her mission.

She put the thought aside as the crowds began to part before her and she saw the towering figure of Kor Phaeron for the first time in real life. He was just as he had appeared in her vision. Standing behind the crumbling remains of the font, the massive, power armoured warrior-god looked down on the little infant seer and laughed.

'AND SO IT *was that the seer-child, the ehveline of Kaelor, walked hand in hand with destiny, taking it with her like a crippled caradoc, guiding it through the quagmires of the present like a farseer. She passed slowly through the ugly confusion of the basilica, parting the congregation like water around a finely honed blade. Until finally, ancient before her time, and possessing the prescient fortitude of her forebears, the infant seer stood her ground before the monstrous form of the Dark Apostle.*

And looking down upon her tiny and frail figure, the giant warrior of Chaos roared with ridicule and mirth, throwing back his head and yelling his laughter into the crude Blood Dome above. His daemonic patrons had warned him of the power of the Sons of Asuryan, whispering promises of carnage and bloodshed on an epic scale, pushing thoughts of legions of Aspect Warriors and of the Avatar of Khaine himself into the roiling fury of the Apostle's mind.

Yet, in the place of these blood-drenched legions came Ela.

There were none to witness the events that transpired before the mutilated altar of the Emperor of Man, and yet it was there and then that the myriad futures of Kaelor resolved into a single path. The decisive moment had nothing to do with the thwarted plans of the decadent and treacherous few, which burned like the fires of Vaul in the plaza beyond the great gates, smouldering in the corpses of the valiant Warp Spiders.

The moment came in the blink of an eye.

As the mirth of the daemon-warrior subsided, and he cast the gaze of his blazing eyes down onto the hooded form of the ehveline, mocking her with his intensity of purpose, the once and future farseer of our fate reached up her hands and slid the hood from her head.

And that was the moment.

Ela of Ashbel looked up, with her glittering sapphire eyes shining with the radiance of the eyes of Isha herself, and she met the cursed gaze of the monstrous Apostle.

It was a transfixion.

In that instant, the great gates of the basilica slammed shut and sealed with powers beyond the whit of any to open, leaving the infant and the monster alone in the cavernous space within. They stood unmoving, like a grand fresco from the golden era of legends, holding each other's will in the clutches of their souls.

The moment stretched out of time as the fury of battle rose and abated in the plaza outside. What passed as a fraction of an instant passed simultaneously as an age – the deep and mysterious minds of the two adversaries amplifying time into impossible durations.

It cannot be known what the darkest of Apostles saw in the soul of little Ela. It has been conjectured that the visions she gave to him challenged his faith to its core, riddling the Master of Faith with doubts and uncertainties that turned his will against itself and drove the perverse mon'keigh to new heights of fury and rage.

Whatever it was that Kor Phaeron saw in the glittering, sapphire eyes of the ehveline, it turned his laughter into fury and drove him ranting from the surface of Tyrine on that very day.

But this victory came at such a cost.

When the infant seer finally lowered her eyes from the font, there was only darkness in her sight. Even the ruddy, red light that flooded down from the Blood Dome had vanished from her view. There was nothing.

Reaching her hand to her face, Ela traced her fingers over her cheeks and found them slick with liquid. Blood was seeping out of her ruined eyes like a torrent of tears.

Kor Phaeron's twisted mind had lashed at her soul and her eyes, granting her visions of such horror that her very being had rebelled against them. Her senses had striven to shut out the sensations, shielding her soul from the insanity that the Apostle had held out to her like a gift, as though tempting her with sheer terror.

She saw visions of the future. She saw Kaelor rebuilt and glorious. She saw it burning and in flames as mon'keigh warriors and daemonettes of the Great Enemy stormed through its boulevards and forests – she saw an Apostle like Kor Phaeron himself standing in the heart of the Circular Council with the broken and battered corpses of the courtiers strewn around him. And she saw that Apostle throw back his head and laugh at the ruination of the ancient craftworld. He held out his hand towards Ela, and she saw that it was overflowing with the spirit-stones of her people. As she looked back up into the Apostle's face, a name smashed into her mind: Erebus. But then the face morphed and twisted, transmogrifying into the visage of Slaanesh itself. In a slow, deliberate and mocking gesture, the Great Enemy brought its hand to its face and pushed the waystones into its mouth, chewing slowly as drool poured over its lips.

And it was with these horrors in her mind that Ela of Ashbel, the ehveline of Kaelor, struggled back through the warp portals of her fallen Warp Spiders, stumbling and staggering under the weight of her efforts and under the ineffable, terrible pressures of the future.'

– The Tears of Blood:
The Chronicles of Ela'Ashbel, vol.2
by Deoch Epona, Craftworld Kaelor

CRACKS OF WARP lightning lashed through the distant wraithbone ceiling of the Styhxlin forest sector, flickering vividly into the fecund zone and rendering the atmosphere into a rainless, electrical storm. The lashes of the Maelstrom whipped against the vast form of Kaelor as it skirted the fringes of the massive warp tempest. Tendrils of daemonic power scraped over the ancient structure, riddling it with flecks of daemonic energy as it pitched and yawed on the very cusp of its own damnation.

Farseer Ahearn Rivalin stood uncertainly amongst the vegetation, his staff sinking slightly into the moist earth as he leant his weight onto it. He did not enjoy these trips out towards the Styhxlin perimeter – it was not the danger, although that had been considerable recently, but rather it was the organic filth of the forest zones that appalled his cultivated sensibilities. Even debris, flame and rubble seemed to have a pristine quality in comparison.

Besides, the Warp Spiders of Exarch Aingeal had been particularly unsympathetic to the needs of the Rivalin court, and they had been the first to end the long tradition of political aloofness by the Aspect Temples of Kaelor when the Prophecy Conflagration had first started to simmer. Aingeal was now called the odai-exarch – the Great Exarch – by those who had been loyal to his cause.

Trust the little abomination to pick this place as her point of return to Kaelor: she had not even communicated it to the court – one of the seer covens of House Yuthran had forewarned the court of her imminent arrival and the farseer had been forced to hasten to this distasteful place to await her, entrusting the earnest Uisnech Anyon with his security in transit.

Thankfully, Ela'Ashbel was on time.

The grand warp portal of the Spider Temple, half hidden amongst the singed but still-lush foliage, shimmered with power. A curtain of mercurial energy in-phased within the circular frame, glistening with reflections like the surface of a lunar pool.

Ahearn peered into the sparkling images, seeing himself and his honour guard distorted in the reflections, rendered ugly and misshapen by the power of the warp. For a moment, he wondered whether this was how he actually appeared to the other, more innocent eldar of Kaelor – those still committed to the overbearing Eldar Paths. As he turned the thought in his mind, playing with it like a flawed gemstone, a shiver of unapologetic superiority thrilled through his spine. Why should he care what others saw?

'She is coming,' said Maeveh, leaning down to whisper into the farseer's ear, her voice edged with excited dread. Her scheme to remove the little abomination and ease Kaelor's passage towards its destiny had been thwarted. For just a moment, she wondered at the incredible power that Ela had revealed through her ordeal.

'Yes,' answered Ahearn, letting sibilance draw his reply into a hiss.

The curtain of warp energy rippled suddenly and violently, bubbling as though a child were blowing air into it. Then a spot appeared in the middle – a point of darkness in the centre that grew gradually into a circle and then a void, pushing the energy curtain into a furious, boiling frame of light. After a few seconds, a tiny, female figure appeared in the darkness.

Little Ela'Ashbel, the abominable infant seer, stepped out of the warp portal and back into the sanctity of the forested grounds of the Spider Temple, where she had spent her earliest years. She was quite alone – her Warp Spider escort having been wiped out on the surface of Tyrine. She was stooped with exhaustion and weariness. And she was bleeding.

Farseer Ahearn shuffled forward, reaching out his hand for the suffering child. 'You have saved us from a great enemy, my little morna. The eldar of Kaelor owe you a great debt of gratitude – their souls are their own, for a while longer at least.'

Maeveh's lips snarled in undisguised disgust and disappointment, making Ahearn turn to encourage her decorum. But then he realised something wonderful: the blood that cascaded down Ela's face was coming from her eyes. It looked as though she was weeping tears of blood. She had been blinded. She could no longer see the decadent ugliness of the farseer's visage; she could no longer discern the snarling disparagement of Maeveh. She would now rely on her caradoc even more than before. Perhaps things had worked out rather well after all.

'My little morna,' he continued, with a moist smile creasing his wrinkled face. 'Come with me. I know a wonderful place where you can rest and gain distraction from your pain. Come with me and Maeveh Yuthran – we will look after you.'

Stumbling with fatigue, pain and sensory disorientation, Ela'Ashbel reached out her hand into her world of absolute darkness and grasped what felt like the old, dry fingers of Ahearn. Too weak to say or do anything else, she simply nodded and let him lead her away.

ABOUT THE AUTHORS

DAN ABNETT

Dan Abnett lives and works in Maidstone, Kent, in England. Well known for his comic work, he has written everything from the Mr Men to the X-Men in the last decade, and is currently scripting Legion of Superheroes and Superman for DC Comics, and Sinister Dexter and The VCs for *2000 AD*. His work for the Black Library includes the popular comic strips *Lone Wolves*, *Titan* and *Inquisitor Ascendant*, the best-selling Gaunt's Ghosts novels, and the acclaimed Inquisitor Eisenhorn trilogy.

DARREN-JON ASHMORE

Darren-Jon Ashmore is said to be an anthropologist, and is rumoured to bi-locate between Sheffield and Kobe at will. However, his girlfriend maintains he is just one of her bad dreams, and apologises profusely for inflicting him on the Black Library.

CS GOTO

C S Goto has published short fiction in *Inferno!* and elsewhere. His work for the Black Library includes the Warhammer 40,000 Dawn of War novels, the Deathwatch series and the Necromunda novel *Salvation*.

MATT KEEFE

Matt Keefe has worked extensively in the movie and games industries and was one of the developers who worked on the latest edition of *Necromunda*. He lives in Sheffield, England.

MIKE LEE

Mike Lee was the principal creator and developer for White Wolf Game Studio's *Demon: The Fallen*. Over the last eight years he has contributed to almost two dozen role-playing games and supplements. Together with Dan Abnett, Mike has written three Darkblade novels, with more to come.

GRAHAM MCNEILL

Hailing from Scotland, Graham McNeill narrowly escaped a career in surveying to join Games Workshop, where he worked as a games developer for six years. In addition to seven novels of carnage and mayhem, Graham has also written a host of short stories. He lives in Nottingham, UK.

STEVE PARKER

Steve Parker lives and works in Tokyo, Japan. He divides his time between writing, shootfighting and teaching English. He grew up on John Blanche artwork and just about anything else that included monsters, aliens, spaceships or ghosts, which would explain his deep-rooted psychological problems. Yoroshiku!

DARK MILLENNIUM
The WARHAMMER 40,000
Collectible Card Game

Go deeper into the action with Dark Millennium – The Warhammer 40,000 Collectible Card Game. Take up the struggle as the defenders of the Imperium or one of the many alien races wanting to destroy it!

With participation events that actually change the fate of entire planets, YOU are in command! What will you do with such power?

Check out *www.sabertoothgames.com* for more information!

Sabertooth Games